Senior Sisters

Book Five
of the
Sister Circle Series

Nancy Moser

Mustard Seed Press
Overland Park, KS

Senior Sisters

ISBN: 978-1-961907-08-9

Published by:
Mustard Seed Press
Overland Park, KS

Copyright © 2023 by Nancy Moser. All rights reserved.

This book, or parts thereof, may not be reproduced, stored in a retrieval system, or transmitted in any form or by any means, electronic, mechanical, photocopying, recording, or otherwise, without the written permission of the publisher.

This story is a work of fiction. Any resemblances to actual people, places, or events are purely coincidental.

All Scripture quotations are taken from *The Holy Bible, New Living Translation*.

Front cover design by Mustard Seed Press

The Books of Nancy Moser

www.nancymoser.com

Contemporary Books

If Not for This
An Undiscovered Life
Eyes of Our Heart
The Invitation (Book 1 Mustard Seed)
The Quest (Book 2 Mustard Seed)
The Temptation (Book 3 Mustard Seed)
Crossroads
The Seat Beside Me (Book 1 Steadfast)
A Steadfast Surrender (Book 2 Steadfast)
The Ultimatum (Book 3 Steadfast)
The Sister Circle (Book 1 Sister Circle)
Round the Corner (Book 2 Sister Circle)
An Undivided Heart (Book 3 Sister Circle)
A Place to Belong (Book 4 Sister Circle)
Senior Sisters (Book 5 Sister Circle)
The Sister Circle Handbook (Book 6 Sister Circle)
Time Lottery (Book 1 Time Lottery)
Second Time Around (Book 2 Time Lottery)
John 3:16
The Good Nearby
Solemnly Swear
Save Me, God! I Fell in the Carpool (Inspirational humor)
100 Verses of Encouragement — Books 1&2 (illustrated gift books)
Maybe Later (picture book)
I Feel Amazing: the ABCs of Emotion (picture book)

Historical Books

Where Time Will Take Me (Book 1 Past Times)
Where Life Will Lead Me (Book 2 Past Times)
Pin's Promise (novella prequel to Pattern Artist)
The Pattern Artist (Book 1 Pattern Artist)
The Fashion Designer (Book 2 Pattern Artist)
The Shop Keepers (Book 3 Pattern Artist)
Love of the Summerfields (Book 1 Manor House)
Bride of the Summerfields (Book 2 Manor House)
Rise of the Summerfields (Book 3 Manor House)
Mozart's Sister (biographical novel of Nannerl Mozart)
Just Jane (biographical novel of Jane Austen)
Washington's Lady (bio-novel of Martha Washington)
How Do I Love Thee? (bio-novel of Elizabeth Barrett Browning)
Masquerade (Book 1 Gilded Age)
An Unlikely Suitor (Book 2 Gilded Age)
A Bridal Quilt (Gilded Age novella)
The Journey of Josephine Cain
A Basket Brigade Christmas (novella collection)
When I Saw His Face (Regency novella)

Dedication

To the Senior Sisters in my life...

Crys, Lois, Wendi, Sheree, Nikki, Suzy, Brenda, Karen, Janie, Jane, Nancy, Carolyn, Lynn, Jill, Kris, Sue, Debbie, Echo . . . and so many more.

I thank God for letting us grow up together as we grow old together, sharing the complicated (but always fascinating) trappings of our hearts.

I love you all and will cherish our sisterhood forever.

Note to the Reader: Before we get started . . .

When we last left the ladies of the Victorian boarding house, Peerbaugh Place, it was 2005. Their stories were told in the first four books of the Sister Circle series.

A funny thing happened between then and now. In 2023 I suddenly realized I was 68 years old! How in the name of sisterhood did that happen? Since I now have first-hand experience in many of the joys and challenges of aging, I decided to check in on the Sisters of Peerbaugh Place. And so *Senior Sisters* was born. Technically, it's set in 2015 . . .

Why 2015, you ask? Because in 2020 I wrote a book called *Eyes of our Heart* that showed some of the ladies living at the Happy Trails Retirement Home. So *Senior Sisters* is a book slipping BETWEEN the first four Sister Circle novels and *Eyes of Our Heart*.

Don't be confused (it takes too much work and life's too short) just enjoy the books! The ladies' issues, relationships, and emotions are timeless.

One last thing . . . if you'd like to get together with some of the sisters in your *own* life, you might enjoy *The Sister Circle Handbook: Balancing the Joy of Friendship with Your God-Given Gifts*. Inside are Bible studies, discovering-your-gifts studies, recipes, and ideas for fun group activities.

Above all . . . remember what good ol' Abraham Lincoln said: "In the end, it's not the years in your life that count. It's the life in your years."

If not Abe Lincoln, how about Star Trek's Mr. Spock: "Live long and prosper." Can I have an Amen?

Chapter One

Evelyn

Autumn 2015

> God will generously provide all you need.
> Then you will always have everything you need
> and plenty left over to share with others.
> 2 Corinthians 9: 8

Evelyn and Wayne Wellington stood on the porch and waved as their latest tenant drove away.

"I can't believe she was here a whole month," Wayne said. "That's a long time for someone who's just staying here while family is in the hospital." He opened the front door for his wife and they went inside their boarding house, Peerbaugh Place.

"I thank God her husband is finally going home." Evelyn started up the stairs to the second floor.

"Where are you going?" Wayne asked.

Evelyn paused on the stairway she'd traveled a million times in the past four decades. She stooped down to pluck a thread from the carpet, and put it in the pocket of her jeans. "I need to clean their room, then start a load of laundry."

He gazed up at her from the foyer. "Uh-uh. You do not *need* to do that."

"Of course I do. We never know when we'll get a call from someone about a room."

"My point is, you don't need to do those things right this minute." He extended his arm toward her. "Come with me. We could both use some swing-time."

She knew he was right. Wayne was usually right about such things.

Evelyn backtracked to the foyer and they went outside to the porch swing. With an *oomph* they sat down.

Wayne laughed. "I can tell I'm old because of the noises I've started to make in the past few years."

"I make them too," Evelyn said.

"I'm louder."

"Because you're older."

He rolled his eyes. "Thanks for reminding me."

She felt bad about that. "*I* will be seventy this year."

"I'm still seven years ahead of you. It's a race you'll never win."

Evelyn slipped her hand around his arm and enjoyed the cool breeze of the Kansas autumn. Although she and Wayne had only been married nine years, they'd been the best years. He was the answer to a dream she'd never thought to dream.

She'd met Wayne and his late wife at a cooking class. Evelyn had been a new widow who'd opened her Victorian home to boarders in order to make ends meet. Her first husband had died in a car accident, leaving her a miniscule amount of life insurance. And yet—as often happened—God brought good out of bad. Because of Peerbaugh Place she'd met dozens of fabulous people over the years. Some were her best friends. The house was blessed that way.

Wayne put an arm around her shoulders and she inched closer, smelling his favorite "Old Spice" aftershave. Good out of bad . . . out of Aaron's accident and Wanda's illness, God had brought Evelyn and Wayne together. He was everything she'd ever wanted in a husband: kind, attentive, loving, honorable. The opposite of her first husband.

Evelyn knew what *she'd* gained from their marriage, but was far less certain what Wayne had gained, for his wife had been a charming, godly woman—hard to beat. Yet whatever she gave him seemed to be enough for they were happy in a contented, slow to ruffle kind of way—which suited Evelyn just fine. They were in complete agreement that family was their focus. Let other couples have their world cruises and golf memberships. If being homebodies made Evelyn and Wayne fuddy-duddies, so be it.

Evelyn let Wayne control the swing, his anchored feet creating a rhythm that matched the flutter of the geraniums hanging in a basket nearby.

"I don't mind having empty rooms for a while," Wayne said. "Before we know it we'll be full up."

That was true. "For now the house is empty—except for Accosta, of course."

"And she's no bother."

"She's a sweet woman. But she's—"

"Ahhhhyyyy!" came a scream.

They jumped off the swing and ran inside. Accosta was sprawled on the stairs.

"Are you okay?" Evelyn asked.

"I'll be fine. I was heading upstairs and my foot slipped."

Wayne helped her up, effectively lifting her down the last four steps to the foyer and leading her toward a chair in the parlor.

He eased her frail body onto its cushions. "There now," he said. "Do you think you broke anything?"

"No, no. Fiddle-dee, don't fuss." She waved the notion away. "I'm fine. I'm just clumsy."

This was not the first time Accosta had experienced balance issues. At age ninety-three it wasn't surprising. But she did look pale.

"Like I've said before, we need to get you a walker," Wayne said.

"We could get two," Evelyn said. "One for upstairs and one for down here."

Wayne added to the scenario. "When you want to go up or down you just ask someone for help."

Accosta shook her head. "I will not be a burden like that. You two have busy lives and the hospital renters have sick family on their minds. No one needs to be bothered with an old woman like me."

They weren't bothered, but they were concerned. They loved Accosta as a mother and loved having her as a permanent resident of Peerbaugh Place.

Accosta started to stand.

"No, you don't," Wayne said. "Whatever you need we'll get it for you. Give yourself a few minutes to just *be*."

"If you're going to be that way . . ." She relaxed in the chair. "I need my Bible and the Bible study book that are next to my bed. And a pen and my magnifying glass."

"You got it," Wayne said. "I'll be right back."

Evelyn arranged a floor lamp so Accosta would have good light for her studies. "Would you like some tea?"

"No thank you, dear."

Wayne returned with the items. "Here you go."

"You two spoil me so."

Evelyn leaned down and kissed her cheek. "Glad to do it."

Wayne glanced toward the stairs. "Evelyn and I are going upstairs to change the sheets."

Evelyn gave him a *'We are?'* look.

He nodded and said, "Call if you need us."

They left Accosta to her reading and went upstairs into the newly vacated bedroom. Wayne closed the door.

"You said to wait on the cleaning," Evelyn said.

"The statement stands." He nodded toward the window seat. "We need to talk."

Evelyn could guess what about. "Accosta?"

He nodded and sat beside her. "The time is fast approaching when we can't give her the help she needs."

Evelyn had been thinking about this for some time. "She's done so well these past ten years."

"She has, but I think we're borrowing trouble. What would happen if she fell down the stairs and broke a hip?"

Evelyn shuddered. "I don't even want to think about it. I've heard about elderly people falling and not recovering because surgery is too risky."

"At least she's still mentally vibrant—which is a blessing to everyone."

"*She* is a blessing to everyone. Our sunshine."

Wayne nodded and braced his hands against his knees. "But it's time. I don't like this anymore than you do, but she needs to move to a facility that can take care of her."

What would they do without Accosta in the house? She was a five-foot tall, ninety-pound rock of their existence. Why couldn't time stand still? Why did it insist on marching onward. And onward.

"Ev? What do you think about a facility?"

Evelyn nodded. "I know you're right. Happy Trails?"

"That's what I was thinking. I know some of her friends are there. Our friends."

Evelyn's thoughts moved from the emotional drain of it to a bottom-line issue. "It's expensive."

"That, it is."

"She doesn't have any money beyond her social security. Even with us not charging her rent, she doesn't have anywhere near enough to cover it."

"And assisted living—which she probably needs, or will need soon—is even more expensive." Wayne sighed deeply.

"Does she need that extra care? She gets along fine with her cane, and will do even better with a walker. With the stool we put in the shower she doesn't need help bathing."

"That's a plus." He turned sideways on the seat to look out the window. "There is another consideration. One day you and I might want to move there. Grab ourselves some one-level living."

Evelyn shook her head adamantly. "No way. I am not leaving this place. Ever. You'll have to carry me out feet first."

He smiled and squeezed her knee. "Don't be pig-headed about it. And don't tell me you haven't thought of it."

She shoved the idea away. Again. Peerbaugh Place would always be her home. "I'm not being pig-headed, it's what I feel. I've lived in Peerbaugh Place since Aaron and I got married—and it was in his family before that. I can't discard it so flippantly."

Wayne touched her arm. "I'm not being flippant, I'm being practical." He pointed out the window at the orange maples in the backyard. "Face it, Ev, we moan when we get on and off the swing. And—if you'll be honest—going up and down stairs wreaks havoc on my knees and on your lower back. Am I correct?"

Evelyn didn't want to agree, so she ignored his question. "It's too soon. Because to do such a thing means . . ." Her throat tightened and she couldn't continue.

He scooted closer and wrapped an arm around her shoulders. "It means we're older than we'd like to admit."

She was shocked when she started to cry. It was embarrassing. Not that Wayne hadn't seen her cry over a lot of things—including Christmas commercials and online clips of delivery drivers returning a blown-down American flag to its proper place. But crying over age was silly—and fruitless.

"Sorry," she said, taking a deep breath. "It's not like it's a sudden surprise. We've been feeling age creep up on us for years."

"Agreed. We've known we were getting older, but when it really hit me was when I realized *other* people saw me as old too."

Evelyn perked up. "That's it! It's like hearing a young clerk answer a question by saying, 'Yes, ma'am.'" She put a hand to her chest. "When did I become a *ma'am?*"

Wayne nodded. "The first time it hit me was when a fast-food place gave me a senior discount—"

"And you didn't ask for it! I know!"

"Not that I didn't mind the discount . . ."

"Exactly." Evelyn laughed, enjoying their moment of playful commiseration. She paused as she heard Accosta singing downstairs.

"'All to Jesus, I surrender, all to Him I freely give . . .'"

Wayne spoke in a whisper. "I love hearing her sing that song every day."

"She has such a clear voice." Evelyn said. "And I like that she sings it when she thinks no one else can hear."

"Like it's between her and Him."

They sat close on the window seat while Accosta's hymn wove its peace around them.

Chapter Two

Evelyn

> "For I know the plans I have for you," says the Lord.
> "They are plans for good and not for disaster,
> to give you a future and a hope."
> Jeremiah 29:11

Evelyn poured two cups of coffee and a cup of tea while Wayne arranged freshly baked scones on a plate. She set the cups on the kitchen table and put the sugar and creamer close. "I'm nervous," she said.

Wayne got the orange marmalade from the fridge. "Me too. But the conversation has to happen. Soon."

Just because he was right didn't make the upcoming discussion any easier.

Wayne added three plates to the table, then looked at her. "Your fully transparent, what-I-feel-is-on-my-face expression looks petrified. Can you relax it a bit, Ev?"

"I'll try, but my emotions usually refuse to listen."

Wayne took her hand and peered heavenward. "Lord, give us the right words."

"Amen to that." She liked her husband's short-and-sweet prayers. He'd once told her that God didn't give brownie points for the length of a prayer or fancy words. The Almighty appreciated heartfelt, to-the-point prayers.

"Ready?" he asked.

"As we'll ever be." She looked toward the door, biting her lip. "Will you go get her?" she asked. "She's reading on the porch."

He saluted. "We'll be back in a jiff."

Evelyn sat at her place and drew in a deep breath, hoping the extra oxygen would stop her from feeling like she was on the edge of a cliff. This wasn't going to be an easy conversation, yet it was a common one. And Wayne was right, it was a needed one.

She bowed her head but words refused to form. Where Wayne was good at short prayers, Evelyn usually trusted God to fill in the blanks.

She heard Accosta's approach before she saw her, her cane adding an extra beat to their footsteps.

Accosta's eyes lit up when she saw the table set with scones. "My favorite!"

As planned.

Wayne held out her chair and she got situated.

"And marmalade too? What are we celebrating?"

Uh . . .

Evelyn was glad when Wayne answered. "It's not exactly a celebration. It's more of a graduation."

Ooh. Good word, Wayne!

Accosta spooned sugar in her tea. "The last graduation I celebrated was nearly eighty years ago." She cocked her head. "Unless you're talking about my final graduation to heaven. Is there something you're not telling me?"

"No, not that!" Evelyn said with a chuckle. She glanced at Wayne and he nodded his encouragement. "It's the graduation to a new milestone. From how you've been getting along, to what we need to plan for."

"Again, is there something you're not telling me?"

Obviously it was best they got to the point. "We are concerned about you getting hurt on the stairs," Evelyn said.

"I'm doing fine. I just need to take my time."

Wayne touched her hand. "There's more to it than that. We don't want to wait too long."

"To do what?"

"That's what we need to figure out," he said.

Evelyn made it plain. "We don't want to wait until you really hurt yourself to have a plan. Then we'd feel bad and have regrets and—"

"We've thought of a few options," Wayne said.

Accosta looked wary. "Such as?"

"That's what we're going to find out," Evelyn said. "Ringo is going to stop by this morning and help us figure it out."

Accosta's fiddled with her spoon for a few moments before looking up again. Her face was firm and set, not in disagreement but in acceptance. She nodded once. "Sounds like a plan. Now let me get to the scones while they're hot."

Evelyn was shocked with how well she'd taken it—whatever *it* might turn out to be.

** ** **

Ringo Fitzpatrick's long hair was pulled back in a ponytail which made him look like he was still a roadie for a rock band, rather than being the owner of a construction company. Besides being the son of her best friend, Mae, Evelyn knew he had a great reputation around Carson Creek for doing remodel work.

Upon entering Peerbaugh Place, he kissed Evelyn on the cheek. He shook Wayne's hand and said hello to Accosta. They hadn't seen him in months.

Evelyn led everyone to the parlor and knew the polite thing was to start off with a little chit-chat. "How's the family?"

"Real good. Soon-ja loves her job at the tile store, and the kids are busy with fall soccer. Let me say that watching Ricky's team of ten-year-olds is much more enjoyable than watching Zoe's team of six-year-olds. That one's total chaos."

Evelyn had always enjoyed going to her son's ballgames. "How's your sister doing in New York?"

Ringo rolled his eyes. "You know Starr. Busy as always. Still at the publishing house."

"Good for her," Evelyn said. Wayne nodded at her, so she got down to business. "We're so glad you could come over."

"Happy to do it." He scanned the room. "You mentioned remodeling?"

"We did," Wayne said. "Accosta's bedroom—all four bedrooms—are on the second floor and we don't like the idea of her going up and down those stairs anymore."

"I can do it," Accosta said with a nod. "I do it multiple times a day." She lowered her voice. "They're just worry warts, that's what they are."

"Call us what you want," Evelyn said. "But one misplaced step and you're in for a lot of agony." *If not worse.* The thought of Accosta in pain was unbearable.

"So you want to install a chair lift on the stairs?" Ringo asked.

"We talked about it," Wayne said.

Accosta's eyes gleamed. "That sounds like fun."

Evelyn wasn't sure about that. Accosta would still need to get in and out of the seat. And buckle herself in. "How safe are they?" she asked.

"Very safe," Ringo said. "But there are construction limitations for the install. First off, I need to measure the width of your stairs." He got out a tape measure and did just that. "Well," he said, coming back in the parlor. "That's a bummer. The minimum width for a lift is twenty-eight inches and you have twenty-six. So that's not going to work."

It was a huge disappointment for they knew that would've been the easiest solution. "On to another idea . . . we thought about turning a first-floor room into a bedroom," Evelyn said. "Like the sunroom."

Ringo stood. "Let's take a look."

"I'd get to sleep down here?" Accosta asked.

Wayne helped her up. "Maybe."

As they headed to the sunroom Evelyn felt like apologies had to be made, "I'm afraid we're behind with modern updates."

"That's okay," Ringo said. "I like old houses. They have character."

Evelyn agreed, yet couldn't help but notice the scuffed baseboard, the worn wood flooring, and the leaky windows.

Wayne and Ringo measured the sunroom, then everyone took a full walk-around of the first floor to put the room in context. It was a simple layout: the dining room and kitchen were on one side of the house with the sunroom and parlor on the other. Between the kitchen and the sunroom was a bathroom that had a tiny shower.

Ringo stepped into the bathroom and had to close the door to stand in front of the sink or reach the shower. "I'm not sure this is big enough for Accosta to maneuver in." He lowered his voice and spoke just to Evelyn. "Does she ever use a walker?"

"Not at the moment, but it's probably the next step," Evelyn said.

Ringo shook his head. "This bathroom would definitely have to be expanded for a walker."

"Or for someone else to be in there to help," Evelyn said.

"That too." He exited and checked the spaces on either side of the bathroom. "We'd have to take footage from at least one—if not both the kitchen and the sunroom."

"That sounds like a lot of work." And a big mess. And a big expense.

"You're right about that."

They returned full-circle to the parlor and sat down.

"We know it's quite a job . . ." Wayne said.

"But doable." Ringo adjusted the papers on his clipboard. "Yet there may be a few more issues."

"Such as?" Evelyn braced herself for the "more."

"Would you want a ramp to lead to the front door? If a wheelchair was ever involved, I'll make sure the bathroom has turn-around space and a wide-enough doorway." He pointed toward the sunroom. "Luckily, that room has double doors so it's not a problem there."

Accosta shook her head. Repeatedly.

"What's wrong?" Evelyn asked.

"Number one, I don't have a walker, and I'm certainly not in a wheelchair, so all these changes for things that don't even exist are ridiculous."

Wayne reached over and touched her arm. "It may seem so now, but conditions change. Needs change. We want to make sure everything is remodeled to accommodate all contingencies."

Accosta kept shaking her head. "That aren't a reality yet."

Evelyn knew how hard change could be—for all of them.

"As far as the time frame?" Ringo said, "I'd have to get something drawn up and approved by the city—which would take a few months. Then I'd like to give myself another month to do the work."

Evelyn hadn't thought much about the timing. "I'm sure that would work out," she said. "We don't want to wait until we have no choice. Planning ahead is the prudent thing to do."

Accosta clasped her hands in her lap. "It is not prudent to spend money on me. I'm fine where I am. You talked about getting me a walker for each floor, and me waiting for help on the stairs. If that's what it takes to stop this madness, I'll comply." She waved her hand at the clipboard. "Besides, all this will cost a lot of money."

They all looked at Ringo, who nodded. "She isn't wrong."

"How much money?" Wayne asked.

Ringo did some figuring, then sighed. "It might be forty to fifty thousand. I'll crunch the numbers more, but that's my initial guesstimate — *if* I don't find larger plumbing or electrical issues."

Evelyn felt a huge weight settle on her shoulders, making her feel tight inside. Deflated. The drop of Wayne's shoulders told her he felt the same. They had money saved away, but the improvements would inflict a big crack in their piggy bank.

Ringo seemed to read the room. He stood. "I'll do some more calculations and get back to you with a firm price." He leaned down and kissed Evelyn's cheek. "No problem either way," he whispered.

"Thank you," she said.

Wayne saw him out. Accosta sat there, shaking her head. Evelyn didn't know what to say. She'd hoped Ringo would offer some doable solutions, but instead, everything was more complicated. And *not* doable.

When Wayne got back to the parlor, Evelyn stood. She needed to escape. "I've got laundry to do."

"Oh no, you don't," Accosta said. "Sit back down. Both of you." They exchanged a look and sat. "I will not allow any of this." Accosta's finger flitted between Wayne and Evelyn and her voice was more adamant than Evelyn had ever heard. "You are not going to desecrate this beautiful home for me. I will not allow it."

Although Evelyn didn't like the idea of it either, Accosta meant more to her than a few walls. "We are willing to do whatever it takes to keep you safe."

The clock on the mantel struck half-past one.

"I am safe." Accosta pushed herself out of her chair. "Now who's going to drive me to my quilt club?"

Wayne stood immediately. "I'll do it."

Evelyn got Accosta's purse and sewing bag.

On the way out the door Accosta turned and pointed at each of them in turn. "Promise me that nothing is going to happen until we all pray on it for a good long while. Jumping ahead of the Lord always ends in disaster."

They promised.

Actually, Evelyn appreciated the reprieve. She hated making big decisions.

Chapter Three

Kay

> I am suffering and in pain.
> Rescue me, O God, by your saving power.
> Psalm 69: 29

Kay Volkov sat on the tiny balcony of her tiny one-bedroom apartment and hated her tiny life.

To pass the time she flipped through social media and watched one of her favorite influencers trying out the newest and best foundation that would even out even the worst skin and make wrinkles disappear.

If only.

Actually, Kay had bought a bottle, but it had made her skin look fake and heavy, like it used to when she'd been in theater productions. From 20-feet away, it might look good, but close up? Disgusting. The foundation had been yet another $70 wasted in her quest to look younger than seventy-two.

She heard the doorbell ring and called through the screen slider, "Come on in."

Her best friend, Sharon, entered, made her way to the balcony, and claimed the other chair as her own—which it virtually was. No one else visited Kay.

A twenty-something revved his motorcycle in the parking lot below them, making conversation impossible.

"Why do they think that's cool?" Sharon asked.

"I haven't a clue. Wally used to do the same thing. Never grew out of it."

"Maybe that's why Janice was attracted to him."

Kay scoffed. A year ago she might have taken offense at any mention of the forty-eight-year-old woman who'd stolen her husband of nearly fifty years. But now the pain had callused over.

Sharon stood. "I want coffee."

Kay raised her empty cup. "Hit me again, please."

Sharon went inside and Kay heard the Keurig whooshing. Within minutes Sharon returned to her chair and the aroma of chocolate macadamia coffee filled the air.

"So then," Sharon said. "Glad to see you and all that, but why have you called this meeting?"

Kay got right to the point. "I want to move."

"You've only been here a year."

"A year next month. But I've had enough."

Sharon nodded. "So apartment living isn't the Nirvana you thought it would be?"

"More like hell."

"Isn't that over-stating just a smidge?"

Kay had thought about it a lot. "No."

Sharon took a sip of her coffee and set it beside her chair. "I know you hate the noise but is it that bad?"

The noise was probably number one on her list. "Between the revving of engines, the kids playing in the hall, the loud music, and the sheer chaos of it all. I can't do it." She tapped her chest. "The incessant bass beat makes me want to jump."

"I get it. It bugs me too."

"But you don't have to live with it." Kay drew in a breath, trying to calm her breathing. "It's not just the music, it's the insensitivity—the total cluelessness—of the perpetrators. They have to realize other people will be bothered. Don't they?"

"Nah," Sharon said. "They live in their own little worlds that are focused on me, myself, and I. Actually, I'm surprised you lasted this long."

Kay held the coffee under her nose and inhaled, but didn't take a drink. "I thought this was the right choice. Wally and I got married right out of college. I went from my parents' house to being a wife. I never got to live alone, so when Wally left me, I had the stupid idea that I could start new, just like him. I'd regain my youth and have the apartment experience. It was my great experiment and it failed." She scoffed. "I actually thought I could make friends here but they're either college students, working couples, or people with kids. I think I've only seen two people over fifty."

"Did you try to make friends with *them*?"

"Both of the oldies are men who didn't even say *hi* back." She finally took a sip of coffee. It was still too hot so she set it on the floor beside her chair. "Have you ever felt invisible?"

"Sometimes I've *wished* I was invisible . . ."

"That's because you still have Hank, and your kids live close. You're busy. You're not alone."

"Gee, Kay. You're making me feel guilty for being happy?"

Kay touched her arm. "Sorry. I didn't mean to do that."

Sharon patted her hand. "I know you didn't. And I know what you mean. In our day, you and I turned heads and now people look past us or turn away."

"Exactly! I thought I'd feel younger living here, I thought I'd have something to offer. I'm an expert seamstress and if anybody needed me to make them something, I'd do it in a minute, but when I mentioned that I sew to someone, they brought me a button they needed sewn on."

"No one sews anymore," Sharon said. "Not like we did."

Kay shook her head. "I got asked to babysit a few times, but changing diapers? And dealing with kids who don't want to go to bed? My two grandkids are teenagers so my toddler skills are long gone." She thought of something. "The one good thing to come out of babysitting is that the mom showed me how to use Pinterest. I've got over 3200 pins already."

"Of what?"

Kay thought for a moment. "Mostly recipes. Decorating tips. Cute sayings."

Kay hooked a thumb toward the inside of the apartment. "Not much need for any of those here, is there?"

"None." Kay got out her phone and went to Facebook. "To make matters worse . . ." She pulled up Wally's profile. "Take a look at his pictures from last week."

Sharon took the phone and swiped through pictures of Wally and Janice on a cruise. "Where are they?"

"The Mediterranean. Off Sicily."

Sharon whistled. "Didn't you want to go there?"

"*We* were going to go there for our fiftieth."

"Yikes. Low blow."

The lowest.

Sharon took another look. "It looks like they've both lost weight."

"And he's dyed his hair." Wally's new younger look was as hurtful as the cruise. He wasn't supposed to improve after their divorce. Kay hadn't. She'd put on ten pounds and had stopped styling her hair. Once her "new friends" attempt had failed, she'd had no reason to care.

Sharon handed Kay the phone back. "I seriously advise you *not* to go down the rabbit hole of social media. All it does is make you feel bad about your life; the places you aren't going, the parties you aren't attending, the food you're not eating, and the fun you're not having."

She was right.

"What do *you* post, Kay?"

"Nothing."

"I rest my case."

Kay felt a familiar wave of hopelessness. "No one around here has ever asked what I do—or did."

"You wanted to impress them by saying you were the manager of customer service at Kohl's for twenty years?"

Ouch. "I get it. Even if they *had* asked, it's not a very glamorous resume. And I've been retired for over a year—since the divorce."

"You should go back to work—if not there, somewhere else. Just for something to do."

She'd thought about it. Kay missed having a purpose every day. She missed talking to people and having co-workers. She even missed making meals for Wally, washing his clothes, cleaning their house...

Kay shook such thoughts away. They were the *past*. She'd brought Sharon here to talk about her future. It was time to tell her the details of her news. "I may not have had anything to post before, but all that's going to change."

"Aha. The surprise you told me about." Sharon angled her chair to give Kay her full attention.

"I don't just want to move, I *am* moving."

Sharon blinked. "Where to?"

Kay retrieved a pamphlet from under her chair and handed it to her friend.

Sharon read the front headline. "Start your Happy Life at Happy Trails." She looked up. "Sounds like a dude ranch."

It kind of did. "Open it up."

Sharon opened the trifold flyer that was filled with pictures of older people smiling, eating, playing cards, swimming . . . "It's a retirement home?"

"A retirement community," Kay corrected. "I wouldn't be surrounded by young people, but people my own age."

"Old people."

Kay didn't like her disparaging tone. "In case you didn't notice, *we* are old people."

Sharon shrugged. "You can call me 'old' — which is a matter of years — but don't ever call me 'elderly' — which is a matter of capability." She shuddered.

Kay had never thought of the difference, but had to admit there was one. "Fair enough."

Sharon skimmed the entire brochure. "You think *this* is going to impress Wally?"

"I'm not trying to impress Wally."

"Aren't you?"

Was she? She hadn't seen him in person since the divorce, except for one time at Price Chopper in the ice cream aisle.

The doorbell rang.

"Hey, maybe you do have friends," Sharon said as they both went inside.

Kay peered through the peephole. Her stomach clenched. She opened the door.

To Wally.

"Hey, Kay," he said. He was carrying a box. "Can I come in?"

No. Absolutely not! She stepped aside and let him in.

"Oh, hi, Sharon," he said. "Long time no see."

"Can't say it's been long enough," she said.

He held the box out to Kay. "We were unpacking from our cruise and Janice was rearranging things to make room for our souvenirs, and she found a bunch of your old frou-frous."

Kay couldn't imagine what they were. "If I haven't missed them by now . . ."

"Maybe. But I thought it would be nice to bring them by." He looked past her and scoped out the apartment. "Not as big as you're used to, huh."

"Really, Wally? And why is that?" Kay grabbed the box away from him.

He put his hands up in feigned surrender in a way she'd seen a hundred times. He knew very well his words would hurt. "Just sayin'."

Sharon stepped forward. "I think you've managed to overstay your welcome in record time. Go."

"That's what I get for doing Kay a favor?"

"I don't need any favors from you." Kay nudged him toward the door. "You haven't seen fit to visit me in the past year, and we've barely spoken, so why the visit now?"

"I told you." He nodded at the box.

Kay handed Sharon the box to hold, ripped the lid off, and took out a pair of brightly-colored fish candleholders she and Wally had bought on a trip to Cancun thirty years previous. "These? You came over here to give me these stupid, ugly candle holders?"

"You bought 'em."

"In the Eighties." She shoved the candleholders into his hands. "Sharon was right. It's time for you to go. Get outta here." She pushed him the final few inches out the door and shut it in his face. A moment later she opened the door and tossed the box into the hall.

Then Kay leaned against the closed door, totally spent. "The gall of that man."

"Those fish things were really ugly."

Kay shook her head. "He didn't come to give me those, or even to see where I live. He came to show off his weight loss, his hair, and his tan."

"Aww, Kay." Sharon pulled her into an embrace. "Don't give him the power to hurt you. You're done with all that."

Kay nodded against Sharon's shoulder. "I thought I was, but it still hurts."

Sharon took a step back and held Kay's shoulders at arm's length. "You *will* be happy again. I know it."

"How?"

Sharon grinned. "Happy Trails. 'Start your happy life' and all that."

It *did* seem like the logical next step.

** ** **

After Sharon left, Kay spent the rest of her Saturday watching TV. She flipped from sappy romances, to crime shows, to watching a chef making raspberry cheesecake, to a shopping channel offering wigs and makeovers.

The only show that caught her eye more than a few minutes was the old Disney cartoon, "Cinderella." She tuned in just as the Fairy Godmother turned the ragamuffin Cinderella into a stunning princess. Bibbidi-bobbidi-boo.

"If only I had a Fairy Godmother to change the ragamuffin Kay into a princess."

On impulse she turned back to the shopping channel and was drawn into the promises of "A new you!"

A new me. A better me.

Suddenly, she sat forward on the couch. Since nobody liked the old Kay, why not make herself over into a new Kay?

Kay. It's such a boring name.

The woman getting the makeover was named Katerina.

Katerina.

It sounded exotic, like someone who'd gone on dozens of cruises around the world.

Someone who would own a wig.

Or maybe more than one.

Happy Trails promised to be the perfect place for a new beginning. But Kay Volkov wouldn't be moving to Happy Trails, Katerina Volkov would.

Chapter Four

Accosta

God has come to save me.
I will trust in him and not be afraid.
The Lord God is my strength and my song;
he has given me victory.
Isaiah 12: 2

The last of the congregation filed past the jam and jelly table that was set up in the narthex every Sunday.

"That appears to be the last of them," Accosta said.

Accosta's friend, Tessa Klein, stacked the money into neat piles. "Do an inventory of what's left," she said.

Accosta counted each flavor and handed the totals to Tessa. "We're getting low on cherry-rhubarb."

"That's always a favorite, but people will have to wait until spring for Mary Jo's garden to grow some more."

Wayne approached the table and began putting the leftovers in a box. "In June we had six boxes and now we're down to one. Well done, ladies."

Tessa put rubber bands around the different denominations, her knuckles as swollen with arthritis as Accosta's were. "We've made over $1200 for the Sister Circle House. Whatever jams we have left after next week we'll donate to them."

Evelyn joined them, overhearing the last sentence. "What are you going to sell after that?"

Accosta answered because it had been her idea. "We're going to sell spice packets to put in apple cider."

"And pumpkin butter," Tessa added. She pushed back from the table and hooked her ever-present handbag over her arm.

Evelyn chuckled. "The way you hold your purse . . . you remind me of a Black Queen Elizabeth."

Tessa stood up straighter and touched the rim of her orange brimmed hat. "I saw her wear a hat like mine too."

"Ever classic," Accosta said. "The both of you."

Wayne got out his phone. "Come out from behind the table and let me take a picture of you two. You're like ebony and ivory."

Accosta and Tessa exchanged a look, then smiled. "I guess we are," Tessa said. They posed arm in arm, the same height and nearly the same age. Then Tessa added, "I need to loan you some of my hats, Accosta."

"I have never worn hats."

"It's never too late to start. You'd look good in a hat."

"Hats do make a woman look regal," Evelyn said.

"As intended." Tessa held her chin high.

Accosta had never, ever felt regal. She'd lived a very unregal life. If Evelyn and Wayne hadn't bought her dilapidated house ten years ago and turned it into a woman's shelter, it probably would have fallen down around her.

Tessa held the zippered cash bag against her chest. "I need to take this to the front office for safe keeping."

Wayne lifted the box of jam. "I'll be right behind you."

A few minutes later they headed out to their cars. Wayne offered Accosta his arm—which she gladly took. But then Tessa stopped her with an invitation. "Why not come with me to Happy Trails, Accosta? You can be my guest for the Sunday buffet and then you can pick out a hat or two to try on."

Accosta checked with Evelyn. "Would that be all right?"

"Of course," Evelyn said. "We're just having leftovers. Enjoy."

"You two are welcome as well," Tessa said.

"Thank you, but no," Wayne said. "Another time."

Tessa flipped her hand at them. "Your loss." She extended her hand to Accosta. "This way, Ivory."

** ** **

The buffet was grand. Accosta had never seen so much food. Although Evelyn was a good cook, the meals at Peerbaugh Place were classic home-cooking like meatloaf or tuna and noodles, with a little apple crisp for dessert. Accosta had never seen—or eaten—chicken cordon bleu or orange roughy in dill sauce. And she had never tasted French coconut pie, or lemon tarts. She did her best to try a little of everything. She wished she could bring a doggie bag back to Evelyn and Wayne.

After eating they walked to Tessa's apartment. Even the hallways at Happy Trails were lovely, with Queen Anne chairs in little alcoves, and a much-appreciated handrail. Tessa had lived here six months, but Accosta had never been past the dining room.

Once inside her apartment, Tessa got right to the subject. "I can't believe you've never worn hats," she said. "It was a part of our generation."

Tessa made it sound like a character flaw, but Accosta didn't take offense. Being tart as a lemon tart was Tessa's way. But she did remember one time . . . "I did wear a hat with my going away suit after our wedding."

"Of course you did. It was essential." Tessa led Accosta into her bedroom and motioned to a chair. "I bet it was a fascinator with a veil."

"I haven't heard that term in years, but yes, it was! My mother made me a plum velvet suit with a matching hat that perched on my head just so. It had a veil that barely covered my eyes."

"That sounds beautiful. Do you still have it?"

She shook her head. She hadn't thought about that hat in years. "I'm not sure what became of it." Accosta felt guilty for losing track of it. And her wedding suit.

Tessa took a hatbox down from a shelf in her closet, but didn't open it. "Of course you know. Choices were made. When your house flooded and Wayne and Evelyn found you sleeping on your porch, you sold the house. You had to do some drastic downsizing to move into a single room at Peerbaugh Place."

Accosta nodded. "You're right. Things had to go." She didn't like to think about the negatives. The whole crisis had turned into a wonderful positive. "Evelyn and Wayne saved me." She smiled. "I was underwater in more ways than one."

"I suppose you were."

Accosta pushed any pesky regrets away and drank in a deep breath of peace. "God supplies all my needs from His glorious riches."

Tessa paused a moment with her fingers resting on her lips. Then her eyes brightened and she said, "Philippians four-something, right?"

"Four-nineteen." Accosta chuckled.

"We should have a verse-off some time," Tessa said.

"A contest?"

"I'm always up for some friendly competition."

Maybe Tessa was, but Accosta disliked competitions—especially spiritual ones. She hated the idea of displaying Bible knowledge in order to win something in an I'm-more-godly-than-you display. She changed the subject by pointing to the hat box. "You wanted to show me a hat?"

Tessa whipped the lid off the ornate box as though unveiling a treasure. "Look at this one. It's really something."

Accosta caught herself before a chuckle escaped. "My, my. You are right about that."

Tessa took the purple pillbox hat out of the box. The front was swept with large white and purple feathers. "Let's see how it looks on you."

On me?

Before Accosta could object, Tessa placed the hat on her head. "Oh yes. Oh my. Come to the mirror and see."

Accosta didn't have to see her reflection to know that she would never ever wear such a flashy hat. But she humored Tessa and looked in the large mirror above the dresser.

I look like a 1920s flapper girl.

Tessa adjusted Accosta's wispy silver hair around the hat. "It's just lovely. You should wear it to church on Sunday. Do you have a dress to match?"

Absolutely not. Which might be her way out. "I'm afraid I don't own anything purple."

"Something black perhaps?"

"You know me. I'm more of a pastel granny. I don't do bold colors—or black" She decided to turn her rejection into a compliment. "It's definitely a Tessa hat. Dramatic and bold. Even a bit audacious."

Tessa nodded in agreement, then took one last look at Accosta's reflection. "You're right. Let's find you something else."

If we must.

** ** **

Accosta stepped out of Tessa's boat of a car, ducking a bit to accommodate the white wide-brimmed hat Tessa had decided was perfect for her.

Evelyn came out to the porch to greet her. "Look at you," she said.

No, don't look at me. Please.

Evelyn came down to the sidewalk to help Accosta navigate the steps. Tessa called out the car window, "You should come over next, Evelyn. I have the cutest tilt-hat with pink feathers."

"Don't do it," Accosta said under her breath.

Evelyn glanced over her shoulder and gave Tessa a brief wave. "We'll see you soon."

Wayne met them at the door. He grinned.

"Don't you dare," Accosta said to him.

He chuckled anyway. "It's quite becoming."

"It's *becoming* a nuisance." Accosta turned to Evelyn. "Please help me get it off. There are hat pins . . ."

They stood in the foyer and Evelyn found the two pins and lifted the hat from Accosta's head. "It *is* beautiful."

"I'm not saying it isn't." Accosta smoothed her hair in the hall mirror. "And it's better than the beret, the purple feather pillbox, and the lacy straw hat Tessa tried on me before we got to this one."

"She means no harm," Wayne said.

Accosta took a deep breath and smoothed her dress. "And no harm was done," she said. "Some people—like Tessa—are hat people. I, however, am not." She headed to her rocker.

Evelyn nodded toward the kitchen. "Are you hungry?"

Accosta shook her head vehemently and lowered herself down. "Fiddle-dee, I won't be hungry for a week. That Sunday buffet could feed a third-world country." She rocked up and back. "All I need is a rock and a read."

Wayne and Evelyn exchanged a look. "Before you get started on your book, we need to discuss something with you."

Uh-oh. She tried to read their expressions—especially Evelyn's—but they looked non-committal. "Is it good news or bad?"

"It's not bad news," Evelyn said. "It's just—"

Accosta suddenly felt tired. "I'd prefer you just say it."

Wayne took over. "We got the estimate for the remodel and it's more than we're comfortable spending."

Accosta closed her eyes for a brief moment of acceptance. She had guessed as much. She was a little disappointed that the remodel of a bedroom and bath on the first floor wasn't going to happen, for it would have been nice to avoid the stairs. But she wasn't going to let them know how she felt. "It was nice of you to look into it, but obviously, God wants me to get my exercise." She made a bodybuilder's pose. "I'm stronger than I look."

"We'll get you the walkers for up and down, and Wayne and I are very willing to help you navigate the stairs."

She hated to bother them any more than she already did but had little choice. "We'll work it out."

Wayne stood and moved to the mantel—which through the years was *the* place for anyone to make big announcements.

This time was no different.

He cleared his throat and said, "How would you like to move into an apartment at Happy Trails?"

Accosta was taken aback. "I've honestly never considered such a thing. It has to be expensive." She imagined it would cost hundreds of thousands of dollars. "I don't have much money."

"I know," Wayne said. "And we're not promising anything, but if you're game, we want to look into it. It won't hurt to be informed."

Evelyn piped up, "We want to make sure we cover all the bases. You're a dear woman, and we want you to be safe."

Accosta wanted to be safe too, and the idea of Happy Trails was kind of exciting. She'd gain weight eating like she had today. And Tessa's apartment was really nice.

But being so close to Tessa? And more hats?

Yet even if it was fun to think about, Accosta knew it wasn't going to happen. She vowed to be extra careful on the stairs.

Chapter Five

Accosta

> The Holy Spirit helps us in our weakness.
> For example, we don't know what God wants us to pray for.
> But the Holy Spirit prays for us with groanings
> that cannot be expressed in words.
> Romans 8: 26

This time when Accosta entered Happy Trails was different from other times. She took in the welcoming foyer with fresh eyes.

This could be my new home.
It probably wouldn't be.
But maybe . . .

She, Evelyn, and Wayne were greeted by the executive director, Mrs. Halvorson. She shook their hands and looked at each of them, eye to eye. Accosta was impressed.

"We are so glad you're here," she said. "Would you like to take a tour?"

"Maybe later," Wayne said.

As much as Accosta wanted to see everything Happy Trails had to offer, they had agreed to talk money first. If it wasn't financially feasible for her to move in, that would be that. Otherwise it would be like showing Accosta her presents under the Christmas tree, then telling her she couldn't have any of them.

"We'd like to know some specifics first," Evelyn added.

"Very well," Mrs. Halvorson said. "Let's go into my office and discuss options."

Accosta took one step toward the office, then stopped. "If you don't mind, I think I'd like to wait out here."

Evelyn gave her a confused look. "But we're discussing *your* life."

Accosta shook her head. "I trust you and Wayne to represent me well." She made it a point to smile so they knew she was okay with it.

And she was. Mostly.

Evelyn smiled back wistfully, and ran her hand up and down Accosta's upper arm. "We'll be back soon."

Accosta took a seat in the large foyer area and declined a bottle of water that was offered. She had work to do. Praying work.

Luckily, she could concentrate as there wasn't much traffic going in and out. She closed her eyes and called on the Almighty to handle things. *If You want me to remain at Peerbaugh Place, let us know. If You want me to move here? Let it work out. If You want me to move somewhere else . . . ?*

Accosta opened her eyes. She was out of practice making big decisions. She hadn't made many decisions at all in the past ten years other than what sweater to wear or which book to read next. When Wayne and Evelyn came into her life, she'd happily relinquished the decision-duties to them. Did she want them to fix up her old house? Sure, if they thought that was the way to go. Have it be used as a safe house for abused women and kids? Perfect. Move into Peerbaugh Place permanently? Sounds good.

For all those years, Accosta had let Wayne and Evelyn make the meals, do the laundry, and wait on her every need.

They hadn't even been married at the time. Which meant . . . Accosta suffered an inner gasp. Which meant, they hadn't been alone as a couple since they got married.

That was unacceptable! Accosta closed her eyes and amended her prayers. *Lord, I just realized how selfish I've been by accepting the kindnesses of my friends while offering little in return. And now that I need more help getting around? I can't add to their burden. I really need to move out and give Evelyn and Wayne their freedom and privacy.* She glanced toward the office door — which was still shut. *Please let there be a way for me to move into Happy Trails, for their sake as well as mine.*

Accosta's prayers meandered from front to back and around the sides to start over again, leaving her head spinning. She trusted God to finetune the desires of her heart to match His.

She was startled when she heard a door open. Wayne and Evelyn came out — without Mrs. Halvorson.

That couldn't be good.

Accosta leaned on her cane and stood. "So? How did it go?"

Evelyn had a transparent face, so Accosta knew the answer immediately. "Not the best," Evelyn said.

Wayne nodded toward the entrance. "Why don't we—?"

"Well done!" They heard a familiar voice. They looked down the hall and saw Tessa walking with a woman who carried a purse and a notebook. She was clearly on her way out.

Tessa continued her conversation. "I'm glad you got the measurements you needed, Katerina. I can't wait to have you move in. We'll have a grand old time." Tessa stopped talking when she spotted Accosta, Evelyn, and Wayne. "Have a good day. I'll see you soon."

The woman left and Tessa headed toward them, her cane marking her speed.

"Well, well. It's a small world. First I spot Katerina, a newbie I met during her first tour of the place. And now you three? What are you doing here?"

Evelyn slipped her arm around her husband's. "Just checking the place out."

"For you and Wayne?"

They seemed surprised as they both shook their heads. "Of course not. For Accosta."

"That would be marvelous!" Tessa said. "I can't wait for you to move in. Why didn't you tell me your plans when we were trying on hats?"

"It wasn't . . ." Accosta said.

"I'm going to have to stop you right there, Tessa," Wayne said. "Unfortunately, it isn't going to be possible." He looked at Accosta. "First off, there are no vacancies at the moment, and secondly . . . I'm sorry, Accosta. We tried to make it work, but the finances just don't jibe."

And there it was. She'd been wise not to dream about it, yet she was a little disappointed. But trust in God she would. The Almighty always knew best.

Accosta felt their gaze, waiting for her reaction. She couldn't let them feel bad about the money. She knew the facts. So she drew from a deep place in her heart and touched Wayne's arm. "Well fiddle-dee. Don't either of you worry about it one minute," she said. "While you were in the office I prayed for God's will in the matter." She spread her hands. "And here it is." She gave Evelyn an encouraging smile. "I am ever so grateful for your gracious hospitality all these years, but it seems you're going to have to put up with me a while longer."

"Oh you," Evelyn said. "We love having you with us. I'd already told Wayne the house wouldn't be the same without you."

"God's will or not," Tessa said. "I'm sad you're not moving in."

Me too. Accosta tried not to be disappointed with God's will, but she was. She really was.

** ** **

Accosta was glad Evelyn and Wayne didn't spend the rest of the day talking about what *wouldn't* happen at Happy Trails. She appreciated the mindset of "what's done is done."

Instead, they sat around the kitchen table and worked on a puzzle that pictured boxes of cereal.

"My favorite was Captain Crunch," Wayne said.

Evelyn made a face. "The sugar coated my teeth something awful."

"Exactly. How about you, Accosta?"

She pointed to a box of her favorite. "Tony the Tiger. Frosted Flakes."

"A good contender," Wayne said.

"You two have such a sweet tooth," Evelyn said. "I liked Honey Comb."

"And that *doesn't* have sugar?"

Evelyn shrugged just as the phone rang. She got up to answer it. "Well hi Tessa . . . now? I don't know. We were just there . . ." She got quiet and started nodding her head as Tessa talked through the phone. "I suppose. We'll see you soon."

"What was that about?" Wayne asked.

"Tessa wants the three of us to come over. Right now."

"Why?"

"She didn't say. But she was very adamant."

Wayne pushed back from the table. "When is Tessa *not* adamant?"

"I hope it doesn't involve hats," Accosta said.

** ** **

Tessa answered the door of her apartment before Wayne could rap his knuckles for the second knock. She was beaming.

"Come in, come in!"

They went inside and, at Tessa's instruction, sat in the living room.

"What's going on?" Evelyn asked.

Tessa remained standing—all five feet of her. She was clearly excited about something because she couldn't stop smiling.

"Tell us before you burst," Wayne said.

She sighed, then extended her hand to Accosta. "Oh I can't decide how I want to say it. I have changed my mind so many times about how to tell you." She looked toward a door and grinned. "Let's do it this way. Accosta? Come with me."

Tessa led Accosta into a room filled with all sorts of souvenirs, maps, and pictures from Tessa's trips around the world. Was she announcing another trip?

"You have quite a collection here," Wayne said. "Your time creating the Sister Circle Network led you to a lot of different countries."

"Thirteen, to be exact." Tessa looked around the room proudly.

"Are you leaving again?" Accosta asked.

Tessa huffed. "No, I'm not. This has nothing to do with the Sister Circle Network. Can I speak now?"

Evelyn chuckled. "Sorry. Yes. Tell us what's on your mind."

She linked arms with Accosta. "Accosta, imagine all of these mementos packed away. Clean walls. Open space."

That didn't make any sense. Tessa had always been proud of her travels. "Why would you do that?"

"To empty the room so your things can be moved in."

"My things?"

Tessa beamed. "This would be your bedroom. You'd move in here. With me."

"What?" Accosta stared at her, trying to process it all.

"What are you talking about?" Wayne asked.

"I'm asking Accosta to move into this apartment with me. Accosta, what do you think?"

"Share your apartment?" Evelyn asked.

Tessa huffed again. "You people. It's not a difficult concept. Yes, she would share my apartment."

"We'd be roommates?" Accosta asked.

"Exactly."

"Is that allowed?" Wayne asked.

"It most certainly is. After you left I came into this room to get something and suddenly had a revelation that it could be Accosta's room. After all, I don't need all this space. So I hurried to talk with Mrs. Halvorson and she said Accosta can most certainly move in! We'd share a 'companion apartment.'"

Accosta pressed her hand against her heart, which was pounding with excitement. "Really?"

"Really, old friend."

"What would you do with all your souvenirs?" Accosta asked.

Tessa left Accosta's side to walk into the room. "I figure we can put a bed here with a bedside table . . . a dresser over there, and a chair . . ."

Accosta put a hand to her mouth, fighting back tears. "You'd give up this room for me?"

"Of course I would, silly." She shooed everyone away from the doorway. "Let's go back in the living room and I'll tell you what we worked out."

As they discussed finances, it became a reality. Tessa was very generous and explained that all Accosta would have to pay for was her food plan and a small portion of the monthly fee. "It should easily be covered by your Social Security check."

Accosta felt like she was in a dream. Moving into this fabulous place? She just sat there, her head shaking back and forth.

"What's wrong?" Tessa asked.

"It's beyond understanding. Your generosity, the room . . . I prayed God would let me live here, but when it wasn't possible I accepted that as His will, but now . . ."

"Now, it's clearly His will that you live with me. When do you want to move in?"

Suddenly big decisions seemed possible again. Accosta looked at Wayne and Evelyn. "Next weekend?" she asked.

"I can get Collier to help," Wayne said.

"And Ringo," Evelyn added. "He has a pickup."

"I don't have that many things," Accosta said.

"Furniture!" Evelyn exclaimed. "You can have the furniture in your room and—"

"But what about renters?" Accosta said. "You need that furniture for them."

Wayne waved off her concern. "I have a better idea. Leave the old stuff behind and buy new furniture."

It was too much to fathom. "I haven't shopped for furniture in . . . sixty years?"

"Then it's about time," Wayne said.

After discussing what she would need, Tessa announced it was time they went home because she had handbell practice. "You could join the Jingle Bells too, Accosta," Tessa said. "Can you read music?"

"Not a note."

"Then . . . maybe not. But you can listen to us practice. And I'll help you check out all of the other activities around here." She led them to the door and put her hand on Accosta's arm. "I just thought of another special bonus of moving in with me."

"What's that?"

"You'd have unlimited access to my hats."

Joy.

On the drive home they all talked at once, amazed and astounded by the way God had worked everything out.

Wearing a few hats was a small price to pay.

*** *** ***

That night, Accosta lay in bed and admired how the moon cast interesting shadows across her bed. The same bed and shadows for ten years. She'd been content in this room. Happy and thankful. But now . . .

She smiled and clasped her hands in prayer. "It's best I just quote Your own book, Lord. Ephesians, I believe . . ." She took a fresh breath and recited two of her favorite verses. "'Now to him who is able to do immeasurably more than all we ask or imagine, according to his power that is at work within us, to him be glory in the church and in Christ Jesus throughout all generations, for ever and ever!'"

Amen.

Chapter Six

Evelyn

Let us run with perseverance
the race marked out for us.
Hebrews 12:1

Wayne brought a box up from the basement of Peerbaugh Place. "This is the last of them." He set it on the kitchen table.

Evelyn read the label. "It says 'Old Photos.'"

Accosta rubbed her hands together like a child getting a cookie. "Of all my boxes, this is my biggest treasure."

Evelyn removed the lid expecting to find photo albums. Instead she found hundreds of photos tossed willy-nilly. "Oh my."

"What's wrong?" Accosta pushed herself to standing to see. "Phew. They look fine. You made me think they were ruined."

"Sorry. I just didn't think they'd all be loose."

Accosta took a handful and sat down. "I always planned on putting them into albums, but never got around to it."

Wayne took a handful and glanced through them. "I understand never-got-around things. Everybody has some of those." He focused on a photo. "Is this you and your son?" He angled it so she could see.

She beamed. "That's me and Eugene when he was about three." She checked out the back of the photo. "See here? Eugene Rand 1960. I may not have put them in albums, but I was pretty good about writing names and dates on the back of them."

"It's good you did," Evelyn said, digging deeper in the box. "Grandma Calhoun, 1923."

"My grandmother. She came over from Ireland. And this one here is their house in Kansas City." Accosta showed Evelyn the next photo.

Wayne tossed a few pictures back in the box. "Well, ladies, if that's all the help you need right now, I have my Meals on Wheels deliveries to make."

Evelyn gestured for him to lean down to her so she could give him a quick kiss. "You're a good man, Wayne Wellington," she said.

"All in a day's work, ma'am."

He left them with a smile.

As Evelyn dug through the box a little deeper she got an idea. What if she could organize the photos, scan them, and make one of those hardbound photo books for Accosta? As a surprise.

Toward that end . . . "How about we divide the photos according to decades? That would make them more meaningful when Eugene gets them some day."

Accosta looked up from a photo. "He won't want them."

Evelyn knew they weren't close, but . . . "That's harsh. He might."

Accosta's hands fell to her lap. "As a trucker he's on the road most every day of the year. *Things* don't matter much to him. His wife works full-time and his kids are in college. They all lead busy lives. They don't want my old stuff."

"But your grandkids might."

She shook her head. "They're focused on the here and now. They have no interest in any long-passed relatives."

How about a still-here grandmother? "If memory serves, they haven't been to see you in a couple years."

"Four years. Carson Creek was near one of his routes, so Eugene stopped by on that Christmas Mae made the popovers that deflated?"

"I remember that year."

"He stopped in but didn't stay for dinner."

He'd only stayed long enough for eggnog, then had handed his mom a box of peanut brittle—that she couldn't eat because of her dentures. After less than an hour, he'd left Accosta with an awkward hug and a "Merry Christmas."

"Even if they don't get here often, they might really appreciate the pictures. Some of them are of Eugene. And his dad."

Accosta shuffled through a few more photos, without really seeing them. It was so sad.

"Did Eugene have cousins? They might appreciate the pictures."

"Yes to the cousins, but as for them wanting pictures? Again, I'd guess no. One lives in Canada and another in Florida. And their parents are gone." Accosta sighed deeply. "I've outlived my generation. Do you know how lonely that feels?"

"It must be very hard." Evelyn wanted to say something to comfort her. "You're part of what people call the Grand Generation."

"I don't know about that."

Evelyn touched her hand, needing Accosta to cheer up. "Your generation lived through the most drastic changes in society, from not having electricity and running water in your house to—"

"That's the truth. Life on the family farm was hard. I hated using the outhouse in the winter."

"Exactly. You lived through half a dozen wars, rationing, the development of television, the Internet, microwaves—"

"And men walking on the moon. I remember watching that on TV like it was yesterday."

Evelyn was glad to see her mood lighten. "You should be proud of all the changes you've endured. You were forced to adapt." She touched the box of photos. "If no one else in your family wants these photos, I want them."

"Why?"

"Because you're you, and . . . I love you."

Accosta bumped her shoulder into Evelyn's. "I love you too. You're a dear friend, but so much more."

"Sisters forever," Evelyn said.

"And ever." Accosta gazed at the box. "I do need to tell Eugene my new address."

"Would you like to call him?"

Accosta hesitated.

Evelyn retrieved her own address book. "I have his number in here."

Accosta's hesitation changed to a no. "You know I'm not a phone person. I've never been comfortable with chit-chat. Eugene's not good at it either so it's nothing but awkward."

"Then drop him a line and let him know. And invite him to bring the family by."

"We'll see."

** ** **

The entirety of Accosta's worldly possessions were packed in the back of Ringo's pickup with room to spare. The only piece of furniture was the rocker from the parlor—a gift from Evelyn. A new set of bedroom furniture had already been delivered to Happy Trails.

Before Accosta got in Evelyn and Wayne's car, she paused to look back at Peerbaugh Place. She cupped her hand against the glare of the sun and lifted her gaze to her bedroom windows.

Evelyn watched her close her eyes for a few moments. She could only imagine the emotions flowing through her. Not only had she lived here ten years, she was moving to Happy Trails in what would probably be her last move. That fact was the very large elephant in the room.

Wayne helped Accosta in the car, closed the door, and got in the driver's seat. "All right, ladies. Are we ready for a new adventure?"

"We are." Accosta's voice was surprisingly strong.

As they pulled away, Evelyn said, "You seem to be doing so well. I find it hard dealing with *lasts*. This morning was your last breakfast in Peerbaugh Place. It makes me sad." She quickly added, "Even as I'm happy for you."

Accosta shook her head slowly. "I stopped keeping track of *lasts* a long time ago."

"Why?" Wayne asked.

"Because they hurt too much and don't do a body any good whatsoever."

"That's probably true," Evelyn said.

"It is true. That's why I refuse to think of *lasts* until after-the-fact. Until I'm already living in a *first* or at least a *next*. By then, the pain has faded."

Evelyn was impressed. "That makes sense."

"Try it." Accosta pointed toward the front windshield. "Don't think about what was, think of what's next. I'm moving into a new apartment—my first apartment ever!" She slapped her hands together and looked upward. "God be praised!"

When she put it that way . . . Evelyn agreed. God be praised.

** ** **

That evening Evelyn and Wayne walked into a dark Peerbaugh Place.

"I can't believe we didn't leave the lights on," Wayne said, as he switched on the lamp in the foyer.

Evelyn hung her jacket on the coat rack. "It was good we got Accosta settled. But I never expected to be gone all day."

"I never expected we'd stay long enough to eat dinner there too."

"At least I didn't have to cook." The older Evelyn got the less she liked cooking. She provided the hospital guests with breakfast choices, but the rest of the meals were on their own. "And now, with Accosta gone, it's just the two of us."

Wayne led her to the couch. He put an arm around her shoulders and she nestled into the crook of his arm. "That's not so bad, is it?"

"I didn't mean it like that, it's just . . ." She sat upright and faced him. "Do you realize this is the first time we haven't had a tenant since we got married?"

He studied the ceiling as though he saw a calendar there. "You're right. I moved in right after our wedding. And at the time I think Accosta, Ursola, and Jody were here?"

"Jody had just moved out when her daughter's surgery was over and she was able to go home."

"That's right."

"And then Ursola left and began running the Sister Circle House." She paused, remembering all of the different life stories that had come through the house. "If I let myself, I could feel really tired thinking of the revolving door of tenants and guests."

"Too many to count."

She shook her head. "Thirty-four."

"You *did* count."

"I did. I listed them in a three-ring binder, and have notes on all of them."

"Wow. Look at you."

She shrugged. "I may occasionally complain about the work but I do love having people around. So many different women, so many stories. There were so many I could write a book."

"Maybe you should do just that?"

Evelyn put a hand to her chest. "I am not a writer."

"You could be."

The idea was kind of fascinating, but Evelyn shoved it aside. "I need to concentrate on the present, not the past."

"Mmm," Wayne said. "I guess *presently* we can open up Accosta's room for another hospital guest."

At the moment the thought of that was too much to bear. "I can't do it," Evelyn said. "Not yet. What if Accosta isn't happy at Happy Trails?"

"Who wouldn't be happy at Happy Trails?" Wayne said.

"What if she isn't happy being Tessa's roommate?"

He hedged. "That's something else entirely." But he quickly added, "You saw her at dinner. Laughing, smiling . . . she'll be very happy there." He flicked the tip of Evelyn's nose. "She's not moving back here, Ev. And that's a good thing."

Evelyn sighed and snuggled into her husband again; her favorite place in the world. Her safe place. "You're right. But my logical self lags behind my emotional self. I don't like change."

This time Wayne sat upright, gently forcing her to sit on her own. "You, don't like change? You, who's run a boarding house for over twelve years? You, who's dealt with thirty-four tenants. Tenants who were ever changing. You handled tenants who were prima donas, angry, willful, disrespectful, annoying—"

All true. "But most were kind, sincere, and considerate."

"Them too. The point is, you've dealt with change every day."

He was right. "My daily life *has* been full of changes."

"Which you've handled with grace and generosity."

She shrugged. *If he said so.*

Wayne would have none of it. "No shrugging. Repeat after me, 'I handle change with grace and generosity.'"

Evelyn knew he would pester her until she repeated the words. "I handle change with grace and generosity."

"Exactly."

But she didn't quite believe it, no matter how many times he made her repeat the words. "I accept change, but that doesn't mean I like it."

"Oh you." He pulled her back under his arm.

Evelyn loved the sound of his heartbeat and the smell of his aftershave. "Did *you* mind?"

"Mind what?"

"Not having a house of our own? Moving in here with me?"

"Anyone can have a house of their own. It's so . . . done."

"But I pulled you into my complicated life."

"That, you did. But I *didn't* mind, Evelyn Peerbaugh Wellington, because Peerbaugh Place is a part of you. I knew that when I met you. Your kind heart and chutzpah is one of the reasons I fell in love with you."

"Ditto." She wrapped her free arm across his chest, claiming this lovely man as her own. *That* would never change.

Chapter Seven

Kay

> They delight in deception
> even as they eat with you in your fellowship meals.
> 2 Peter 2: 13

Kay—Katerina—Volkov watched the moving truck pull away from the curb. It was a weird sensation to know that the sum of her life's possessions could be packed in one not-so-big truck and her car. It was disconcerting. Shouldn't there be *more*?

More of so many things.

Kay went back in the apartment that had been her home for the past year. Sharon knelt in the empty living room beside a box marked *Breakables*. She taped it shut and stood. "This is the last of the stuff you didn't trust to the movers. But I have a question."

"Shoot."

"Why is it labeled 'Katerina Volkov'? I've never heard you use that name."

She hadn't told Sharon about her intricate plan to become someone completely new at Happy Trails, and now wasn't the time. Instead, she made up a lie. "My grandmother used to call me that. I like it. Don't you?"

Sharon shrugged. "Sounds a bit hoity-toity."

As planned.

"I'll put the box in your car—your *new* car." She paused at the door. "I still don't understand why you traded in your SUV."

Kay drove an SUV, Katerina drives a Mercedes. "I've always wanted a Mercedes. And it's used."

"You've never cared one whit about cars, but . . . whatever floats your boat."

As soon as she left, Kay hurried to the bedroom to slip on one of her wigs. She *did* value Sharon's opinion—not that it would change her mind about anything. The course of Kay's transformation was already in motion.

When Sharon returned, she did a double take. "What did you suddenly do to your hair?"

She didn't sound enthused. Kay ran her fingers through the tips of her tousled wig. "Do you like it?"

Sharon shrugged. "The color is nice. But a wig?"

"Wigs. Plural. I've bought several to wear wherever the wind takes me." She almost sounded eloquent but quickly came back to earth. "You know I have zero talent doing my hair."

"So that's the reason you cut it so short?"

"Exactly. Now I can easily wear my wigs."

Sharon made a face. "I agree you needed a new 'do, but isn't this going a little far?"

"Happy Trails is a new beginning, so I thought it was appropriate to be a new me."

"I like the old you."

"I'm the old me too. But don't begrudge me for a few changes, Shar. I need to do it this way. Don't give me grief about it."

Sharon shrugged. "Life's put you through the wringer the past few years. If you have to wear wigs to move on, knock yourself out." She checked her watch. "We'd better get going or the movers won't know what to do at the other end."

Now came the tricky part. "Actually . . . I think I'd like to handle the other end by myself. You've been so much help to me, but starting over means I need to do this on my own."

Sharon eyed her suspiciously. "Why don't you want me to see your new place?"

"I do want you to see it. I definitely do." Kay slipped a hand around her arm. "Let me get my feet set and then I'll have you over."

"I wish you weren't moving ninety minutes away. I'll never see you."

Unfortunately, distance from her old life was a necessity.

** ** **

After changing into a crisp pair of chinos, a Tommy Hilfiger shirt, and new Gucci mules she'd found at the outlet store, Kay drove to the Happy Trails Retirement Village in Carson Creek, Kansas—just south of Kansas City. As she pulled up to the building, she was met by Mrs. Halvorson, the smiling representative who'd sold her the unit. Two male underlings stood nearby, like servants at the ready.

Mrs. Halvorson opened Kay's car door and helped her out. "Welcome, Mrs. Volkov. Welcome to your new home."

"Thank you so much." She saw the moving truck idling in the parking lot. "Can someone instruct my men, please?"

"Of course." The woman waved at one of her workers and he jogged over to the truck. "Well then, if you get me your keys, I will have Ted park and unpack your car. Is that agreeable?"

"That's very nice of you." She flashed Ted a smile and handed him the car keys to her Mercedes. "Take care of her," she said.

"Yes, ma'am."

Mrs. Halvorson swept her hand toward the front door. She pushed a button and the double doors opened for them.

She introduced Kay to a few of the office people whom she'd met before. They were all very friendly and accommodating.

Kay received her key and Mrs. Halvorson accompanied her to the top floor, to her one-bedroom apartment.

"And here we are," she said as she unlocked the door.

Kay had seen the apartment twice, once before the sale and once to take measurements for furniture. She'd been pleased to see that they'd replaced the carpet and a faulty faucet in the bathroom. It certainly was in better shape than her old apartment.

Kay wandered through the small kitchen, eating area, and living room, ending up in the bedroom and bath. She nodded and kept her smile steady. "It's very nice."

They backtracked to the kitchen where Mrs. Halvorson pointed out a welcome basket with a bottle of water, a Happy Trails mug, snacks, and fruit. "And here is your Happy Trails packet with information about activities, meals, and amenities." She gave Kay her card. "Please let me know if you need anything at all. We have staff who will assist you in hanging pictures or shelves. Again, just call." Her eyes darted to the door. "I believe the first load is arriving."

She was right. The woman exited with a few words to the movers and Kay was left to handle it.

"Where do you want this?" was asked and answered too many times to count.

Her head began to spin but eventually settled down.

There was no turning back now.

** ** **

Within an hour the movers finished, leaving Kay alone with mountains of boxes. If only Sharon was there to help.

But no. Kay had carefully planned this new beginning. She couldn't risk having someone from her past call her out on the new and improved details she'd created for her new life — details that went far beyond a name, a car, and a wig. There were only three life-facts Kay was keeping. Number one, her last name *was* Volkov — a name she'd always enjoyed because it sounded foreign and rich. Number two and three, were the names of her children, Tiffany and Connery. Never mind that her daughter insisted on rejecting the glamour of the jewelry store she was named after by being called Tif. Or that her son, Connery — named after the most ravishing man of all time, Sean Connery — had embraced the tragic nickname "Con" after he became one.

Other than those three names, her life and identity were totally new and had been created with great care. Kay had been set aside as old and of no use to anyone. Katerina had been born, fresh, new, classy, and ready to take on the world.

She stretched out on the couch, much in need of a nap. A year ago when she'd moved, Sharon, Hank, and another friend had done most of the work at her command. Now . . . her eyes wandered around the room, settling on those pesky boxes. They were totally her responsibility and they wouldn't unpack themselves.

There was a knock on her door. A visitor already? "Coming." She stood and smoothed her pin-striped shirt and adjusted her wig.

She opened the door to Tessa Klein, a woman she'd met both times she'd seen the apartment.

Tessa held out a potted cactus. "Happy housewarming from the welcome committee." She pointed her cane toward the interior so Kay had no choice but to step out of her way. She was one hundred pounds of feisty-Black-grandma-spunk. She walked in, her animated eyes scanning the place. "I like this layout because it has space for a small dining table," she said. "However . . . your table is a might large, don't you think?"

It was. Although Kay had measured and planned for furniture placement she'd taken a chance on her table and six chairs—and had obviously miscalculated. "You're right. I should trade it out for something smaller." She placed the cactus on the table.

"Good decision," Tessa said. "But that's a chore for another day." She finally looked at Kay. "So, Katerina. I know moving is a whirlwind, but how are you faring?"

Kay stood taller to suit her newly chosen name. "I'm tired, but I'm doing well, thank you. I am very glad to be here."

"A good attitude. That's the ticket," Tessa said. "I'll let you get back to it, but I wanted to invite you to have dinner with me tonight so you can meet a few of my dearest friends." She turned toward the door. "Five-thirty sharp, in the dining room. We'll see you then."

And she was gone. It took a moment for the air to stop spinning behind her.

** ** **

Kay dressed carefully for dinner because she knew first impressions were lasting. She wore black pants, a black tunic with gold buttons at the shoulders, and gold jewelry to match. Her makeup was done just the way the makeup clerk had shown her— including false eyelashes.

To finish her look, she unlocked the doors of the curio cabinet in her bedroom. Inside were three head-mannequins sporting two of her three wigs. She carefully removed the tousled one she'd worn all day and put it on the empty head. In its place she chose her classy wig that was the same length but sleekly styled. She stood at her mirrored dresser and pulled it into place. With a few practiced moves with fingers and comb she was set. She locked the wig cabinet and placed the key under a porcelain cardinal. A quick spray of Estee perfume and she was ready to go.

"Knock 'em dead, Katerina," she told the mirror.

** ** **

While waiting for Tessa outside the dining room, Kay saw a stunningly handsome man walk down the hall. He was tall with silver hair, and had an elegant look about him. He oozed confidence as though he was used to garnering respect. She smiled at him and he nodded at her.

The hostess said, "Good evening, Mr. Stockton. How's your day been?"

Mr. Stockton. Kay would have to keep track of that one. Kay had given up on any thought of men and romance. But Katerina . . .

"Katerina!" Tessa approached, walking slowly beside a tiny woman who had to be in her nineties.

"Katerina, I'd like you to meet my roommate, Accosta."

Ack-what?

"Accosta, Katerina Volkov."

Katerina knew she would never remember the odd name. She could usually remember the first letter of a name, but quickly forgot the rest. Wally had made fun of her for it. At least he couldn't do that here.

Before the three of them could begin the chitchat, a high-school girl with long blonde hair came to take their drink and appetizer orders.

"Oh Summer, you know we always get the same thing on Wednesdays," Tessa said. "I'd like to introduce you to our newest resident, Katerina Volkov."

"Nice to meet you, but I'll need just a minute to choose what I'd like." Kay checked out the menu.

"Take your time. Nice to meet you too," she said. She turned to the oldest woman. "You're not the newest tenant anymore, Accosta."

Accosta. Accosta. Kay repeated the name in her head.

As soon as the girl took her order of iced tea and a relish tray Tessa rambled on about how Summer had lived in a boarding house called Peerbaugh Place with her mother at the same time Tessa had lived there. "I've known her since she was five. Actually, her mother Audra married the owner's son, Russell. He's a banker and she makes wedding dresses, and..."

Blah de blah de blah.

Kay certainly had no use for a wedding dress, and since she knew she'd never remember any of the names Tessa was spewing off, she nodded when it seemed appropriate but mostly studied the rest of the menu—which was impressive. It should be for what Kay was paying per month.

When Tessa was done talking, Accosta said, "I can't believe you just moved in today, Katerina. I mean, look at you. Not a hair out of place."

"You do have commendable style," Tessa said.

Kay smiled. Mission accomplished. "The movers did the hard part. And I'm far from being completely moved in."

"No one expects you to be," Tessa said.

"I hope to have a little soiree after I am settled."

"A soiree?" Tessa's eyes brightened. "We accept."

"I have no idea what a soiree is," Accosta said. "But I always enjoy a party."

Their iced tea came, and then the expected questions began. "So, Katerina?" Accosta began. "Your last name of Volkov . . . are your ancestors Russian?"

"My husband's were. Nicolae." She looked down as if in grief. "My husband passed away from a heart attack when we were on a Mediterranean cruise."

"How horrible for you," Accosta said.

"How long have you been a widow?" Tessa asked.

Kay tried to remember her story. "Three years last July."

"How did you end up here?" Accosta asked.

Kay had her answer ready. "Nicolae and I had discussed moving to a retirement community and we researched many of them. I know he'd approve of my move here."

"But why here in tiny Carson Creek?" Accosta asked. "Tessa mentioned you're from Lee's Summit—that's over an hour away, and I know there are many nice facilities closer."

Too close. She thought of the perfect answer. "I chose Happy Trails after meeting Tessa when I first had the tour."

"Me?"

Kay nodded. "You were so vibrant and friendly. You were interested in me. We had a good, long discussion." *Too long.*

Tessa pressed a hand to her chest. "If I had something to do with your move, then I'm glad. Actually, we might not have met at all that day except for me missing my ride to women's group. I was headed back to my apartment and saw you in the hall outside what ended up to be yours, and then Mrs. Halvorson was called away and . . ."

Kay gladly let Tessa take over the story of their first meeting.

It was always good to have a front man paving the way.

Chapter Eight

Evelyn

> The generous will prosper;
> those who refresh others will themselves be refreshed.
> Proverbs 11: 25

Evelyn stood at the kitchen sink and washed a coffee mug. And kept washing it, over and over.

Wayne brought his cereal bowl to the sink and stood there, watching her. "Was your mug filled with mud this morning?"

She blinked and looked at him. "Mud?"

He nodded at the mug. "I think it's clean now."

She snapped out of it, rinsed the soap off, and set it on the rack. "Sorry. I'm a little preoccupied."

"With what?"

"Life."

"Can you narrow it down?"

She wiped her sudsy hands and faced him. "I feel like I've lost my rudder. I coast through the days but I don't have any direction."

"Without Accosta here?"

Evelyn nodded. "I'm doing the same things I've always done, but without her here . . ."

"It can't be that different. She didn't demand that much of your time."

"I know, but she was *here*. My friend was *here*. I miss her so much."

"It's only been two weeks."

"Fifteen days."

Wayne pulled her close. "Why don't you go visit her today?"

Evelyn shook her head against his chest. "She and Tessa have an outing planned to the Sister Circle House. She's busy."

"And you're not."

She turned back to the sink and washed his cereal bowl. "I'm not. Being here for her was a big part of my purpose. I need to help people. It's who I am."

"You're helping the two new hospital guests."

She put the dish in the drying rack. "Barely. We give them a place to crash, and a few muffins and coffee."

"You take care of me."

"You're easy."

He made a face and pulled her close. "If it would help, I could become a demanding husband who insists you wait on me every waking moment." He paused a moment, smirking at her. "I truly could do that. As a favor to you."

She snickered. "Actually, you could *not* do that. That's not who *you* are."

"Well then." Wayne sighed dramatically. "What are we going to do to solve your problem?"

"I have no idea."

He took her hands in his. "Want to go to the hardware store with me? I need some screws to fix a cabinet door that's wonky." He made his eyebrows dance and his next words came out in a singsong. "It will be pretty exciting."

Evelyn loved how he could make her smile. "I think I'll pass. Thanks for the offer though." She heard her neighbor's car driving away. Everybody knew when Collier was coming or going because of the bad muffler on his ancient Chevy. "Actually, I think I'll pop over to Mae's while you're gone."

"Sounds like a grand idea." He kissed her cheek. "How about I bring you something? Maybe a wire-cutter or some light bulbs? Or a new toilet plunger?"

"Surprise me."

** ** **

Evelyn could always count on her best friend Mae to lift her out of a bad mood. For there was nothing dull or stagnant about Mae. Ever.

Mae went through life like an aging hippie waiting for the next Woodstock. She wore Indian-printed skirts or caftans, and flip-flops in all but the coldest Kansas weather. Her gray hair was still long, like she was 23 not 63. It had a mind of its own and Mae was as lenient with *it* as she'd been with her kids, Ringo and Starr. Evelyn admired her courage to be different. Evelyn was mired in the status quo, but was okay with that. As Mae would say, "Gracious jean skirt, Evie! Be yourself!"

After hearing her knock, Mae drew Evelyn inside her 1920s bungalow like a mighty wave overpowering a stream. Evelyn could depend on Mae to flood the absurdities of her problems until they were cleansed. She counted on it.

Mae put the kettle on for tea, then sat at the kitchen table across from Evelyn. "Now then, Evie . . . what's got you looking like a lost puppy?"

Evelyn hated her inability to hide her feelings. "It's silly. But I miss Accosta."

"Gracious gobstoppers. That *is* silly. She's not dead. Go visit her."

"I've done that already. And I'll go again. Soon."

"Is *she* having trouble with the transition?"

Evelyn couldn't miss the emphasis. "*She's* doing well. She likes it at Tessa's."

Mae scoffed. "Meaning she's one in a million. But the point is, Accosta is thriving, yes?"

"Yes."

"So . . . what's the problem beyond you missing her?"

Wasn't that enough? "I miss having her around the house to . . . to talk to, to cook for, to care for."

"So me calling you a lost puppy isn't that far off—except Accosta is the lost puppy?"

"No! I don't think of her like that." She tried to make her emotions sound less pitiful. "I liked being there for her. Helping her. Interacting with her."

"You still have the hospital people and Wayne. Aren't they enough?"

"Of course they are, it's just . . . I like to be needed."

Mae slapped her hand on the table. "You, Ms. Evelyn Wellington, are definitely suffering from a servant's heart, heart attack."

Evelyn had often been told she had a servant's heart because she liked to help people. "What's the solution?"

"Helping more people, of course."

"And where would I do that?"

"I haven't a clue."

Evelyn was taken aback. "You have to have some sort of idea for me."

"Not offhand." The teapot started whistling. "See who shows up. God's not going to let you be stagnant very long."

"I hope not."

"In the meantime . . ." Mae got up to pour two cups of her favorite Moroccan Mint tea. "I do have another sort of idea. Let's plan a party."

Mae was always up for a party.

"Fill Peerbaugh Place with tons of your friends so you'll be so overwhelmed with the noise and chaos and work of it all that you'll be happy when they leave."

Evelyn dipped a tea bag up and down in her cup. "That's not a bad idea."

"You doubted me?" She retrieved a notepad and a pen. "Let's start with the guest list."

Chapter Nine

Scranton

Love the LORD, all you godly ones!
For the LORD protects those who are loyal to him,
but he harshly punishes the arrogant.
Psalm 31: 23

Scranton Stockton stood at the hostess podium in the dining room at Happy Trails. The hostess was seating a group. And chatting with them. And chatting. And chatting . . .

A couple came up behind him, waiting their turn.

"Hello, Scranton," the husband said.

"Hello." He didn't know their names and had no wish to know.

Finally the hostess returned. "Where would you like to sit, Mr. Stockton?"

"No where. I want to order my dinner as take-out."

"I'm sorry, but that's not possible, sir."

"Why not?"

Her eyes flitted between Scranton and the couple behind him. She wasn't going to be able to concentrate on his needs until they were seated.

"Go ahead and seat them first."

She seemed relieved. "Mr. and Mrs. Benson. Your usual table?"

"Yes, Frani. Thank you."

She showed them to a table near a window and returned. "Now then, Mr. Stockton. You were asking about take-out?"

"I was. I've determined that it's an inefficient use of my time to spend hours dining every day. I'm paying for the meals so I want to pick them up, or better yet, have them delivered to my apartment." It wasn't a difficult concept.

Frani nodded, but something in her downcast eyes told him she wasn't going to give in. "I understand your request, Mr. Stockton, but an important part of independent living is being part of a community. That's why we don't allow in-apartment dining unless there's good reason, such as illness." She smiled, eyeing him up and down. "You seem to be enjoying very good health, sir."

"Don't be so sure. I feel my blood pressure rising as we speak."

He saw a twinge of panic cross her face. "I'm sorry you feel that way. Would you like to be seated?"

He turned and stormed away, mumbling to himself.

Part of being independent was having the choice to walk away.

** ** **

The halls were empty when Scranton went to check his mail — which was just how he liked it. Chit chat was totally pointless. And annoying. All the "Hello" and "Good morning" chatter was forced courtesy. He didn't want to make friends because he didn't want to be one.

He opened his mailbox with a key and stood there sorting through it, depositing most of it in a wastebasket nearby.

A woman approached the mailboxes, her bracelets clanking as she walked. Scranton angled himself so he didn't have to say hello.

But the woman moved into his view. "Hi there, I'm Katerina Volkov. I just moved in."

"Good for you."

Scranton saw her head jerk back. His words *had* been incredibly rude — even by his standards. He turned just enough to finish their conversation. "I'm Scranton Stockton." He braced himself for the usual question: *How long have you lived here?*

But the woman surprised him.

"I've heard there's an indoor pool here."

He paused, looking her over. She was the definition of high maintenance with lavish makeup, perfect hair, and red nail polish. She wore a navy blazer with a Ralph Lauren crest, and far too much jewelry. She was definitely trying to impress.

Someone. Not him.

"There is a pool," he said.

"They showed me where it was during my first tour but I've been so busy settling in I can't remember. Can you show me where it is?" She looked toward the entrance. "There's no one at the front desk, and I'd really like to see it. If you have time, that is."

Scranton was caught off guard. He knew he couldn't claim he was busy. "I suppose."

"Excellent," she said. "Lead the way."

"It's in the lower level." They walked to the elevator and were taken down.

"How long have you lived here?" she asked. The question always came around eventually.

"A year."

"Do you like it here?"

"Yes." Any other answer would require more discussion.

The elevator doors opened and he let her exit first. "This way." They wove their way right, then left. "It's a long way," he said.

"I don't mind. It's good exercise."

He didn't remember it being so far. He hoped he hadn't taken her in the wrong direction. Then he spotted a sign. A few steps more and . . . "Here you are."

She waited for him to open one of the glass doors for her. He did, and she paused in the doorway. "It's lovely. Do you swim?"

He didn't want to leave the door open and let the awful humidity and stench of chlorine escape to the hall, so he motioned her inside. "I do not. Ever."

Her forehead dipped as she laughed. "You act as though swimming is something distasteful."

Not at all. He thought of his Olivia. She loved to swim laps. She'd tried to teach him different strokes, but he'd never taken to it. She'd been a fish to his flounder.

He needed to leave because he wanted to keep all the memories of his wife intact without adding to them. He opened the door to leave. "To each his own."

"Or her own." When she passed by him he noticed she was wearing false eyelashes. The right one was slightly askew.

He let the door swing shut and motioned toward the elevator. He checked his watch. "I don't have time to swim. I still work."

Her penciled eyebrows rose. "Oh. I assumed you were retired."

"Only partially. I am still involved in the firm."

Her eyes widened. "The firm . . . are you a lawyer?"

"I am a partner at Burroughs, Blake, and Stockton."

She gave him a blank look.

"We're located in Kansas City. Surely you read about the Dutton murder case?"

She shook her head.

"He was accused of shoving his wife off a cliff."

"Oh my. I do remember hearing something about that on the news. She had a lot of life insurance?"

Of course this woman would remember one of the main bits of evidence against Scranton's client. "I got him acquitted."

She seemed surprised. "Was he innocent?"

"That doesn't really matter, does it? A jury of his peers decided he was."

She nodded weakly. "You must be very good at your job."

Indeed I am. He punched the button on the elevator. Luckily, the doors opened. He let her get on first. "I represent my clients to the best of my ability."

Her expression changed and she peered at him through the fake lashes. "I'm sure you have many abilities, Mr. Stockton."

He was taken aback by her blatant flirting. As soon as the elevator doors opened he said, "If you'll excuse me, I need to be going. I assume you can find your way back?"

She blinked. "Of course. I don't mean to keep you. Have a good day."

The sooner he could get home the better.

** ** **

Scranton turned the last corner before his apartment. He spotted an acquaintance named Rosalie on her knees, trying to gather a dozen or more magazines that had fallen to the floor.

She gazed up at him. "I'm so clumsy."

"Let me help you with that."

Her expression showed her relief. "Thanks, Scranton. I appreciate it."

Scranton handily picked up the bulk of them.

Then Rosalie tried to get up, but faltered. She chuckled. "Either you help me up or I'm going to embarrass myself by doing an awkward and very unladylike contortion to get to my feet again."

He liked her honesty and offered his hand. She leaned heavily on it and stood. "Thank you for saving me." She added a single magazine to his pile.

"No problem." He'd noticed the covers: *Fishing Unlimited, Woodworking Digest,* and *Conde Nast Traveler.* "Where are you taking all these?"

"To Lonnie. He gets bored with daytime TV."

"I don't blame him." Scranton remembered hearing that Lonnie Clemmons had suffered a stroke and was recuperating in assisted living.

She held her arms out. "Here, I'll take them from here."

She was a bitty thing and Scranton couldn't imagine her carrying the stack for any distance. "Let me carry them for you."

"Well, thank you. You're such a gentleman."

Olivia used to call me that. I used to be that.

They walked toward the assisted living wing. "How's Lonnie doing?"

"He's a fighter. He's trying hard to improve so he can come home to me."

Scranton remembered his wife's battle with cancer. He still cringed at the memory of her pain—and his own, at seeing her suffer. She'd been gone two years now. A year ago he tried to start fresh at Happy Trails but still found his new life stale and confining. He felt like he was in a bad play, a reluctant actor refusing to learn his lines.

When they entered the assisted living wing, Scranton felt his body tense at the sight of people being helped down the hall, and the sound of a metal cart holding medicines making its rounds. There was a palpable smell of anguish here.

He must have hesitated because Rosalie stopped and put her hand on his arm. "Was your wife ever here?"

"No. But she was in the hospital a lot, and the atmosphere..."

"Of course. I'll take the magazines from here."

He chastised himself for being weak. "Nonsense, I'll take them the rest of the way. I'm fine."

She smiled a knowing smile, and he resented that she'd seen his weakness. Yet he appreciated her doing just that. She was a kind woman. Olivia would have liked her.

Rosalie led him to a small apartment. It consisted of a tiny living room with a two-person table, a small kitchen area with a fridge, a microwave, a sink, and virtually no cupboards. It had one bedroom with an attached bath. The window offered a view of sky and treetops. Better than one overlooking the parking lot.

Lonnie was sitting in a wheelchair, reading a book with a magnifying glass. Rosalie gave him a kiss on the forehead. "Look who helped me carry your magazines. You remember Scranton, don't you? You and I shared a few meals with him."

Lonnie nodded. "No coo-tons."

His words were slurred. "Excuse me?" Scranton said.

Lonnie made a picking motion with his right hand.

Rosalie smiled. "You picked the croutons out of your salad."

Scranton felt his eyebrows rise, but nodded. "I guess I did." He didn't appreciate Lonnie pointing out this idiosyncrasy.

"Tanks for helfing Rosie." Only the right side of his face moved.

Scranton grimaced, but tried to smile at the same time. "Glad to help," he said. "Where would you like them?"

Rosalie touched the table next to the wheelchair. "Here would be great."

Scranton stacked the magazines on the table, dividing them into two piles so they'd be less likely to fall. "I hope you feel better soon." It was such a trite thing to say but he couldn't think of anything else. Then he gave a small wave and stepped into the hall.

Rosalie came after him. "Will we see you at the Friday Fling?"

Scranton hated the forced frivolity of this weekly activity. "Probably not." He had never attended. Not once.

"Oh, do come," Rosalie said. "I'm bringing Lonnie."

If Lonnie was willing to attend in a wheelchair, Scranton didn't have any viable excuses—except that he didn't want to. It occurred to him that he was acting like a grumpy curmudgeon.

"I'll think about it," he said.

"We look forward to seeing you."

Maybe.

65

Chapter Ten

Accosta

We should help others do what is right
and build them up in the Lord.
Romans 15: 2

Accosta drifted from sleep into wakefulness and whispered the first words she said every morning, "Thank You for this day, Lord." She opened her eyes and immediately marveled once again that she was in an apartment at Happy Trails. She was safe and felt peace about being in a place that could care for her through the rest of her days.

She had fond memories of her lovely bedroom at Peerbaugh Place. It was far more homey than this room. And she missed seeing Evelyn and Wayne every day, but she knew moving had been the right thing to do. One of the disadvantages of getting old was the necessity of making alternative choices to the ones she wanted to make. She would have loved staying where she was, but the frailties of her body made it impossible. And so she thanked God for this wonderful—miraculous—alternative.

The luscious aroma of coffee spurred her to fold back the covers and dangle her legs over the side of the bed. Accosta remembered getting up without a pause in her younger days. But with years adding to years she found it was safer to take the process one step at a time, letting her body get used to each position before risking the next. Everything took a little longer.

So it was.

When she emerged dressed and ready for the day, Tessa was already sitting at the table, two cups of coffee poured, two Bibles at the ready, and the devotional they were reading opened to the proper page.

"Good morning," Accosta said.

"That it is," Tessa said. "Shall we get started?"

Absolutely.

** ** **

Accosta followed Tessa into a large room that held two sewing machines, an ironing board, and a large table for cutting out fabric. There were cabinets and shelves brimming with craft supplies. It made her wish she was creative.

Tessa set a bin of fabric on the table and began to separate the colors. The sewing club was meeting in a few minutes and Accosta was going to be their newest member — even if she hadn't sewn in thirty years. "Go with the flow" was her new motto.

Accosta was happy to swim in Tessa's wake. As an active member of the welcome committee, Tessa knew everyone at Happy Trails and was more than willing to share her opinions of all the available activities in and away from the property. To Accosta it was like going on a trip with a tour guide leading her from here to there, addressing any hiccups along the way. With Tessa taking care of the details of her life, Accosta could relax.

She knew Evelyn, Mae, and many others thought Tessa was domineering and bossy — and she was — but Accosta realized those traits originated with Tessa's willingness to be a leader. Her knowing a lot about a lot was a gift from God. Tessa was a teacher at heart.

Accosta had learned to ignore the times when Tessa used her gift without restraint. At age 83 Tessa wasn't going to change and suddenly become mellow, just as at age 93 Accosta wasn't going to change from mellow and become a firebrand. It was God's desire that everyone use their gifts to help the whole. Accosta knew that Tessa and their friend Mae had the gift of gab while she and Evelyn were the listeners. The arrangement worked well. They balanced each other out.

Tessa finished getting out scissors, pincushions, and thread just as three ladies strolled into the room. They introduced themselves to Accosta. *Nice to meet you too.*

Tessa moved along to the task at hand. "Now then, ladies. Let's begin making the patchwork blankets."

"Nap blankets for kids," Betty explained to Accosta.

"That sounds wonderful," Accosta said. "How can I help?"

"Would you rather cut, pin, or sew?" Mildred asked.

Accosta hadn't used a machine in years, and her hands were arthritic so she wasn't sure about cutting. "Pin. I should be able to pin pieces together." She would go slow and get it right.

"That's perfect," Tessa said. "Let's get started on a blue one."

They divided the fabrics into groupings of four patterns that looked good together. There was a rhythm to the work as the ladies alternated sewing and lively conversation. They shared stories about their families before asking Accosta about hers.

She regretted not being able to think of any funny stories to tell. "My husband has been gone for many, many years," she said. "But he was a lovely man. He used to make me laugh."

"A sense of humor is important," Tessa said.

"Did your husband have one?" Accosta asked.

"Not one whit," Tessa said.

They all laughed.

But Tessa put up her hand. "I don't say that to disparage Alfred, for he was a kind, generous man — albeit a serious man. He was also a forgiving man."

By the shadowed look that clouded Tessa's face, Accosta guessed she was referring to something specific. "Forgiving of what?"

Tessa shook her head as if shooing the answer away. "It's a long story made short by saying . . ." she hesitated, then after a deep breath let it all out. "I didn't believe he was sick and told him to snap out of it. Then he died."

All the women's heads pulled back.

"Whoa," Helen said. "That's harsh."

"That's me — or the me I used to be," Tessa said. "God's forgiven me, and I know Alfred has too. I take comfort in knowing no one on this earth deserves heaven more than him. And — believe it or not — since then, I have tried to be less blunt."

The ladies hesitated just a second before chuckling. Tessa pretended to take offense. Somehow personality flaws were easier to take when the guilty party acknowledged them. Laughed at them.

Just then, another new resident stepped into the room. "Hello, ladies," Katerina said.

"Morning," Accosta said. "Are you joining us?"

"Oh, heavens no. These fingernails are not meant to do stitching of any kind." She wiggled her long, red-painted nails.

"You could cut them shorter," Tessa said.

"My manicurist would kill me."

Accosta looked at Tessa and could guess she was about to ask, *"Then why are you here?"* So Accosta jumped in. "Would you like to sit with us and visit?"

"Perhaps for a minute or two." She pulled out a chair.

The ladies didn't smile and looks were exchanged. It was like they had something against Katerina. She was new. Surely she hadn't rubbed them wrong so quickly.

The ladies went back to their work, but the conversation lagged.

Katerina glanced from one to the other, then said, "Who will be the proud owner of this blanket?"

"We don't know yet," Helen said. "We bring them to the Sister Circle House to give to the kids who come there with their mothers."

"That sounds like a good cause," Katerina said. "My late husband, Nicolae, and I were big advocates for a particular Ukrainian orphanage. He and I traveled there to see the facilities. We were welcomed with open arms. Those children," she sighed dramatically, "were so precious."

Accosta was surprised when no one said anything in response to Katerina's story. It's like a switch had been turned off. "Did you get to know any of the children?" Accosta asked.

Katerina seemed confused, then stood to leave. "It's been nice seeing you ladies, but I have an appointment. Carry on."

A few seconds after she left, the ladies scoffed.

"'Carry on,' she says." Helen rolled her eyes.

"Of course it was a *Ukrainian* orphanage," Mildred said.

Helen put a hand to her chest. "And they welcomed her with open arms." She sighed dramatically.

Accosta was confused by their reaction. "It's admirable she and her husband giving aid to an orphanage."

"It is," Betty said. She looked confused too.

"*If* it's true," Mildred said with raised eyebrows.

Accosta was baffled. "Why wouldn't it be true?"

Helen smoothed a piece of fabric. "After only being here a few days, it's become clear that Katerina has one mission: to impress. She always has a story—an exotic story."

Mildred nodded. "According to her, she's been everywhere and has seen everything. She told me she chose Happy Trails because she longed for a simpler life." She scoffed. "But that doesn't jibe."

"No, it doesn't," Helen said. "She's the least simple person I've ever met. All the makeup and clothes and jewelry." She shook her head in disgust.

Accosta didn't like how they were talking so badly about Katerina. "But maybe she's just—"

Tessa interrupted. "Have you seen how much furniture she's stuffed into her apartment?"

Accosta shook her head. "But isn't that a problem for a lot of people who move here? Downsizing is difficult."

Tessa acquiesced. "You're right about that. It's just . . . "

"And doesn't downsizing come in phases?" Accosta asked.

Betty thought for a moment and bobbled her head. "It did for us. There's the first wave, then the second."

"I think I'm on the tenth wave," Helen said.

They laughed.

"How about you, Accosta? What wave are you on?"

"Thankfully, I don't have a wave. I downsized to a few clothes and boxes ten years ago."

"That's what made your move here so easy," Tessa said. "You didn't even fill the closet in your bedroom."

"I've never cared much about clothes," Accosta said.

"That certainly makes life easier," Mildred said.

Accosta wasn't sure whether she should take offense or not. She decided *not*.

Helen picked up two contrasting squares. "Does the daisy floral come after the stripe or the check?"

And just like that they moved on.

As Accosta pinned she said a quick prayer for Katerina—and for all the ladies who disparaged her.

Chapter Eleven

Evelyn

> Tune your ears to wisdom,
> and concentrate on understanding.
> Cry out for insight,
> and ask for understanding.
> Proverbs 2: 2-3

Evelyn piped the filling into the deviled eggs. She had to stop halfway through because her hands ached from the repetitive movement. Her doctor said she had arthritis. Her hands and Wayne's knees. It was what it was.

Wayne came in from the backyard and washed his hands in the sink nearby. "I got the chairs wiped off and the firepit is ready."

"Thanks." She went back to her piping. Only nineteen to go. The piping was not as pretty as it showed in the cookbook. Nothing was ever as pretty as it showed in the cookbook.

Wayne swiped his finger through the yellow filling. "Yum." He put his finger out to swipe more.

"No double dipping." She stood upright, feeling the burn in her back. Was that arthritis too?

"Do you want me to finish?" he asked.

"You could probably do a better job with the piping than I'm doing." Nevertheless, she persisted. "I have this to finish, the cider needs to be put in a pretty pitcher, the meatballs need to be stirred in the crockpot, the brownies are in the oven, and I haven't even started the hot cheese dip." She thought of something else. "Would you make sure the powder room is clean? I meant to do that, and make sure there's enough toilet paper, and—"

He slipped behind her and put his hands on her shoulders. "Stop."

"I can't stop. I have too much to do."

He made his voice soft and gentle. "Stop, Ev. Take a breath. Or three."

But with a few trembling breaths, tears fell. Her shoulders sagged for a moment before they began to shudder with her sobs.

Wayne took the piping bag away and set it on the counter. He pulled his wife into his arms. "It will be all right. I promise."

Evelyn leaned hard against him, needing to tap into his strength. "I'm getting too old for this. I'm exhausted and the party hasn't even started. I used to do this so easily." She pulled back to look at his face. "Does this mean I really am old?"

"Yes."

"Uhh!"

"Do you want me to lie to you?"

"Maybe." She pouted for just a second. "The point is, I haven't had a party for this many people in ages. I think there will be fifteen? Or is it sixteen counting you and me?" Her mind began to go through the counting process again.

Wayne pulled her back into his arms. "And all fifteen or sixteen people are family and close friends. People who don't care if the deviled egg filling is a bit uneven, or if you serve the cider right out of the jug. Though they might care if there's not enough toilet paper."

She laughed and felt the tears retreat. She stood on her own and mimicked Wayne as he drew in two exaggerated deep breaths.

"Better?" he asked.

She nodded.

"I thought of something else that will help ease your mind."

"What's that?" she asked.

"Isn't everybody bringing something to share?"

"I forgot about that. Yes, they are."

He spread his hands. "As I said, everything's going to—"

"Be all right."

Wayne flicked the tip of her nose. "I'll go check the toilet paper."

Evelyn went back to her piping, very grateful to have a husband who took up the slack and made "all right" possible.

** ** **

Mae stood at the fireplace and finished her story. "So right there in the grocery store I opened the box of Cheerios to keep Ringo happy, but then the whole box tipped over in the cart and spilled all over the floor."

Her husband Collier cupped his hand against his mouth. "Clean up in aisle five!"

"And then three-year-old Ringo pointed at it and said—" Mae looked expectantly at Ringo, who was sitting on the couch. eating a brownie.

"'Mommy made a *big* mess.'" Ringo rolled his eyes. "How many times have you told that story, Mom?"

"Not *that* many," she said.

Ringo raised his hand. "I need a show of hands: how many of you have heard the Cheerios story?"

Ringo's wife Soon-ja raised her hand. "I think I'm up to fourteen times."

"Don't be rude, Soonie," Mae said.

But everybody else also raised their hands—except Accosta, who said, "I don't think I've heard it."

Summer raised her hand. "I don't think I've heard it either."

"Then I tell it for the two of you," Mae said with a bow. "Gracious cheese dip, people. A good story is timeless."

Tessa leaned forward in her chair. "Settle in, everyone, you know she's got a million of 'em."

Evelyn was glad for Mae's ability to entertain with witty stories. Evelyn was an observer. She was content to stand in the background and let the sounds of the families weave around her. She loved seeing her son Russell and daughter Piper chat and laugh with each other's spouses. And then all of her grandkids ran in and out of the room with Mae's until Summer herded them all into the backyard. All *this* was worth some sore muscles and tired bones.

Her cup runneth over.

** ** **

As with most parties, toward the end, people started to trickle out. Ringo and Soon-ja agreed to drop Tessa and Accosta at Happy Trails. Russell's family left, and Piper's husband took their kids home. Mae and Collier signed off and went to their house across the street, finally leaving Evelyn and Wayne alone with their daughter.

Everyone had helped clean up so Evelyn wasn't as tired as she could have been. Still, she gladly accepted Wayne's invitation to sit with Piper by the firepit to decompress.

It was dark and the light on the back deck made the branches of the trees cast odd shadows.

"Want to make s'mores?" Piper asked.

Evelyn moaned. "I couldn't eat another thing."

"Me either," Wayne said.

"It was just a thought."

They sat without talking, at ease in each other's company.

Piper broke the silence. "It was great seeing everyone. We all get busy and forget how special it feels to get together."

"I agree," Wayne said. "Your mother's really been missing Accosta."

"I don't doubt it. She lived here a long, long time. But she seems to like Happy Trails."

"She does," Evelyn admitted. "Though she's a quiet sort, I think she likes being around more people every day."

"Even Tessa?"

"Especially Tessa," Evelyn said. "They're an odd couple, but it works. I think Accosta will be good for Tessa too. She might soften her a bit."

Wayne chuckled. "I'm not sure that's possible."

Piper smiled. "Tessa wouldn't be Tessa without being . . ."

"Tessa?" Evelyn asked.

"Exactly." Piper slumped down in her lawn chair and gazed at the back of Peerbaugh Place. "I do love this house," she said.

"We do too," Wayne said. "But it's a lot of work to keep everything ship-shape."

Evelyn rarely took time to look at the house from this angle. The windows of the sunroom glowed with lamplight. She saw a window blind cocked oddly, probably the work of some grandchild messing with it while they played Monopoly and Chutes & Ladders. The two second-story windows were dark, but without blinking an eye Evelyn remembered them alive and bright with delightful tenants. A row of autumn-colored mums marked the path from the kitchen door to the firepit where they sat. She liked what she saw. "This house does take a bit of work but it's been my home for all of my adult life."

"And *that* is a very long time," Piper said—but she said it with a smile.

"I can't dispute the fact," Evelyn said.

They listened to the sound of crisp leaves skittering over the grass. Which made Evelyn think of the raking that should be done. She hated raking and it made Wayne's knees—

"I could sell this house for you," Piper said.

Evelyn was taken aback at the abrupt segue. She turned sternly toward Piper. "I'm sure you could, but it's not for sale." She looked at Wayne and was surprised he was just sitting there, neither nodding nor shaking his head. "Wayne?"

He said, "It's not for sale," but added a shrug.

"A shrug?" Evelyn sat forward.

Wayne did it again. "It's not out of the question, Ev."

Evelyn's heart started pumping. "It most certainly is! I told you the only way you'll get me out of this house is feet first!"

The new silence quivered with tension.

Way to kill a party, Evelyn.

** ** **

Lying next to Wayne, Evelyn's thoughts refused to calm down. It had been exhausting enough helping Accosta move out, but the idea of moving *their* stuff out to claim another place as home? It was beyond comprehension.

She lay on her back, staring at the ceiling.

"I can hear you thinking," Wayne said into his pillow.

"I can't help it."

"Then think of something else."

"How do you know what I'm thinking about?"

He turned on his side to face her. "You don't often react to ideas the way you reacted to Piper's."

She turned on her side to look at him in the moonlight. "Most ideas don't involve my home. Plain as I can say it: I don't want to move."

"We don't have to."

"But you shrugged. Twice. That means you'd consider it."

He moved a strand of hair away from her face. "One day we'll need to move, Ev."

She hated to hear it. "That is *not* a given. A lot of people stay in their homes until . . . the end."

"I want you to be realistic. Accosta needed to move because of physical limitations, so it follows that those issues might become our issues."

"Fine." She punched a corner of her pillow into the space beneath her chin. "When we're ninety-three I'll agree to move. That gives me twenty-three more years in this house."

"But what if—?"

"I don't want to talk about it anymore, Wayne. I'm going to sleep." She turned her back to him and closed her eyes.

But sleep eluded her.

Chapter Twelve

Rosalie

Encourage those who are timid.
Take tender care of those who are weak.
Be patient with everyone.
1 Thessalonians 5: 14

Rosalie Clemmons sat beside her husband and squeezed his arm. "They're going to come take you for your bath soon, Lonnie."

He cupped her cheek with his good hand and smiled a half-smile. "I sorry I a 'eak ole 'an."

His words were slurred and took a lot of effort. "Nonsense," she said. "You're *my* weak old man and I love you."

One of the staff in assisted living entered the room with a smile and a bright attitude. Rosalie was always amazed by them. How could they be so upbeat all the time?

Lonnie shooed his wife away. "Go. I call 'oo 'en I squeeky c'ean."

Rosalie kissed him on the head and left. She nodded at the other workers as she passed, but kept her head down so they didn't talk to her. The sooner she could get back to their apartment the better.

Her avoidance of any kind of interaction was a new development since Lonnie's stroke. When they'd told her he had to temporarily move out of the apartment they'd lived in the last two years, she'd thought it would be all right. It was the best plan to get Lonnie the care he needed. But without Lonnie around to be her other half, Rosalie discovered she was *just* half. And never whole.

Without him being the witty, capable, and outgoing better half she felt unable to fully function. She had lived decades in his shadow, a place of cool relief from the uncomfortable heat of daily life. Occasionally Lonnie had tried to pull her into the light with him, but she always quickly withdrew. She was content being Lonnie's "other half."

Rosalie purposely took the stairs so she didn't have to talk to anyone in the elevator. Once she reached the third floor she paused to catch her breath. When she heard voices in the hall she waited until there was silence again. She even peeked out the door to make sure the hall was empty.

The coast was clear.

Only it wasn't.

"Rosalie!"

She'd almost made it home free. She stepped fully into the hallway and waited for Tessa to reach her. "Good morning, Tessa."

"Back atcha." Tessa pointed her cane at the stairs. "Why in the sake of sore muscles are you using stairs when there's a perfectly good elevator a few steps away?"

"I like the exercise." Her words came out sounding like a question.

"You've lost weight. If I were you, I'd do more eating and less stair-climbing." Tessa only paused a second before asking, "How's Lonnie?"

Rosalie gave her usual answer. "He's doing all right."

"Having a stroke is no small matter. I've never seen him smoke. Is he a smoker?"

Rosalie wasn't sure why Tessa was asking the question. "Never."

"That's in his favor. Smoking can cause strokes and certainly would make recovery harder. How long does he have to stay there?"

"Hopefully not long." Rosalie glanced toward their apartment. Longingly. "I should go. I have a book to read and — "

Tessa slipped her hand around Rosalie's arm. "I have a better idea. Come with me."

Without violently shaking Tessa's arm away Rosalie had no choice but to go with her.

** ** **

Tessa led Rosalie to the Game Room. Rows and rows of bookshelves were on one end, tucked around a grouping of comfy reading chairs. On the other end were four game tables in front of a long cabinet full of boardgames, puzzles, and cards.

A couple sat at a table. The man was shuffling cards.

"There she is," the woman said.

"Sorry I'm late," Tessa said. "I captured a fourth player in the hall. Have you three met each other?"

The man stood. "Rosalie is it? I think we rode with you and your husband to a concert once or twice. We're Neil and Lucy."

Rosalie barely remembered them but said, "It's nice to see you again."

Neil helped Rosalie and Tessa with their chairs. Lonnie had always done that for her. The gesture from someone else made her miss him all the more.

Tessa slapped the table. "Now then. Let's play Pitch."

"Do you know how to play, Rosalie?" Lucy asked.

Again, it was Tessa who answered. "She does. I taught both her and Lonnie." She pointed at Lucy. "Switch chairs with me so Rosalie and I can be partners." After Rosalie sat down Tessa waggled a finger at her. "I want you to be bold this time around. No four-bids."

Four bids? Rosalie's mind went blank. She desperately wanted to leave. Lonnie was the good card player in their family, and now Tessa wanted her to be bold? It was not a word in her vocabulary. And so she said, "I'm not sure I'm up to cards today."

"Sure you are," Tessa said. "We'll just—" Tessa looked to the right, which meant everyone looked in that direction. She quickly turned back to the table and whispered, "Rosalie, you're staying."

A woman approached the table. She was slim and pretty, but overdressed for Happy Trails with far too much jewelry. Yet Rosalie admired her style—maybe because she herself didn't have any.

"Hello, Tessa," the woman said.

Tessa didn't look up but quickly began dealing the cards. "Hello, Katerina."

"Can you introduce me to your friends?"

Neil stood and shook Katerina's hand and introduced his wife. There was silence and Rosalie realized they were waiting for her to introduce herself. "I'm Rosalie."

"Nice to meet you. My name is Katerina. I'm new here and I just love to play cards. I really enjoy playing Napoleon. Nicolae and I learned it when we were in Paris."

"I can't say as I've ever heard of it," Neil said.

"I mention it because it can be played with five people. But I'm sure I can learn whatever game you're playing. Can you deal me in?"

"Too late," Tessa said, as she finished the deal. "Maybe another time." She spoke to the players. "Neil, you bid first. Four is minimum bid."

Katerina blinked a few times, and said, "Well I guess that's goodbye for now," and left.

After she was gone, Lucy said, "Pardon me, Tessa, but you were rather harsh with her."

"That woman needs some harsh."

Rosalie was shocked. She knew Tessa could be blunt, but she'd never seen her this rude.

"Katerina said she was new," Neil said. "What's she done to make you dislike her so quickly?"

Tessa un-fanned her cards and leaned forward. "She's not new to me. I met her when she was first shown her apartment. She was nice enough then, but since moving in I've heard a great many people complain that she's a braggart, always talking about her rich husband who died on a Mediterranean cruise, and—"

"How sad for her," Rosalie said.

"Yes, I suppose it was, but apparently she's always telling stories that make her out to be better than everyone else."

"That's too bad," Lucy said.

Rosalie agreed with Lucy, though she didn't say anything.

Suddenly Tessa sighed deeply, shaking her head. "Oh dear. I *was* rude. I'm on the welcoming committee, yet here I am, talking like I'm talking . . . I'm not being very welcoming. I apologize to all of you, and I'll apologize to her."

"We appreciate it," Lucy said. "And that's a good idea."

Rosalie thought so too. Why couldn't everybody just get along?

"Enough about her," Tessa said. "Let's play."

Rosalie had only played cards with Lonnie as her partner. She knew Tessa would not be as forgiving.

When Neil bid four and it was Rosalie's turn to bid, she knew Tessa wanted her to bid five, but her cards were awful. "Pass," she said.

Tessa did not look pleased.

Chapter Thirteen

Kay

> The prudent understand where they are going,
> but fools deceive themselves.
> Proverbs 14: 8

Kay left the card game that never happened, and wandered the halls of Happy Trails. She smiled at everyone she saw, and most everyone smiled back. But she needed more than smiles. She needed friends. Or even just one friend. Like Sharon.

She missed Sharon horribly. Sharon knew the real Kay and loved her anyway. Maybe it was time to invite her —

Mrs. Halvorson waved at Kay and came to greet her. "How are things going for you, Mrs. Volkov?"

In a split second Kay suppressed an impulse to tell the truth. "Very well, thank you."

"Have you found some activities you enjoy?"

"Not yet, but I will."

"Don't miss the dance tonight. Our Friday Fling is always a big hit. Do you like to dance?"

"I love to." *That* was true.

"Very good then. See you tonight at seven in the Gathering Room. Let me know if there's anything you need."

"Thank you."

A Friday Fling. That sounded fun. But it also meant she needed to take extra care getting ready.

She headed home.

*** *** ***

Kay answered a knock on her door and was shocked to see Tessa. "Hi."

"May I come in a minute?"

Kay stepped aside but felt like she was letting in the enemy. She did not offer Tessa a seat.

The older woman stopped just inside the door and steadied herself with both hands on her cane. "I came to apologize."

Kay could have fainted right there. She feigned ignorance. "For what?"

"For treating you so rudely at cards. And . . . and at sewing, too. I know I can be brusque at times — it's a lifelong struggle — but when I'm wrong, I say so. And I was wrong."

"Why . . . thank you, Tessa. I appreciate that." She wanted to ask why people weren't warming up to her, but Tessa had already turned to leave.

"Will I see you at the Friday Fling this evening?" Tessa asked.

"You will."

With a nod she left.

An apology from Tessa Klein. Kay felt the faintest glimmer of hope that her new life could be a good one.

** ** **

Kay started her Friday Fling preparations late-afternoon, skipping dinner. Since moving, she'd been disappointed that people didn't dress up for meals. But actually, their laissez-faire attitude about their appearance worked to her advantage. It made her style and newly-honed fashion sense stand out. By playing the wife of the late Nicolae Volkov — a ridiculously successful international banker — she'd already stepped onto the top rung of the Happy Trails social ladder. If only someone like Scranton Stockton would climb up with her.

She didn't know why she couldn't stop thinking about him. He'd given her zero encouragement — if anything, he'd been dismissive. If she was smart, she'd move on.

She never claimed to be smart.

Kay held an old bottle of cologne to her nose. It smelled more alcohol than scent. Not surprising since she'd bought it eons ago when she'd been an Avon lady. Twenty years ago? She did the math real quick. 40 years ago.

I guess I am that old.

She tossed it in the trash and tried a newer one that Wally had bought for her. It still smelled nice so she sprayed some in the air and walked into it like she'd seen influencers do online. One of the first things she wanted to buy when she found a rich husband was a bottle of real perfume, something in the hundred-dollar range, not twenty.

She carefully did her makeup, leaning into the magnifying side of a mirror. Once her eye liner was in place, she flipped to the regular mirror. Staying too long on the magnifier was a blast to her confidence. No wrinkle could hide under such scrutiny.

She opened up her wig cabinet and chose the tousled style. She hoped it made her look pretty and carefree and . . . fun. The people at Happy Trails needed a large dose of that.

Finally it was time to put on her gold sequin dress. She'd bought it on a clearance rack at Nordstrom's—which was the only way she could ever afford anything from that store. She'd asked the clerk what jewelry to wear with such a dress and had been told to pare it down to simple gold hoops or perhaps a couple gold bangles. Kay had opted for both because more was always more. Lastly, she put on the gold spiked sandals that had only been twenty-five percent off, but were too yummy to pass up.

She stood in front of her full-length mirror and shimmied a little to get the sequins to sparkle to their fullest extent. She looked good for seventy-two. If this didn't make people notice, she didn't know what would.

She spread her arms wide. "Watch out Happy Trails, here I come!"

** ** **

Kay knew she was *way* overdressed before she even reached the elevator. A few women wore skirts, but most wore pants. And the men wore khakis and plaid shirts. They were way too middle-class. They were everything she'd left behind.

She felt the eyes of a woman in the elevator.

"That's a very pretty dress."

She wanted to say, '*Oh, this old thing?*' but the line had been overused in way too many movies, so she opted for a simple, "Thank you."

They exited the elevator and walked down the corridor to the Gathering Room. Kay loved having every eye. She walked — no, she strolled like Marilyn Monroe making an entrance.

She scanned the room for Scranton, but didn't see him. She did spot Tessa and Accosta at a table. They both smiled — which was a relief.

She walked toward them. "Hello, ladies."

"Well then, Katerina. I'm not used to needing sunglasses for an evening party," Tessa said. "You are shimmering."

Thank you?

Accosta grinned. "You look like a movie star."

"Thank you. What a dear woman you are." She looked around the room. "Where can I get something to drink?"

Tessa nodded to the right. "At the bar there's red and white wine, and sparkling cider for those who don't wish to imbibe." By her amber colored beverage, Kay knew which way Tessa's wind blew.

"I don't mind if I do." With a turn on her heel — to best show off her sequins — Kay made her way to the bar. Two men approached and offered to get her a drink. One was skinny with face wrinkles like crumpled brown paper, and the other was fat and saggy. But she smiled and let them get her some white wine.

"Why haven't we met?" asked the saggy one.

"Just unlucky I guess."

"You new here?" Wrinkles asked.

"I am. I lost my husband on a cruise, and he'd suggested I simplify my life by moving here."

"Wise man. Sorry about your loss," Saggy said. "What did he do for a living?"

She noticed he hadn't asked what *she'd* done — not that she would have told them the truth — working at Kohl's would not impress. "He was an international financer. We spent much of our time overseas."

Saggy made a face. "Then how did you ever end up in Carson Creek?"

Since this seemed to be a popular question, she'd come up with an answer that sounded plausible. "A great aunt used to live here and I occasionally spent time with her. She used to drive us into the countryside to watch the amazing sunsets."

"You came for our sunsets?" Saggy asked.

"Don't you appreciate sunsets?"

"Sure, but I'm pretty certain I'd appreciate the sunsets in Paris or Monaco more."

She decided to change the subject. She glanced around the room. "It appears I'm overdressed."

"Not at all," Saggy said. "I appreciate a woman who knows how to flaunt . . ." he paused and let his eyes reach the sequins before looking away. He seemed to be trying to think of a better word.

She helped him out. "A woman who knows how to carry off a designer dress?"

His cheeks reddened. "Exactly."

Wrinkles chuckled. "Go easy, Nate. Don't overpower her with your charm."

"As if you could do better, Joe?"

Joe waved them off and moved on to another group.

Kay did *not* want to be stuck with Saggy all night. If only she could spot —

And there he was.

"If you'll excuse me, Nate?"

He glanced behind himself and saw Scranton coming into the room. He turned back to her, resigned, "Of course."

She sashayed toward Scranton, but was surprised when he veered to Tessa and Accosta's table. He began to talk with two new additions: the mousey woman from the card game, and a man in a wheelchair.

"Good evening," she said to Scranton.

He stood to greet her. "Evening."

She waited for him to compliment her dress, but instead he said, "Katerina, have you met Rosalie and Lonnie Clemmons?"

"I met Rosalie earlier today, but I haven't met Lonnie." She did her duty and shook hands. The man must have had a stroke because only half of his face smiled.

She waited for one of them to offer her a seat, but when they didn't, she said, "May I?"

"Of course," Accosta said. "Join us."

Kay sat down. She noticed Rosalie holding her husband's hand. It was touching. Would she ever feel a connection like that with anyone? She certainly hadn't with Wally. If only she'd left him years ago when she'd first caught him cheating she wouldn't be past her prime.

The MC of the event took the mike and got everyone's attention, announcing that the dance floor was open. Actually, it wasn't a dance floor at all, just a space where dining tables had been moved back. The voice of Frank Sinatra filled the room. "'I've got you under my skin...'" Four or five couples began to dance. Kay looked at Scranton. He was still talking to Lonnie and Rosalie. Then she heard Lonnie say, "Dans if' 'y 'ife, San'on."

Rosalie's face lit up as she looked to her husband to make sure he was serious. "Go," he said with his half-smile.

Scranton seemed uncertain, but offered Rosalie his hand. They walked to the dance floor. They were good dancers.

That should've been me. Surely Scranton wouldn't dance every dance with her. After all, she was married.

Just then Kay saw Saggy walking toward her. She fended him off by pretending to listen intently to Tessa and Accosta as they tried to talk with Lonnie. She was relieved when Saggy went elsewhere. She kept watching Scranton and wondered when it would be proper for her to cut in. *Would* it be proper? Kay would never do such a thing, but would Katerina?

The choice was made for her as the song ended and Scranton and Rosalie came back to the table. Kay sat up very straight and smiled at him. *Come on, ask me to dance!*

Rosalie pressed both hands against her chest. "That was fun. Thank you, Scranton."

"You're welcome." He took a seat near Lonnie.

"I love to watch people dance," Accosta said. "My husband was a good dancer."

"And you?" Rosalie asked.

"Not so much."

Tessa watched the group of dancers. "You know who I miss seeing out there? Reggie and Sadie Watkins."

"Who are they?" Kay asked.

"They were Happy Trails' version of Fred Astaire and Ginger Rogers," Rosalie said.

"Light as a feather," Tessa said with awe in her voice.

"They couldn't be here tonight?" Kay asked.

Looks were exchanged, then Tessa answered. "They died in a car accident earlier this month. A drunk driver hit them head-on."

"How awful," Kay said. "I'm so sorry."

They all nodded. Rosalie took Lonnie's hand again. "Death can be sneaky. We have to live each day to the fullest."

Kay was uncomfortable with this kind of talk. "I don't like to think about dying, much less talk about it."

"You think by not talking about it you're going to avoid it?" Tessa asked.

"Talking about it helps us remember not to waste the time we have," Rosalie said.

"Talking about those who have passed is a way to remember them," Accosta said.

So much for changing the subject.

Tessa seemed to count the people at the table, "Look here. Four of us have lost our spouses."

Kay was confused. She looked around the table and counted Accosta, Tessa, and Scranton, but then realized Tessa had counted her. "We have," she said clumsily.

Lonnie lifted his wife's hands to his lips. "We lucky, 'osie."

The opening strains to Glen Miller's "In the Mood" played and Kay ached to show her dance moves. The sequins on her dress would tremble.

Scranton stood up. It was happening. But then he leaned forward and picked up his glass. "Would anyone like a refill?"

Her face fell.

He took people's drink requests and walked off.

So much for showing—

Wrinkles walked toward her, his hand extended. "Like to dance, Katerina?"

"I'd love to." Dancing was dancing. At least Scranton could watch.

Wrinkles was a good dancer and twirled her under his arm and back again, making her laugh. Other people on the dance floor smiled at them.

When the song ended, Wrinkles wiggled his eyebrows. "Want another go?"

"Perhaps, but I need to rest first. Thank you . . ."

"Joe."

"Thank you, Joe."

"Until next time," he said.

She returned to her table but Lonnie, Rosalie, and Scranton were gone.

"Where did they go?" she asked the ladies.

"Lonnie tires easily," Accosta said.

"But why did Scranton leave?"

Tessa shrugged. "I was surprised to see him here at all. He mostly keeps to himself."

"Why?" Kay realized it was a blunt question. "I mean . . . is there a special reason?"

"Grief," Tessa said. "Though his wife's been gone a few years, he cared for her at home for months before that. They were obviously very close." She took a sip of cider. "I heard he moved here because being alone in their house became too painful."

"I understand that pain," Accosta said. "But I *didn't* move. I stayed far too long in our house. I lived in the pain."

"Katerina, did you move here to get away from your memories?" Tessa asked.

Memories of an unfaithful husband and *to escape a mundane, mediocre, miserable life.* "I suppose I did."

"I've forgotten, how long ago did your husband die?" Accosta asked.

"Two years." Kay realized she'd messed up. She panicked and quickly added, "Three. It's been three years."

Tessa gave her a slow blink.

Wrinkles was walking toward her again. Kay stood to accept his invitation before it was offered. "If you'll excuse me."

That was a close one.

Chapter Fourteen

Evelyn

> Cheerfully share your home with those
> who need a meal or a place to stay.
> God has given each of you a gift from his great variety
> of spiritual gifts. Use them well to serve one another.
> 1 Peter 4: 9-10

Evelyn was cleaning the mirror in the first floor bath when she felt a drip on her head.

She looked up and saw a large wet spot on the ceiling. *No, no, no, no.* She checked around for any other water spots as she called out, "Wayne!" She met him on the stairs and turned him around. "Water is leaking from our bathroom into the one downstairs."

He beat her to the upstairs bath. "It looks fine. Nothing's overflowing."

"Could a pipe be leaking in the walls?"

He touched the pipe under the sink. "Possibly." He stood. "I'll go turn off the main water valve."

Evelyn looked at the shower faucets and around the toilet. Nothing seemed amiss. When she heard Wayne coming up from the basement she met him in the first floor bath.

He peered up at the water stain. "That's not good," he said.

"I'll call Ringo."

** ** **

Ringo pulled the toilet from its place in the upper bathroom and set it to the side. "I'll replace the wax ring, but I don't see any leakage there, or in the faucets."

"That's what we thought too," Wayne said.

"So it's in the walls?" Evelyn asked.

"Seems so. I'm going to have to cut holes through the drywall to get to the pipes."

Holes? Evelyn didn't like the idea of that.

Ringo must have seen her face because he said, "Holes can be repaired. When I'm done you won't see a thing."

Promise?

"Let me get the right tools from my truck. Don't worry. I'll fix it."

"Could you use an extra set of hands?" Wayne asked.

"Always. I'll be right back."

Wayne headed to the bedroom. "I'm going to put on a work shirt. Don't worry Ev. We'll get it fixed up good as new."

"I know you will." *I pray you will.*

** ** **

Yes, there was a leak behind the walls under the sink.

Yes, Ringo fixed it.

Yes, he made a mess.

And yes, he was patching the drywall in both bathrooms so it would look brand new.

They were lucky to have him at their beck and call.

Evelyn watched as Ringo smoothed drywall spackle on the taped seams of a hole in the wet ceiling. "It seems you've done this a time or two," she said.

"A few times or two." He got off the stepstool. "It has to dry before I can sand it so I'll come in and out during the day — if that's all right."

"Of course it's all right," Wayne said. "Come and go as you need."

He pointed at the drop cloth he'd put down. "Don't worry about the sanding mess. I've got a shop vac, so I'll leave everything as I found it."

"I'm sure it will be better than you found it," Evelyn said. "We appreciate you."

He set his tools aside. "I'm going to go grab lunch. I'll see you soon."

"Actually would you like to eat with us? Tomato soup and grilled cheese?"

He smiled. "Actually that's a favorite. Thanks."

They went to the kitchen where soup and sandwiches were put on the stove in a matter of minutes.

Wayne got out plates and bowls while Ringo strolled around the room. He stopped at the Hoosier baking cabinet. "This looks original."

"It is." Evelyn stirred the soup, then went over to show him. "These two bins are for sugar and flour and they tilt down."

"Wow. That's cool."

"As you see, there's storage for spices and bowls and utensils. It was ahead of its time, grouping all the baking items together."

"Clearly." He looked out the backdoor to the yard. "I've always thought this was a great house." He put his hands in the pockets of his jeans. "A big house."

"It belonged to my husband's family before he and I moved into it after our wedding. We brought up Russell here. Actually, at one time it had been a boarding house before I turned it back into one. I found the old Peerbaugh Place sign in the attic."

"When did you turn it back?"

"In 2003, after my husband died and left me with virtually nothing. I had never worked outside the home and I needed income. God led me to the sign, I put it up, and an hour later your mom showed up wanting to rent a room."

"Leave it to Mom to be first."

Evelyn touched his arm. "Mae was my first tenant and became my very best friend—close as a sister."

"I know she feels the same about you."

"Actually, most of my close friends are linked to this house. It was all part of God's plan. Because of my need, your Mom, Tessa, and Audra with five-year-old Summer moved in."

"I'd forgotten that's how you all met. At the time I was traveling a lot as a roadie for a band."

"I remember that." Evelyn handed Ringo the napkins to set around.

"Mom met Collier while she was living here," he said.

"Yup. He lived across the street then, as they both do now. Though it was definitely not love at first sight."

He chuckled. "They've said as much. Mom tends to overwhelm."

"In a good way. They definitely fed each other's need for drama. Love came later."

"And Audra living here was how she met your son—and married him?"

"It is."

"Wow. The power of a place, huh?"

Evelyn liked the phrase. Peerbaugh Place had been instrumental in forming many relationships.

She went back to the soup, flipped the sandwiches to check the browning, and turned the heat off on both. "Lunch is served."

Wayne said grace and they dug in. In unison they dipped the tip of their sandwich in the soup. They exchanged smiles. "It *is* the only way to eat it," Wayne said with a laugh.

"How many tenants have passed through here?" Ringo asked.

"Thirty-four. Accosta stayed the longest—ten years. We've had lots of people stay for shorter periods of time. I was never stringent about a lease. If they didn't want to be here, I figured it was best to let them go. And then there were the ones who had—and have—family in the hospital who are just passing through."

"Do those people pay you anything?"

Evelyn shook her head. "Once in a while they slip Wayne a few dollars or leave us a gift, but we figure they have enough on their minds. Letting them stay is our way of giving back."

"You're a good woman, Evelyn."

"I second that," Wayne said.

Evelyn was touched by the compliment.

Chapter Fifteen

Scranton

> Be merciful to me, Lord,
> for I am in distress;
> my eyes grow weak with sorrow,
> my soul and body with grief.
> Psalm 31:9

Scranton skipped breakfast in the dining room and poured himself a cup of coffee. It would have to do. He told himself he wasn't hungry for a four-egg cheese and mushroom omelet, three strips of crisp bacon, and blueberry muffins, fresh out of the oven.

That was his annual birthday breakfast, served to him in bed by his lovely Olivia. And later, after a dinner of chicken parmigiana, she'd carry a red velvet cake to the table and sing "Happy Birthday" in her sweet but off-key voice.

He'd give anything to hear her voice again, to touch her cheek, to look into her pale blue eyes. And to touch her . . . she'd been such a tiny thing she would sit on his lap and he'd wrap his arms around her like a protective shield.

Only he hadn't been able to protect her at all. Cancer was stronger than them both. Vicious. Insatiable. He'd watched her body wilt like a week-old rose. When they'd had to accept that there was no escaping death, she'd wanted to spend her last months at home. He'd taken time away from work to be by her side until the end. That last night he'd lain next to her, holding her hand, synchronizing his breathing to hers. Until he suddenly realized he was breathing alone. He'd drawn her frail hand to his lips, sobbing with angry tears that God had taken her and not him.

Yet in the past two years Scranton realized that God took Olivia because she was more dear to Him than he was. During her illness her faith had glowed like a beacon shining in a dark, invincible forest. She had comforted *him* and had made him promise to move into Happy Trails—as they'd planned. "There's no need to worry about where I'm going to live. God has prepared a place for me in His house and I'm ready to go. And I'll have plenty to do. Plus, I have a few questions for Him."

"Like what?" he'd asked. Scranton had expected her to say she wanted to ask God why He'd let her get cancer. But instead she'd said, "I want to ask the Almighty why He created hedgeapples and fruit flies. For the life of me, I can't figure out a use for either one of them."

Olivia was like that, always thinking thoughts that nobody else would think to think. Always seeing God's hand in everything from a sunrise, to bumping into a friend, to getting a good parking space. Plus, she was always loving over everyone--whether they deserved it or not.

He'd never deserved her love. If only he'd been more loving toward *her*, if only he'd deserved her.

Scranton drew in a breath and pressed the space between his eyebrows, trying to force the tears away. Every time he thought he was cried-out more tears tried to bully him back into the abyss of his pain.

He shook his head and whispered to the bully, "No! You can't have me. Not today." After a few deep breaths, the tears subsided.

Until the next time.

** ** **

Scranton was awakened by the doorbell. With a start he realized he'd fallen asleep in his recliner watching a replay of the Royals winning the World Series the previous week.

The doorbell rang again. "Coming!"

It was Katerina—the over-done, over-cheerful, ever-annoying woman who kept inserting herself in his life.

She smiled at him, holding a piece of cake on a paper plate. "For you," she said. "Happy birthday."

He took the plate. How did she know?

"You missed the First Sunday meeting," she said. "They listed all the people who have birthdays in November. I realized yours was today."

"It is," he said. "Thanks."

She looked over his shoulder toward the apartment. "Can I come in for a few minutes?"

Scranton wanted to say no, but was too drowsy to think of a good reason. "Sure," he said, stepping aside.

Katerina swept past him in an overwhelming wave of floral perfume. Without being invited she strolled into the living room, touched a lampshade, and eyed the Waterford vase that he and Olivia had bought when they were in Ireland. She perched herself on the edge of the couch and said, "I love baseball. Nicolae and I had season tickets."

Good for you. "For what team?"

"Hmm. That's funny. I don't recall."

Not funny. Strange.

Scranton wished the game wasn't on. He had no wish to sit with this woman and watch it. He set the cake on the counter in the kitchen, then retrieved the remote and shut it off. "Sorry to cut this short, but I was just getting ready to go out with friends to celebrate."

She stood. Her frown aged her face dramatically. She changed it into a smile. "That's nice. Where are you going?"

He chose a random place. "Delvecchio's."

"I've never been there. Maybe we could go together some time."

He didn't want to encourage her, didn't want to say "maybe" because she seemed to be the kind of woman who would take that as a "yes." Instead he said, "Thanks for the cake."

She headed toward the door but paused before opening it. "Have a good birthday dinner."

"Thank you. I will."

He shut the door on her. And locked it—which seemed silly. It's not like Katerina was someone to lock out. And yet . . . he did *not* like her. There was something fake and desperate about her.

He collected the cake and went back to his recliner. He turned the game back on and took a bite. It was good.

But it was no red velvet.

Chapter Sixteen

Accosta

Always be joyful. Never stop praying.
Be thankful in all circumstances,
for this is God's will for you who belong to Christ Jesus.
1 Thessalonians 5: 16-18

Accosta had never planned a charity drive and wasn't sure what she could offer the committee. But Tessa had insisted she come along.

Everyone greeted them as they entered the meeting room. Everyone made her feel welcome. Although she had a lifetime of friends in Carson Creek through church and Peerbaugh Place, she'd met dozens of new friends at Happy Trails. It was not something she'd expected at age ninety-three.

Although she was happy for the friends, she was also happy to let Tessa and others take the lead. She knew her strengths. She was a good listener and a good pray-er. Long ago the Almighty had called her to be a prayer warrior. She'd been reluctant at first — after all, who was she to the world and to the firmament of heaven? But as her awareness of the needs of others increased, she surrendered to her calling. God wanted her to pray? She would pray. A lot. No matter where she was, she found herself praying for people's work issues, safe travel, sick family, hurting relationships . . . it was her job.

To facilitate God's assignment He'd given her the ability to send prayers heavenward while listening to earthbound conversations. It was like her mind had two sections, one linked to the people in the here and now, and the other to the Almighty in heaven. She was their intermediary — because far too many people never thought about praying. They were too busy, too proud, too meek, or too skeptical to believe that the Lord of the Universe would want to know about their wants, desires, and the details of their lives. Surely He had better things to do.

Accosta knew He didn't. Even though the God of the Universe always had a lot to do, He also always had time for His children. Each prayer represented a desire to build a relationship. God was all about relationships.

As a prayer warrior her biggest hope was that the beneficiaries of her prayers would feel a spark of God's presence and start their own conversation.

Like now, as the ladies discussed the type of charity event they would hold—whether it was a silent auction, a raffle, or a food or toy drive—Accosta nodded at all the right moments, even as she prayed for the personal lives of the ladies.

Her prayers were interrupted by Katerina tapping a pen against a pad where she was taking notes. "How about a casino night?" she said. "My husband and I loved going to the casinos in Monte Carlo. They had such a vibrant, elegant atmosphere. The house usually wins so we could give that money to charity."

If looks could kill . . . *No one* liked the idea.

"Hmm," Tessa said.

Accosta was glad the idea was quickly overruled, as nothing good ever came from gambling. But Accosta didn't understand why Katerina felt the need to mention visiting Monte Carlo—and so many other fancy, foreign places she'd gone. It wasn't making her any friends. Accosta knew some people had branded Katerina a showoff and a snob—and she was. But Accosta felt there was more to the woman than that. There had to be.

When her suggestion was dismissed, Katerina's jaw tightened and she crossed her arms, allowing her magenta-painted nails to play with her long gold necklace. Behind her proud aura, Accosta sensed a vulnerability. And pain. *Lord, Katerina needs Your special care. Only You know what's behind her obsession with puffing herself up. Replace her insecurity with Your peace. Show me how to help her.*

There was a swell in the decibel level as three of the ladies talked at once.

Tessa got them under control. She was so skilled at being a leader, yet not many knew what a softie she was. For only a person with a generous heart would allow a friend to upset the equilibrium of her well-established life by letting them move in. Accosta was forever grateful for Tessa's generosity. *Bless her, Lord. Thank You for giving me Tessa's friendship. And thank You for giving her this outlet for her leadership.*

A half hour passed and a silent auction was chosen as the vehicle for fund-raising. The discussion moved on to decorations and food. Everyone gave their opinion—even Accosta, who thought potted mums were a great centerpiece choice because they could be sold or planted in the flower beds around the building.

Only one person remained silent. And it wasn't Katerina.

It was Rosalie.

It was like she was there, but wasn't *really* there. She'd separated herself slightly by pushing her chair back a few inches from the table. Her hands kept each other company in her lap. She was attentive, but timid. More than once Accosta saw her raise her finger as if to interject a point, but quickly lower it when the discussion moved on without her. She didn't act frustrated by her inability to be noticed, she seemed resigned, as if she thought very little of her own ideas and was willing to let others take control. The only time Accosta had ever seen Rosalie come alive was in the presence of her husband. Left on her own, she seemed to flounder.

In some ways she reminded Accosta of herself. Accosta had been a dutiful wife who'd lived within the dictates of her roles as wife and mother. Her husband had ruled the roost—which wasn't bad, but in retrospect, Accosta wished she'd been more aware of the basics of their life, such as balancing a checkbook, dealing with taxes, or hiring someone to repair the water heater when it stopped working. When her husband died twelve years ago, she'd been completely overwhelmed by the how-tos of daily living. If not for Evelyn and Wayne she probably would have died in her broken-down house with the electricity turned off due to non-payment, the floors flooded by burst pipes, and the windows broken by bored neighbor kids.

Was Rosalie and Lonnie's relationship similar? She was a generation away from Accosta's age, but that didn't mean husbands didn't still like to be in charge, or wives weren't overly dependent and silent.

Rosalie's busy hands stilled and she clasped them in her lap. Accosta saw her eyes close. Was she praying? With Lonnie in assisted living she had to feel a lot of pressure and uncertainty.

Accosta immediately sent up multiple prayers for both of them. *Lord, Rosalie and Lonnie . . . heal Lonnie so he can return to their apartment soon. Rosalie needs him to be her true north. Help them both find strength and peace.*

Tessa must have noticed the direction of Accosta's gaze because she said, "Rosalie? What do you think about the menu?"

Rosalie gave a slow blink, then said, "I think it's marvelous. Let me know what to bring."

Tessa turned her attention to Accosta. "And you?"

She smiled at Rosalie. "I'm with her. Let me know what to bring."

Rosalie returned a grateful smile.

** ** **

After the meeting Accosta stayed back to talk to Rosalie. "They're quite the group of dynamos, aren't they?" she said.

"I'm grateful for them," Rosalie said. "They have so many good ideas. Lonnie said I should get more involved, but I'm not very good at brainstorming or making decisions."

"Not to worry. They seem very capable of making them without us, yes?"

Rosalie smiled. "Very."

Accosta pointed toward the game room. "I was going to work on a puzzle. Do you want to join me?"

"That would be nice."

They reached the room and took chairs at the community puzzle. It was a picture of an old fashioned general store.

"Well now," Accosta said. "I think I'll work on these candy jars over here."

Rosalie scanned the puzzle. "I'll get the shelf of canned goods."

They worked in silence a few minutes before Rosalie spoke up. "That committee . . . thanks for backing me up. I came from a family that was always *loud*. Mom and Dad loved to argue, and my two brothers wrestled and broke things, and . . ." She shook her head. "I was the only girl, and the youngest, and hated all the commotion and drama. They made fun of me for being so quiet. Papa called me his meek mouse."

Accosta nodded. "'Blessed are the meek for theirs is the kingdom of heaven.'"

She scoffed. "That's certainly not what they thought."

"You're not alone," Accosta said. "I'm more comfortable observing than participating."

Rosalie's eyes lit up. "Me too!" Her expression suddenly changed. "Yet, as much as crowds overwhelm me, I don't actually like being alone."

Loneliness. Accosta could relate. "How is Lonnie doing?"

"Well. I think. But being the weak one frustrates him. I wish I knew what to do to really help, besides visiting or bringing him things to read."

Accosta reached her hand across the table and touched Rosalie's. "Just be you. That's all he needs. He'll be home in no time."

"I hope so."

Accosta went back to work on the candy jars as she raised up more prayers for Rosalie and Lonnie.

Chapter Seventeen

Kay

> If we claim we have no sin,
> we are only fooling ourselves
> and not living in the truth.
> 1 John 1:8

After leaving the charity drive meeting, Kay stormed into her apartment and shucked off her shoes, sending one bouncing against a chair, and the other scuffing the wall. She sailed her notepad over the couch, pages fluttering. Her pen followed, doing an end-over-end against a crystal candleholder on the coffee table.

"Those women! They shot down every idea I had." She stomped into her bedroom, whipped off the wig, her jewelry, the expensive wool sweater that made her itch, and the pair of navy pants whose crease she had pressed with great care. She pulled on a pair of jeans that hadn't seen the light of day since she'd moved in, and her favorite I Love NYC sweatshirt that she'd bought online—having never been to New York or anywhere east of St. Louis.

Kay sat at her dressing table and peeled off her false eyelashes. She raked her fingers through her boy-short hair, letting the mousy salt-and-pepper layers fall where they may.

She peered in the mirror. "If they could see me now . . . "

The bed beckoned and she flipped on the TV, threw the covers back, climbed in, and let the sounds of soap operas compete with the could-have-saids in her mind.

** ** **

Kay checked the bedside clock. She'd been in bed an hour and hadn't slept a minute of it. Her mind raced with thoughts of retaliation against the ladies on the committee, against Scranton and his rudeness, against the shunning of the sewing club, the card players, and against all the people at Happy Trails who gave her disapproving looks and whispered behind their hands. She'd moved out of her apartment because no one had noticed her there, and now people noticed her but didn't like her.

What was she doing wrong?

It was as bad as junior high when the cool kids made fun of her for wearing skirts down to her knees instead of mini-skirts. She still heard her mother's voice: "I will *not* have any daughter of mine leave the house looking like a floozy!" The cool kids also teased her for wearing fake Bardolino shoes instead of the real thing which cost four times as much—too much for her family to afford. It hadn't helped that she'd suffered from a horrible case of acne. The cool kids went to dermatologists for their breakouts while Kay was stuck with Noxzema and told not to eat French fries and chocolate. What was life without French fries and chocolate?

She flung the covers off and sat up. "How can I get them to like me?"

The scene playing on the soap opera got her attention. *"Please come to my party, Carl,"* said the gorgeous TV diva.

Party. She'd talked to Tessa and Accosta about having a party. One that would wow them into liking her.

Not just a party . . . a soiree.

She got out of bed and began to plan.

** ** **

The problem with having an extravagant soiree was that it cost an extravagant amount of money. But it couldn't be helped. Although Kay had money from the divorce settlement, most of her nest egg had gone toward buying into Happy Trails. She was getting monthly alimony from Wally, but it wasn't as much as she deserved for being the woman scorned. She had enough to get by, but had to be careful. She'd already splurged on wigs and clothes. Yet going into debt to gain acceptance would be worth the price.

Although Kay had studied what wealthy women wore she wasn't sure about the details of putting on a fancy party. The biggest party splurge she and Wally ever made was for his sixtieth birthday. They'd bought brisket from a local BBQ restaurant. They'd added buns, potato salad, cole slaw, fries, and beer, and everybody was happy.

None of that would do for her soiree, so she spent hours online getting ideas for fancy appetizers and desserts. She knew next to nothing about wine other than it being red, white, or rosé, and was certain that serving what she could afford—which fit within her box-o-wine budget—wouldn't do anything to win friends and influence people. Instead she chose a champagne punch because it would make the booze go further and seemed upscale. Iced tea and coffee would have to do for those who didn't imbibe—to use Tessa's term. She didn't want to use paper plates so rented goblets, plates, cups, saucers, and silverware. And cloth napkins in a classy ivory.

Invitations caused another big decision. Should she hand out invites to those she really wanted to come? That was the proper way of it, but that number was under a dozen. To make a splash she needed *dozens* to attend. So she hand-delivered invitations to her Happy Trails friends, but also posted an invite in the weekly bulletin. She asked people to RSVP, but was doubtful they would. So there was the added worry that she'd run out of food and drink. Plus, how would she keep up with the punch and refills of the food?

There was no way around it: she needed help.

With less than a week to go before the event, Kay decided to call Sharon. Kay had made a point of talking to her once a week, and so far had been successful in fending off Sharon's questions about when she could come visit.

The time had come.

Sharon answered her phone. "Two calls in a week? You must need something."

Kind of. Sort of. "Actually. . . I need a *really* big favor."

"Does it involve a visit?"

"It does. But with a twist." There was silence on the line. "You still there?" Kay asked.

"It sounds ominous."

"Not at all," Kay said. "I'm giving a big soiree to—"

"Soiree? What kind of word is that?"

"French, I think."

"That's not what I meant. Since when does Kay Volkov talk about having a soiree?"

Kay fueled herself with a breath. "Since Kay Volkov became Katerina Volkov."

Another pause. "The name your grandmother used to call you."

Kay remembered the lie and decided to come clean. "Actually, I got the name from a woman who was getting a makeover on the shopping channel. They were changing her looks with different wigs."

"Wow. I don't even know what to say." There was no way to avoid telling Sharon the full truth. "When I moved here I chose to become another person—with another past."

Sharon huffed. "Okay . . ."

Kay pressed on. "My late husband's name is Nicolae."

"Whoa there. Late husband? I know you wanted to kill Wally a time or two but . . . and why Nicolae?"

Kay had no feasible explanation. She just liked the sound of it. "We're a wealthy couple who have traveled the world. He's an international banker."

Sharon scoffed. "What in the name of crazy are you doing, woman? Do people really believe you?"

"They do." *I hope they do.*

"But . . . you're lying. Big time. I may not know my Bible much beyond Christmas and Easter, but even I know 'thou shalt not lie.'"

Kay began to pace. "It's not really a lie. It's more an embellishment."

"Changing Wally's name to Nicolae, having him be dead, and pretending you're rich is lying. Plain and simple."

Why didn't Sharon understand? After all Kay had been through she deserved to have the lifestyle she wanted. "Here's the why of it, Shar. Up until now I've lived an ordinary life, been married to an unfaithful husband, had one kid end up in prison, and the other move as far away from me as she can get."

"Tif didn't move to Idaho to get away from you. She, Rod, and the kids love it out there."

"Rod's her *second* husband."

"So . . ."

"They run a Dairy Sweet."

"There's nothing wrong with ice cream. It makes people happy. Especially Rocky Road."

Sharon wasn't getting it. "Don't you ever want to be someone different? Someone better?"

"Sure. But I'm not going to change my whole history to do it." She huffed into the phone. "We are who we are because of who we were. There's nothing wrong with that."

There was everything wrong with that. "I don't want to live the rest of my life the way I was living it before. I want it to be different. Nothing turned out how I dreamed or planned."

"Join the club. I wanted to be a ballerina and I'm pretty sure Hank never planned on being a tax accountant. But you don't see us changing our names to Alexandriana and Horace. Tell me this, who are you trying to impress?"

Kay's thoughts flew to Scranton, yet quickly boomeranged back. He was a definite fail.

"Kay?"

"No one in particular."

"Are there a lot of rich people at Happy Trails? Are you trying to fit in?"

"No and no." She wasn't trying to do that at all—in fact, she was trying to do the opposite and rise above everyone else. "Being Katerina makes me happy, okay? Don't I deserve to be happy?"

"Sure, but—"

"But, nothing." Back to the reason for her call. "To be happy I'm giving a big party to impress everyone and make them like me."

"That soir-y thing?" Sharon asked.

"Soir-aye."

"I don't understand why you think your real life was so bad. So you've been through a rough patch? Lots of people get divorced, and lots of people have kids who've gotten off track."

"Prison is more than off-track."

"Yeah. I suppose it is." Sharon changed direction. "Is being this new person why you bought a wig?"

"Wigs."

"Right. Wigs. From the shopping channel, modeled by a woman named Katerina."

Kay didn't know whether Sharon would understand, yet who *but* Sharon would understand? "The divorce forced me to start over and made me question who I was. I mean, after nearly fifty years of marriage Wally left me for frumpy Janice?"

"There's no way either of us can figure out Wally. I mean the guy wears socks with sandals and has a comb-over."

All true. "What kills me is the two of them look better than they ever did before and they went on *my* dream vacation. Plus they're living in *my* house! The one I decorated and made a home."

"Yeah, that was cruel. But Wally paid you for your share, right?"

"He did, but here's the point: my year in apartment hell didn't work out with me being myself. Since I decided to scrap that life, I wanted to start over somewhere completely different, being some*one* completely different."

"I know you didn't find friends at the apartment, but surely Happy Trails is different. Do you really think the people there wouldn't like Kay—just plain Kay who's been my best friend forever? You're a good, kind person. I love you."

Kay appreciated Sharon's nice words, but defending herself was exhausting. She fell back onto the couch. "I love you too, Shar, but don't begrudge me the chance to embellish my past in order to get a better future. I'm not hurting anyone. And to answer your first question about them liking Kay? How can I expect the people at Happy Trails to like me as Kay when *I* don't like me as Kay?"

She heard Sharon's heavy sigh through the phone. "Wow, woman. This is heavy stuff. I'm not sure how to help."

Kay felt a glimmer of hope. "I do. You can—"

"Stop." Sharon said into the phone. "Stop just a minute because I have a big question for you."

"Shoot."

"Do *I* have a place in Katerina's life?"

Kay hesitated. "Of course you do . . ."

"I hear a 'but' in that sentence."

She might as well just say it. "But . . . right now I need you to help with my party, refill the punch bowl and food so I can mingle."

There was a long pause. "Why can't I just help you as a friend attending the party? We've always helped each other when we entertain. It's natural. It's what friends do."

Kay didn't know how to answer her.

"Are you ashamed of me?"

"No, no," Kay said. "Not at all. It's just that I have this scenario in my head about me being able to afford to hire help for my party and—"

"I'm the hired help."

"Just this once." She hurried with an explanation. "You can call yourself the caterer or a waitress or whatever title you want."

"Can I wear a French maid's uniform?"

"Uh . . . doesn't that have bad connotations?"

"Fine. Can I at least wear a little cap and apron?"

"You can wear anything you want—within reason."

Silence.

"You're missing my point completely, but okay. Fine."

Kay blinked. "You'll do it?"

"Of course I'll do it. But I want to go on record that I don't know this new Katerina-person and I miss my best friend. We *were* joined at the hip, Kay. I don't want to lose that."

"I know. And we won't. I'm still here." Mostly. She was too confused to know for sure.

Sharon sighed. "Do you need help making the food?"

"Yes, please." Kay let out the breath she'd been saving. Once again, Sharon had proven herself to be her very best friend. No matter what.

Chapter Eighteen

Evelyn

We can make our plans,
but the Lord determines our steps.
Proverbs 16:9

A new hospital guest stood in front of Evelyn—loomed over her, all six-foot-four of him. "I told you yesterday, Mrs. Wellington, that I do not eat carbs." He picked up a muffin. "This..." He tossed it back on the tray. "Is unacceptable. I need protein."

She had never had anyone complain before. "I could include some hard-boiled eggs..."

He shook his head slowly, back and forth, as if disgusted with her ignorance. "I like my eggs warm."

Wayne came into the dining room from the kitchen. "I'm sorry our continental breakfast doesn't please you, Mr. Moore, but that's what we have to offer so our guests can come and go as they need. Our other guest, Mrs. Sanger, has no objections."

"Good for her." He poured coffee into a foam cup. "And no cream?"

"Cream needs to be refrigerated," Evelyn said. "That's why we bought these other creamers so they are fresh for you any time."

Mr. Moore shook his head. "As if I don't have enough to worry about with my wife's recovery."

Evelyn felt bad. His wife had had major surgery three days earlier. "Maybe *she'd* like a muffin? I could wrap it up for her."

"Don't be ridiculous. No carbs." He stormed out.

Evelyn's insides trembled at the exchange. "What are we going to do with him? I've never met anyone so disagreeable."

Wayne flicked stray crumbs into his hand. "There's no pleasing some people."

But that's what I live for.

Wayne swiped the crumbs into a waste basket. "Collier and I are going to the men's meeting at church. Why don't you go talk to Mae. She'll walk you off the cliff."

It was a great idea. She put the leftover muffins in Tupperware and walked across the street just as Collier and Wayne drove away. She knocked, then opened the door. "Knock knock, it's me."

Mae called from the kitchen. "Come on back. Tea's on."

Evelyn loved how they could come and go in each other's houses with little fanfare or notice. It worked because they knew each other's schedules and didn't abuse the privilege.

Mae had tea poured before Evelyn took her usual place at the kitchen table. She shoved a tin full of rusks toward her. Evelyn took one out and dipped it in the tea.

"You look horrible," Mae said.

"Nice to see you too."

"Just being honest, Evie." She stirred sugar in her tea. "You and hubby have a fight?"

"No. That's not a thing with us."

Mae rolled her eyes. "You two are far too easy-going. Collie and I enjoy an occasional ruckus."

Evelyn shook her head, thankful that both she and Wayne avoided drama.

"So?" Mae said. "Are you going to tell me what's wrong, because if you don't, that crease between your eyes is going to become a crevasse."

Evelyn blew on her tea then took a sip. "It's our newest hospital guest. He's . . . difficult."

"How so?"

Let me count the ways. Evelyn told her about the no-carb fiasco.

Mae made a face. "If he wants his eggs hot tell him to mash a few hard-boiled eggs on a plate, put a pad of butter on top, and nuke 'em."

"Butter on eggs?" It didn't sound good at all.

"Collie likes 'em that way once in a while."

"I suppose it's worth a try."

"Or offer Greek yogurt, meat sticks, or cheese in a little cooler."

"Those are okay for low carb?"

"I think so. I may dress like a hippie but my breakfast preferences fall into the chocolate-chip muffin category or getting my serving of fruit in a Pop-Tart."

"Mine too." Evelyn was thankful for the ideas. "Actually . . . food is just one part of our problem with him."

"Go on."

"Mr. Moore comes in after we've gone to bed . . ."

"That's not unusual for a hospital guest."

"It's not, but he's noisy about it. He stomps on the stairs, doesn't know how to close a door without making everybody hear, and clanks around in his room and in the bathroom he shares with another guest. She's complained about him too."

"Have you or Wayne talked to him about it?"

Evelyn's stomach tightened at the mention of confrontation. "Not yet. Though Wayne did put a list of our house rules in his room yesterday. "

"How did he react?"

"I don't really know, as he got them after he stomped in. I expect to find the paper thrown away."

"Zounds. You should tell him to find more suitable arrangements elsewhere," Mae said. "I know it won't be easy, but if he's not following the house rules or the simple rules of good manners . . ."

Evelyn nodded. It *was* the logical thing to do, yet she knew Wayne wasn't the sort to give ultimatums. And neither was she.

"I can tell you're not getting enough sleep." Mae pointed at the dark circles under Evelyn's eyes.

Evelyn knew her age was showing. "Ever since Accosta moved out, my energy is gone—which makes no sense. We only have the two hospital guests and haven't rented out her room yet, so theoretically I have less work, but physically, I can't seem to catch up."

Mae ate an entire rusk before answering. "Maybe it's time to move on." She looked directly at Evelyn. "Move out."

It took her a moment to understand. "Sell Peerbaugh?"

"Well yes." Mae leaned forward on the table. "Have you considered it?"

"Piper mentioned it at our party. She says she can easily sell the house."

"Then do it."

Evelyn sat back in her chair. "We've gotten the same suggestion from two different people. That's got to mean something."

"Exactly. Hearing something twice is not a coincidence. It's—"

"God." Evelyn nodded. They'd talked about God's nudges many times. "Actually, Wayne and I *have* talked a little about moving to Happy Trails."

Mae clapped her hands together. "Perfect."

"It's not perfect at all. We just started talking about it. It can't be time yet."

"Why not?"

"Because . . ." She thought of a reason. "They don't have any openings. That's why Accosta moved in with Tessa."

"But people move in and out all the time."

"Not really. People generally don't move into a retirement place without realizing it's probably their last move. They move out when they . . . you know. Die."

Mae sat back in her chair. "Gracious wake-up call, Evie, you are so dramatic. Not everyone at Happy Trails is on death's door. You can't think of it that way."

They shared a moment of silence.

Mae took another rusk. "Think of it as a step toward freedom to fully enjoy your life. Freedom to take all the chores off your plate and do what you want to do."

"But what do I want to do?"

Mae tossed her hands in the air. "Sheesh, Evie, I can't do everything for you. That's something you'll need to figure out."

"I just don't know Mae. I'm not ready."

"Ready or not, I still think you should do it," Mae said. "It's a wise choice."

"If it's such a wise choice why don't you and Collier move there?"

Mae got up to pour more tea.

"You're avoiding the question," Evelyn said.

"I most certainly am." She poured, then returned to her seat. "We're just not there yet. This house is about half the size of

Peerbaugh Place, with half the maintenance. We don't have tenants to mess with our lives. And so far, Collie likes to mow the lawn and I like to garden. It's not time. Yet." She reached over and took Evelyn's hand. "Imagine not having to mess with any of that."

It would mean fewer aches and pains. Fewer times of complete exhaustion. "It would be nice." Evelyn could see her point. "And we *are* older than you."

"You're coming up on seventy, but how old is Wayne?"

"Seventy-seven."

Mae spread her arms as if that number clinched it.

"I'm still not sure," Evelyn said. "It's such a drastic step."

"As much as I like to tell people what to do, the final decision has to fall on you and Wayne."

Unfortunately.

** ** **

"You'd really consider selling?" Wayne said at lunch.

"Maybe."

"What happened to the Evelyn who proclaimed, 'The only way you'll get me out of this house is feet first?'"

She hated being inconsistent — or rather, she hated being *caught* being inconsistent. "Selling is just an idea."

"A big one."

"It would take care of our bad boarder problem."

Wayne picked up half of his ham sandwich and pointed a corner at her. "I will not let a bully push us out of our home."

He was right. "And yet . . . it would be nice not to deal with the constant turnover and so many challenging personalities. What if we closed up the boarding house and just lived here?"

He dragged his finger through a glob of mustard on his plate, and licked it. "It's a big house for just us two."

She thought of another good point. "And it's an old house. Remember the leaky pipe? And the windows in the sunroom leak too."

"Only when we have a storm from the south."

"Which is almost weekly in the spring. And the front landscaping is overgrown, the fridge is on its last legs, and the porch needs to be painted—which means sanding first." The to-dos became overwhelming. "It's a lot."

"It is a lot." He pushed his plate away. "So do we really want to consider moving?"

"I don't know." She shook her head, realizing there was another problem: "Even if we wanted to move, there's no room at Happy Trails. That's one reason Accosta moved in with Tessa."

"I am *not* moving in with Tessa," Wayne said.

She rolled her eyes at his humor. "I think the feeling is mutual. The point is, Happy Trails is not an option."

He set his sandwich down. "Give me your hand." He took it and bowed his head. "Father? We are very confused. A part of us wants to move and another part wants to keep things as they are. You know where we need to be. Guide us toward the right decision." He squeezed her hand. "Amen?"

"Amen." Evelyn hoped God would make things clear enough for her sleep-deprived brain to grasp.

Chapter Nineteen

Rosalie & Kay

> The prudent understand where they are going,
> but fools deceive themselves.
> Proverbs 14: 8

Rosalie wasn't sure about going to Katerina's party by herself, but Lonnie had told her it would be good for her. She'd suggested he come with her, but Lonnie said his wheelchair would be in the way, and he wasn't feeling up to it anyway.

And so, she went alone.

She *had* been curious about Katerina's apartment. With all her talk of world travel she'd expected to see exotic souvenirs, yet the décor was pretty normal. The most exotic thing she saw was a set of nesting Russian dolls displayed in a huge hutch. But maybe Katerina had put all her valuables away to prevent breakage.

The apartment was full to overflowing with people. Katerina was in her element, looking gorgeous in a champagne-colored silk top and tailored tan pants. Her hair was perfect — as always — pulled back into a braided bun. She touched her own gray, thinning hair. Rosalie envied Katerina's perfect hair more than the clothes. If she didn't comb hers just right, a bald spot would show.

Katerina had pulled out all the stops for the food. There was a whipped feta dip, a caramel dip with pretzels and apples, baked mac and cheese bites, and a pastry cup full of yummy French onions — way fancier than Rosalie had ever served — or eaten.

There was even a champagne punch. Scranton teased her into having a taste of his but she quickly changed to iced tea. Tea wasn't glamorous, but neither was she.

After a half-hour Rosalie gazed longingly at the couch. She'd had a hard day trying to keep Lonnie's spirits up and needed to sit. But when Accosta and Tessa arrived — both wearing pillbox hats with feathers—she motioned them over and offered up her place to Accosta. Somehow Tessa managed to sit in the space too.

"Can I get you ladies a plate and something to drink?" Rosalie asked.

"You don't have to play the hostess," Tessa said. "By the way, where is she?"

Rosalie spotted Katerina near the punchbowl, chatting with two men she didn't know. "Over there."

"She's certainly popular," Tessa said.

"It's nice she gave the party," Accosta said. "It's a good way for her to meet people."

Tessa shuffled her shoulders. "I suppose it is." She looked at Rosalie. "Well, since you offered, we'd be glad for some refreshment."

"Tea, coffee, or champagne punch?"

"Coffee," they said at the same time. "If it's decaf," Tessa added.

"Cream or sugar?"

"Black," they said in unison a second time.

"Some appetizers?"

"Nothing with mushrooms," Tessa said.

Rosalie realized she'd overpromised, but loaded up two plates with tasty options and got them delivered, then went back for the coffee.

"You're a dear," Accosta said.

An exhausted dear.

They overheard people talking nearby, as they held up photographs of the Eiffel Tower and the Coliseum. Rosalie looked at the far wall, where there were photos of Big Ben and St. Basil's in Moscow.

"Where are Katerina and her husband in the pictures?" said a man. He scoped out the room—which made all of them do the same. "I haven't seen a single picture of her family."

Tessa glanced at Accosta and Rosalie. "It is a bit odd. I like to get people in my tourist pictures."

Rosalie felt a stitch in her stomach. People were insinuating something, yet she couldn't quite figure out what.

She heard someone mention the punch was running out. Rosalie glanced toward Katerina, but she was still occupied being the hostess.

Rosalie looked toward the kitchen, then back to her friends, "I'm going to help the waitress. It seems she's getting behind."

"You don't have—"

Rosalie ignored Tessa and went into the small kitchen that had been set apart with a folding screen. The waitress was pouring a beverage from one wine bottle to another. Why would she do that?

She looked up when she noticed Rosalie. "Oh. Hi." She quickly set the first bottle aside. "Can I help you?"

"That's what I was going to offer you. How can I help?"

The woman sighed. "Just a minute and let me transfer this." She finished pouring from one bottle into another that had a Dom Perignon label. She gave a nervous laugh and poured ginger ale into a pitcher that appeared to be orange juice. "If you want to take that tray of bruschetta out, I'd appreciate it."

The waitress went first and with much applause poured the liquids into the punch bowl. Rosalie replaced the empty appetizer tray with the full one. Other trays needed to be replenished. The waitress picked up one and nodded at the other. "If you would?"

They went back to the kitchen. "You're a godsend . . . what's your name?"

"Rosalie."

"I'm Sharon."

"Nice to meet you."

Together they filled the two trays. "When Kay and I were making all these appetizers I thought we were making too many. Obviously not."

"Kay?"

"I mean Katerina."

"You two made all these?"

"We did. Kay got the recipes off Pinterest. I wouldn't cook much of anything without Pinterest."

Rosalie had heard of Pinterest, but had never used it.

They finished the last tray. "As a guest you certainly are going above and beyond, Rosalie," she said. "I'll make sure Kay knows how much you helped."

There was that 'Kay' name again.

** ** **

If Rosalie had been tired before the party, afterward she could barely walk back to her apartment.

"Gracious, Rosalie," Tessa said after dropping Accosta off. She linked their arms. "Let me help you. You seem done in."

"I'm afraid I am."

"You were working as hard as the waitress. You didn't have to do that."

"I didn't mind. I feel more at home if I'm helping."

"You need to learn how to relax and let others do for *you*."

"I know," Rosalie said, but it was never going to happen. They reached her apartment and she fumbled with the key and dropped it. "I'm such a klutz." When she bent down to get it and stood up, she wobbled. "Whoa. I'm dizzy."

"Did you eat anything?"

"I had a couple nibbles," she said.

Tessa took the key, opened the door, and led Rosalie inside, making her sit down.

"I'm okay. Really."

"You are not okay. I'm going to sit here until you get your bearings. I'll get you a glass of water."

Rosalie hated being fussed over, but she drank most of the water.

Tessa sat nearby. "What did you think of Katerina's soiree — as she liked to call it."

"It was a great success. People seemed to have a good time. Lots of laughing and talking." She took another sip of water. "I'm glad I could help. Sharon, the waitress, was overwhelmed. "

"You're a gem, Rosalie Clemons."

Rosalie appreciated the compliment.

"What catering company did Katerina use?" Tessa said.

"Sharon said she and Katerina made all the appetizers."

"*They* did?"

"I think they're friends. She kept calling Katerina, Kay."

"Hmm. That's interesting." Tessa leaned forward on her cane. "She must have spent a pretty penny on the affair—even if they made the food themselves. I saw five bottles of Dom Perignon being poured in that punch. Even I know that's extremely expensive."

"Oh." Suddenly Rosalie realized what she'd seen.

"What 'oh'?"

She didn't want to tattle. "It's nothing."

Tessa sat up straighter. "It is not nothing. Tell me."

Rosalie knew Tessa wouldn't give up and she was too tired to fight the inevitable. "Sharon kept refilling the Dom Perignon bottle with champagne from another bottle. I know nothing about such things, and yet—"

Tessa nodded knowingly. "Of course. She was passing a cheaper champagne off for the expensive one."

Rosalie felt bad. "I wouldn't want other people to know. I'm sure she saved a lot of money by doing that."

"I'm sure she did. Because no one *needs* Dom Perignon. But I say, just be open about serving the less expensive label—or don't mention it at all. No one really cares." Tessa shook her head back and forth. "'What a tangled web we weave, when first we practice to deceive.'"

"I shouldn't have told you."

Tessa waved away her concern. "The champagne was only part of it. From what I heard buzzing around the room, people were doubting she's even been to all the places in the framed photos. Some of the pictures looked like blown-up postcards. And an antique dealer friend said the console Katerina said was 18th century was more like 1980."

"Oh dear. That's not good."

"That's not good." Tessa perked up. "You said the waitress called her Kay?"

"It's probably short for Katerina."

Tessa shook her head back and forth. "Kat is a nickname for Katerina, or even Rina. Not Kay. Is her name a lie too?" She waggled her eyebrows.

Rosalie pressed her fingers to her eyes. She couldn't think about that now.

"Never mind. Let's get you to bed. We'll worry about Katerina or Kay or whatever-her-name-is in the morning."

* ** **

Kay and Sharon boxed up the last of the rental dishes. "That's it, then," Kay said.

"It's been a long night," Sharon said. "My feet are killing me."

"Me too," Kay said. "Neither of us are used to standing so long."

"I don't know what I would have done without Rosalie helping me."

"Rosalie?"

"Your friend? She helped make the punch and replenish the trays. Surely you saw her helping."

Kay's insides grabbed. She had seen Rosalie—in passing. "Did she help with the champagne?"

"I'm sure she did. We were moving like a well-oiled machine by the end of the night."

"Oh no! Shar, I'm ruined."

"You're over-reacting."

"I'm not."

"Don't worry. Rosalie didn't blink at any of it. And she didn't seem the type to spread gossip. She was a nice lady. I told her how to use Pinterest."

It took Kay a moment to mentally move from champagne to a website. Then it hit her. "You told Rosalie that *we* made the hors d'oeuvres?"

"Was that a secret too? Making your own food shows you're a hard worker—and a good cook. And honestly, Kay, the whole champagne game seemed unnecessary. Nobody but the ultra-rich would use Dom in a punch."

Suddenly, Kay felt a little silly. It had seemed like a good idea at the time. She sank onto a dining room chair. "I'm done for."

"Don't be so dramatic." Sharon touched Kay's shoulder. "You had a great party. People had a good time."

Kay peered up at her hopefully. "They did, didn't they?"

"Of course they did." She took her coat and purse out of the entry closet. "I have got to go. We're having a birthday party for Hank tomorrow afternoon. All the kids are coming."

"Tell him happy birthday for me."

She opened the door. "I'll do that." She turned back to Kay. "You're welcome to come if you want. It's nothing fancy. Not fancy like this party at all."

Kay shook her head. She didn't feel up to it.

Sharon stood in the doorway. "By the way . . . you're welcome."

Kay ran her hands over her face. "Yes. Of course. I'm so sorry. Thank you, Sharon. I truly couldn't have pulled this off without you."

Sharon nodded once. "Can I give you two pieces of advice?"

Kay knew she couldn't stop her. "Go for it."

She leaned into the apartment as though not wanting others to hear. "Number one: Mark Twain had a great quote about honesty. 'If you tell the truth you won't have to remember anything.' You might consider it."

Ouch. "And number two?"

"Just because people eat your food and drink your drinks doesn't mean they're your friends. Night, Kay." With a wave she closed the door and was gone.

Ouch times two.

Kay locked the door. Sharon's advice stung because she wasn't wrong. But Kay couldn't think about it now. She barely had the energy to get undressed and take her makeup off. Finally, she crawled into bed. As she turned over she started to pray. *God? What do I have to do to get people to like me? What —*

She stopped praying. It probably wasn't a good idea to talk to God about her new life—which was based on lies. So she turned onto her other side, pulled a pillow to her chest, and let her prayers fade away.

She hoped the Almighty was too busy to notice.

Chapter Twenty

Scranton

I let them follow their own stubborn desires,
living according to their own ideas.
Psalm 81: 12

Scranton went to breakfast, but the dining room was empty. There was no bread or cereal out. No hard boiled eggs or oatmeal. Nothing.

He stopped a waitress pushing a cart of glasses. "Where's breakfast?"

"There isn't any breakfast today, Mr. Stockton. Being Thanksgiving they have a huge buffet starting at eleven. I guess they expect you to wait until then."

Thanksgiving. He'd forgotten all about it. What a fool he was. He started to walk away.

"I could get you a muffin and yogurt if you'd like," the waitress said.

"Don't bother." It's not that he was against putting her out, but taking her offering would reinforce his mistake.

Back in his apartment he put the coffee on and turned to a new crossword puzzle.

When he thought about it, "Thanksgiving" was a twelve-letter word for "overrated".

** ** **

When Scranton finally looked up from his fourth crossword puzzle of the morning, it was nearly eleven. The buffet would open soon. He should have accepted his daughter Shelley's invitation to go to their house for the day—or he could have invited them all here. He vaguely remembered her asking—and him declining—but hadn't thought of it since.

But now . . . the idea of going to the dining room and seeing all those residents sitting with family — meeting so-and-so's daughter and such-and-so's grandchild — was too much forced friendliness to bear.

He used to be friendly. He used to like holidays. Olivia made each holiday an event with loads of decorations and special foods. She loved pumpkins. They always had nine or ten arranged around the house, inside and out. She always insisted on going to the pumpkin patch and picking them out. And no one made sweet potato casserole like her. Scranton didn't really like sweet potatoes, but even he couldn't resist her recipe.

Anymore, he hated this time of year.

It didn't help that she'd died between Thanksgiving and Christmas. She'd been too sick to go to the pumpkin patch that year, and the only Christmas decorations Scranton had managed was a ceramic tree that had little lights at the tip of each branch. He'd put it in their bedroom — which had become her sick room.

As soon as she passed, he'd put it away. Seeing the happy, twinkling lights was too much to bear.

He'd stayed in the house the next year, but hadn't put up a single decoration. When he'd moved into Happy Trails — which they'd been considering before she'd gotten sick — he'd given all of it away. Except for the ceramic tree.

He sat upright in his recliner. Suddenly, he needed to see that tree.

He knew just where it was. He took it out of a lower cupboard and put it on the sideboard in the living room. With a grunt and a groan, he moved the furniture away from the wall enough to plug it in. He flipped the switch and the lights of the tree twinkled and glowed.

That's so pretty, Scranton. Thank you for setting it up for me.

Olivia had been so appreciative of the small things. The sound of a bird made her hum, an array of clouds could keep her interested for an hour. She loved walking on fallen leaves and smelling the damp mustiness of autumn. She perked up at the sounds of kids playing outside as if their liveliness was fuel to her fire. And ice cream. She would savor a bowl of mint chocolate chip as if it was a delicacy.

He touched the tree's lights. A yellow one, red, blue —

His phone rang. It was Shelley. "Hi, daughter," he answered.

"Hi to you, Dad. Happy Thanksgiving."

"Thank you."

"Are they putting on a big feast for you?"

"They are. How about your family? Did Craig smoke a turkey like he did last year?"

"He did and it came out perfect. I made Mom's sweet potatoes."

He forced his voice to remain even. "Wouldn't be a proper Thanksgiving without them."

He heard voices in the background. "Are Craig's parents there with you?"

"They are."

He heard laughter. They were there, but he was not.

"Would you like to talk to BB?" Shelley asked.

"Of course." His granddaughter was the light of his life.

"Bernadette? Come talk to Grandpa."

When Scranton had first heard her fancy name, he'd vetoed it by calling her BB. She seemed to like it.

"Hi, Grandpa!"

"Hey there, sweetie girl. How's my BB?"

"I'm good. Me and Mama made rolls, and I got to brush butter on them when they were hot. And we put tons and tons of marshmallows on the sweet potatoes."

His stomach growled. "Sounds yummy."

"They are." She paused. "Why aren't you here, Grandpa? Didn't you want to see us? Grandpa and Grandma Miller are here."

Suddenly he couldn't think of a single reason why he hadn't gone to his daughter's house. She only lived two hours away. What was wrong with him?

"I'll come next year, okay?"

"You promise?"

"Promise." He'd held up his right hand as if taking an oath, promising himself as much as BB. "You go eat now and have a good time."

"Mommy says we need to tell everybody what we're thankful for. I'm thankful for you, Grandpa."

He drew in a gasp. "I'm thankful for you too, sweet girl. I'll see you soon."

He hung up and slouched in his recliner. He was such an old fool. Passing up time with his only daughter and grandchild. Sitting alone in his apartment while the rest of the residents were gorging themselves on the buffet.

Then go! It's not too late. Go!

He stood, grabbed his billfold and keys, and a coat. He wouldn't go to the buffet, he'd drive to Shelley's and spend what was left of the day with family. So what if he missed the meal? He needed a filling up of a different sort.

Scranton went out to his car and pulled away from the building. He passed local restaurants that were packed and sported marquees advertising Thanksgiving dinners. Even if he didn't want to drive to Shelley's there were other ways he could have celebrated with his family. He could have taken them out. He could have invited them to Happy Trails. He could have. Should have.

He saw flashing lights ahead. There must've been an accident. All traffic slowed to a stop. He was in between intersections so there was no way out, no side street to detour to.

An ambulance drove through traffic. Someone wasn't having a good day.

Join the club.

As five minutes turned to ten, he realized how hungry he was. He saw Burger Madness to his right. With a little finagling he could drive in. If only the car in front would move up six inches . . .

As if hearing his wish, they did just that, and he turned into the parking lot. He wasn't sure it was even open, but when a car came out of the drive-through, he gave it a shot.

He ordered his usual Double Madness meal. "Happy Thanksgiving," said the worker in the window.

It was then he realized how pathetic it was that he'd ordered fast food. He took the drink and the bag, and pulled out of line, but he couldn't drive anywhere. The street was still backed up. He was stuck.

He pulled into a parking space. The aroma of French fries lured him to take a bite. Before he knew it he'd eaten the whole meal. He crumpled up the wrappers and shoved them in the sack, tossing it in the backseat. Pathetic, pathetic, pathetic.

He saw movement in the traffic. He could leave now and still get there in time to celebrate the day. He drove out of the parking lot. At the light were the remnants of the accident. A cop was directing traffic—to the right. Scranton wanted to go straight but had no choice but to follow the detour caravan.

Was it a sign? *Go home. Go home.*

He had a couple blocks to think about it. When he got to the next intersection where he could head toward Shelley's, he turned back the way he had come.

Back at Happy Trails he parked the car, deposited his fast food trash in an outside bin, and somehow managed to enter without running into anyone.

It was just as well.

He deserved to be alone.

Chapter Twenty-One

Kay

> I will test you with the measuring line of justice
> and the plumb line of righteousness.
> Since your refuge is made of lies,
> a hailstorm will knock it down.
> Since it is made of deception,
> a flood will sweep it away.
> Isaiah 28:17

During Thanksgiving week Kay had navigated the halls of Happy Trails like a miner searching for gold, desperate to mine some positive comments about her party. But she was also wary. Were people talking about it for the wrong reasons? Had Rosalie blabbed about her food secrets?

After two days of testing the gossip waters, Kay relaxed. No one confronted her about anything. A few had even leaned into the season of Thanksgiving, and expressed their gratitude for being invited. They thanked her.

Even as she was lying to them.

The contradiction was not lost on Kay, but by the time Thanksgiving day rolled around she once again felt secure in her lies.

As she was putting on her makeup to go to the Thanksgiving buffet the phone rang. She picked it up.

Will you accept a call from the Pilham Correctional Facility?

"Yes." She braced herself for a call from her son.

"Mom?"

"Yes. I'm here." *And you're there.*

"I wanted to call . . . it's Thanksgiving — or so they tell me."

"Of course. Happy Thanksgiving." Certainly they were having a celebration for the prisoners. "How are you doing, Connery?"

"What do you think?"

Kay closed her eyes against the slew of non-answers that were his pattern. "Did you get the books I sent you?"

"You know I don't read books."

"I just thought with you having time—"

He snickered. "Yeah, time I got. Six years' worth."

She never knew what to say to that. *She* hadn't been a meth dealer, yet he acted like she was at fault.

Kay needed to change the subject. "I'm all moved into my new place."

"I'm happy for you." His sarcasm oozed.

"It was a good move. I was in an apartment for a year, but that didn't suit me at all."

"Whatever."

"I like my new place."

"Again I say whatever. It doesn't affect me."

"So it doesn't matter?" Kay hated how needy she sounded. "Sorry. It's just that—"

"I gotta go, Mom. Things to do, you know."

"*You* called me."

"Just to say happy Thanksgiving. So . . . bye." He hung up.

Kay felt like she always felt after talking to her son: depleted, depressed, and distressed.

She examined her reflection in the mirror. She had one eye made up, and the other was au natural. She yanked a makeup remover cloth from its container and wiped the makeup off. One cloth became two. Three. By the time she was done she was out of breath. She was so tired of—

The phone rang again. Hopefully Connery wasn't calling back. But it was her daughter. "Hi, Tiffany. Happy Thanksgiving."

"Happy Thanksgiving to you too, Mom. How do you like your new place?"

Finally, someone who cared. "It's lovely. They're having a big buffet today."

"We're at Rod's parents' right now."

Kay could hear conversations and commotion in the background, and imagined a traditional holiday meal with turkey and cranberry sauce and all the things *she'd* served when the kids were little. Before they moved away. Before Wally betrayed her.

"I talked to Dad."

Kay was jarred out of her memories. Tiffany had called Wally before she'd called her. "I don't want to hear about it."

"I get it. I only bring it up because he didn't sound happy, which... you know."

Makes me happy. "That brings joy to my heart. So Janice isn't all she's cracked up to be?"

There was a pause.

"Tiffany?" Kay regretted being so harsh. Wally was still her dad.

"Sorry I brought it up."

"Why was Dad unhappy?"

"It's really nothing. Again, I shouldn't have—"

"You tell me this minute."

Tiffany sighed. "Janice's family has a tradition where they make fried chicken at Thanksgiving, not turkey."

That was it? The substitution of one poultry for another?

"Like I said, Mom, I shouldn't have brought him up."

"No, you shouldn't have. Here I am alone on a holiday and you—"

"I'm sorry, okay? I didn't mean... next year we'll make sure we spend Thanksgiving with you."

Kay held back tears by pressing her index finger against a worry line that was carved between her brows. "Promise?"

"Promise. Really."

Kay took a deep breath, hoping her voice would come out strong. "I can't wait a year to see you," she said. "When can you come out?"

"I'm not sure. You know how hard it is to get teenage workers to show up at the Dairy Sweet. We're always having to fill in."

That's what you get for opening an ice cream place. Kay took a page out of Connery's playbook and wrapped things up. "I need to go, hon. People are meeting me at the buffet."

"Yes. Of course. Have a good day, Mom. Love you."

"Love you too."

Kay ended the call then tossed the phone on the dressing table. One child wasn't showing up because he was in prison. The other was unavailable because her business was more important than her mother. And then there was a husband—ex-husband— who was enjoying his life with a new wife, pretending not to like fried chicken—when Kay knew he loved it. He'd never been that keen on turkey in the first place.

The point was, no one was making an effort for her sake. For good reasons or bad, all were fully involved in lives they'd created apart from her.

"Which is why I created a new life for *me.*"

Speaking of . . . she picked up the eyeshadow. Katerina Volkov had her own holiday celebration to attend.

** ** **

Kay had lied to her daughter when she said she was meeting someone at the buffet. She'd talked to Tessa and Accosta about sharing a table, but they had a big group of family and friends coming from that boarding house where they used to live. Seeing the long line to be seated, she wished she'd made arrangements. Kay saw a few people ahead of her who'd been at her party, and waved at one woman, but she merely nodded and turned away.

It was hard being a single in a couples world. She looked for Scranton. Even though he'd made it clear he wasn't interested in her romantically, it would be nice to sit with someone she knew. She spotted Wrinkles sitting with a group. And even Saggy. Everyone had someone.

Except her.

But then she heard her name called. She turned and saw Rosalie pushing her husband in a wheelchair. He looked awful, all slumped over, his mouth slack. Should he be in the main dining room?

"Hi there," Kay said to both of them.

Rosalie studied the line. "It's so busy but I guess good food will do that," she said. Then she waved at a young man coming toward them. He hugged her, and then Lonnie.

"We're so glad you could come, Evan." Rosalie was beaming. "I'd like you to meet Katerina Volkov. Katerina, this is our grandson, Evan."

He held out his hand to shake. "Nice to meet you, Mrs. Volkov."

Kay was impressed by the handshake and the respect he showed by calling her missus.

"Evan goes to college in Kansas City," Rosalie said. "He's going to be a doctor."

"Someday," Evan said.

"That's a lot of hard work," Kay said.

"Yes it is."

"Have you heard from your parents?" Rosalie asked him. "Are they having a good time on their trip?" Before he could answer, Rosalie added for Kay's benefit, "Our daughter and her husband are on a three-week trip to the Far East to celebrate their twenty-fifth wedding anniversary."

"I love the orient," Kay said. "Nicolae and I especially liked Japan and Siam."

Rosalie and Lonnie exchanged a look. Had she said something wrong?"

Whatever it was, was forgotten as Rosalie said, "Do you have someone to sit with, Katerina? You're welcome to sit with us."

Relief washed over her. "That would be nice. Thank you."

A few minutes later they were shown to a table, ordered drinks, and were told to help themselves to the extensive buffet. Rosalie made up two plates so Lonnie could stay at the table.

As Kay filled her plate she saw an enormous table set in an adjoining room with a string of people arriving and hugging each other. Tessa and Accosta sat together at its midpoint. Kay envied their family and friends. The sight of them made her extra glad for Rosalie's invitation.

The food was delicious and Kay enjoyed hearing about Evan's studies. Rosalie and Lonnie were so lucky to have such a bright grandson to brag about. Tiffany had two children, but they were still in high school and Kay wasn't up to date about the details of their lives.

Poor Lonnie. He had trouble getting food to his mouth without spilling and Rosalie had to help him. He added little to the conversation, and looked uncomfortable.

"I know . . ." Rosalie said. "What if we all tell about our favorite Thanksgiving. Evan, you go first."

As Evan told a story about hiding four of his grandmother's homemade rolls in a bookcase to eat later, Kay thought about her own answer to the question. She remembered her first Thanksgiving with Wally. They'd been at his parents' house and Wally had announced their engagement. Everyone cheered. The world had seemed limitless and —

"How about you, Katerina? What's your favorite Thanksgiving memory?"

She took a portion of the truth and embellished it. "My husband Nicolae and I were in St. Petersburg with his family and we—"

"They celebrate Thanksgiving in Russia?" Evan asked.

Kay felt her face redden. "No, of course not. But they were being polite for me. Actually, Nicolae used the day to announce our engagement. Just as he made the announcement the bells of the cathedral began to ring."

"Wow," Evan said. "That sounds amazing."

Yes, it does.

"I certainly can't top that," Rosalie said with a smile to Lonnie. "But I think our favorite Thanksgiving was 1968." She squeezed Lonnie's hand and he smiled a crooked smile. "That's the year Lonnie came back from Vietnam. We were so thankful he was home and safe."

She clumsily drew his hand to her lips.

Will I ever have someone love me like that?

Rosalie let go of Lonnie's hand with a pat. "Tell us about your children, Katerina."

Kay tried to remember the lies she'd created. "Our oldest is Tiffany—named after my favorite store in New York City."

"Oh my," Rosalie said. "How fancy."

"Tiffany is a chef out west. She has two amazing children, Kaylee and Bradley." At least their names were true.

"Do you get to see them very often?"

"Not often enough," Kay said. "And our son is Connery, named after—"

"Sean Connery?" Rosalie asked.

"Exactly! I'm a great fan of his movies."

"Wasn't he in one of the Indiana Jones movies?" Evan asked.

"He was. Among many others."

"He was dreamy," Rosalie said. Which made her giggle and look at her husband. "Sorry, dearest. You're dreamy too."

He shook his head.

"What does your son do?" Evan asked.

"He's in pharmaceuticals." It seemed an appropriate lie.

But Evan perked up. "Where did he go to school?"

Only then did Kay realize the problem she'd created. She couldn't think of a single medical school, so said, "Not here. Back east." She quicky changed the subject. "How long have you and Lonnie lived at Happy Trails?" Kay asked.

Kay relaxed as the subject was suitably changed. She needed to be more careful.

Chapter Twenty-Two

Evelyn

> Look and be amazed!
> For I am doing something in your own day,
> something you wouldn't believe
> even if someone told you about it.
> Habakkuk 1: 5

Evelyn and Wayne parked the car in front of Happy Trails. But Evelyn hesitated before getting out.

"What's wrong?" Wayne asked.

"This is the first time I haven't cooked Thanksgiving dinner in...forever."

"Then it's high time you got a holiday off."

She angled to look at him straight on. "But it's like I'm not doing my job."

He put his fingers under her chin. "How soon you forget being totally exhausted at our party."

Evelyn *had* thought of that. Even ten years ago Thanksgiving meals were exhausting. "I didn't forget. It just seems too . . . "

"Easy? Effortless? Relaxing?"

She raised her hands in surrender. "All of the above." She thought of something else that had been bothering her. "Having this meal away from home won't be the same."

"No, it won't. Is that bad?"

"I don't know." She sounded like a toddler but it was true. "I don't like change."

He nodded. "Here's some change for you. Next year *we* could invite everyone for Thanksgiving dinner. Here."

She was surprised he'd brought it up. "You're assuming we move?"

He shrugged. "I do not presume or assume. I only offer possibilities." He opened his car door. "Shall we?"

*** *** ***

Evelyn was amazed at the number of people who'd come for the buffet. Apparently it was *the* place to be in Carson Creek.

As co-hostesses Tessa and Accosta had asked the staff to put enough tables together to seat nineteen. Evelyn and Wayne made the rounds to greet everyone who was anyone in their lives. Kids, grandkids, friends, kids of friends . . . When Evelyn took her seat, she couldn't help but gaze around the table in awe.

Wayne leaned over and whispered in her ear. "We are very blessed."

"That, we are."

Tessa dinged a spoon on a glass to get everyone's attention. "Welcome family."

"Hail, hail, the gangs all here!" Mae said.

There were nods all around, but Evelyn could tell Tessa didn't appreciate the interruption. When everyone had quieted, she continued. "I think a fitting prayer of thanksgiving comes from Psalm ninety-two." She held out her hands and everyone did the same until all hands were clasped in a circle. Then Tessa gazed heavenward. "'It is good to give thanks to the Lord, to sing praises to the Most High. It is good to proclaim your unfailing love in the morning, your faithfulness in the evening . . . You thrill me, Lord, with all you have done for me!' She smiled at everyone at the table. "All you have done for *us!* Praise the Lord!"

"Praise the Lord!" was repeated round the table.

"Well then," a beaming Tessa said. "Let's eat!"

The families with little kids went first and Evelyn was happy to see Accosta using a walker that had a seat in it — a perfect place to set a plate full of yummy food.

Evelyn and Wayne were just about to take their turn when the head of Happy Trails tapped on their shoulders. "I'm sorry to interrupt your dinner, but may I have a word?"

They followed Mrs. Halvorson out of the dining room to an empty corridor. "Is something wrong with Accosta's arrangement?" Wayne asked.

"No, no. Nothing is wrong with that. She and Tessa make a good team." She smiled at each of them in turn. "I just wanted to let you know that an apartment has opened up. I was going to call you next Monday, but when I saw you here, I just knew I was supposed to let you know right now. That is, if you're still interested?"

Evelyn shocked herself by saying, "Yes." She looked at Wayne. "Yes?"

He nodded. "Yes! But not for Accosta. For us."

"Well now. That's excellent! Consider it yours. Come in next week and we can go over details." She shook their hands. "Congratulations."

As soon as she moved away, Evelyn took Wayne's hand. "What just happened?" She felt herself grinning.

"I think God just happened."

Evelyn gave a joyous chuckle. "I'd asked Him to be plain about it. I don't think He could be plainer than this."

Wayne shook his head. "I can't believe it all fell into place."

"Or that we both said yes, right then and there. We don't even know which apartment layout it is."

Wayne's smile made him look decades younger. "If we trust God to get us here, we have to trust Him to get us in the right apartment."

Evelyn wrapped her arms around him. "I'm so happy."

"Me too."

She suddenly remembered the rest of their family who were probably wondering where they'd gone. "Shall we tell them now?" she asked.

"Let's get a plate of food first and then—"

She knew she was beaming with happiness, but her stomach tightened with the shock of it. "I'm not sure I can eat."

He kissed her cheek. "You can always eat. Food first, surprise second."

Everyone was busy eating when Evelyn and Wayne returned to the table with their plates.

"Where did you go?" Piper asked.

They set their food down and stood behind their chairs. Evelyn looked at Wayne, but he nodded, giving her permission to share the news. "Meet the newest residents of Happy Trails."

A stunned silence was broken by Accosta. "Really?"

"Really," Wayne said.

Tessa said, "I saw you with Mrs. Halvorson. Has there been an opening?"

"There has. So we took it."

Everyone reacted with exclamations, questions, and even applause.

As the room quieted down, Piper stood up. "And so I am ready and eager to sell Peerbaugh Place."

"Are you going to sell it as a boarding house?" her brother Russell asked.

"I don't know," Evelyn said. "We'll have to see what kind of interest we—"

Ringo pushed his chair back from the table and stood. "Before you do any of that . . ." He looked at Soon-ja. "It doesn't hurt to ask. Would you consider selling Peerbaugh Place to us?"

Where Evelyn's announcement had elicited happy chaos, Ringo's words elicited silence.

But not for long.

"*You're* interested?" Wayne asked.

"We've always thought it was a great house, but when I spent time there making repairs I started seeing it with new eyes."

Soon-ja nodded. "He came home and kept talking about it, telling me what he'd do to the place if it was ours."

Evelyn was moved by their passion. "Would you use it as a single-family house?"

"We would." He drew Soon-ja to her feet. "Go ahead."

"Actually, we're going to need a big house . . ." Looks were exchanged as Soon-ja put her hands on her belly.

"A baby?" Mae asked.

They nodded.

Mae jumped out of her chair and rushed to hug them. "I'm going to be a grandma again!" She kissed the heads of her grandkids. "You're going to have a baby brother or sister! Aren't you excited?"

Ten-year-old Ricky shrugged. "As long as I don't have to change diapers."

Six-year-old Zoe raised her hand. "Can I have my own room in the new house?"

"You can," Ringo said. "You both can."

Mae suddenly gasped. "You'll live right across the street from me and Collie!"

Evelyn saw Ringo and Soon-ja exchange a look as if they'd discussed being so close. But then Ringo said. "Ready or not, here we come."

Mae shrieked with glee.

Tessa raised her water glass for a toast. "To a new baby, new life for Peerbaugh Place, and having my dear friends move close. Happy Thanksgiving!"

Everyone toasted. But Tessa had a few more words to add. "As I said before I say again: 'You thrill me, Lord, with all you have done for me!' Praise the Lord!"

When they all sat down to eat, Evelyn whispered to Wayne, "What have we done?"

"We've changed our lives. Isn't it grand?"

"It's the scariest thing we've ever done."

He winked at her. "That too."

Chapter Twenty-Three

Rosalie

> Have you never heard? Have you never understood?
> The Lord is the everlasting God, the Creator of all the earth.
> He never grows weak or weary.
> No one can measure the depths of his understanding.
> Isaiah 40: 28

On Thanksgiving evening Rosalie held the photo album so her husband could see it. "Look at this one from Thanksgiving 1993." She glanced at her grandson. "You were one cute baby, Evan. You were crawling everywhere. I remember when your mom dropped an earring and she had to scramble to get to it before you did." She turned back to Lonnie. "Do you remember that?"

He barely shook his head, and by his droopy eyes Rosalie knew he'd had enough. It was understandable. After the buffet they'd taken a walk outside in the brisk November air, and then had come back to his room to look at old photo albums.

She put her hand on his. "Do you want me to help you get to bed?"

He shook his head no. "Heh-puh."

"Helper? You want a helper to do it?"

He nodded.

"I'll get someone," Evan said.

After Evan left, Rosalie stroked Lonnie's hair behind his ears. "I shouldn't have forced you to go to the big buffet. And then all the visiting. It was too much for you."

He didn't react. His breathing was heavy.

"Are you all right?"

Lonnie gazed at her with pleading eyes. "Tire."

He rarely admitted he was tired. When he closed his eyes she went out to the hall to find out what was taking so long.

Evan was on his way back and met her at the door. "Someone will be here in a minute."

Good. Sooner was better.

Evan came back inside and Rosalie left the door ajar. A wonderful woman named Jessie entered a minute later. She was always so patient with Lonnie.

"Well, say there, Mr. Clemmons. Did Thanksgiving wear you out?"

He gave her a small smile. "Tire," he said.

"That's how everybody feels after a holiday. Let's get you settled for the night." She moved to the back of his wheelchair to push him.

Rosalie bent down and gave him a goodnight kiss and Evan gave him an awkward hug. "Sleep good, Grandpa. I'll see you soon."

Lonnie lifted his hand in a feeble wave as Jessie wheeled him into the bedroom.

"Let's give them some space," Rosalie said.

"Actually, I should be going," Evan said. "I probably shouldn't have stayed so long, but I enjoyed the old albums."

"So did I. So did Grandpa." She squeezed his hand as they moved into the hallway. Rosalie appreciated him so much. There weren't many twenty-somethings who would spend their Thanksgiving with their grandparents. He was a keeper.

She and Evan walked down the halls toward the front door, but at the last minute, Evan made a little detour and drew Rosalie to some chairs in an alcove.

"Before I go . . . I never had a chance to talk to you alone. How are *you* doing living separate from Grandpa?"

Rosalie touched his knee. "You are a dear to ask. I'm doing all right, though once in a while I flounder. Since he retired Grandpa and I were rarely apart, so waking up without him, going on errands, even watching TV without him . . ." She shook her head, thinking of today. "I never should have taken him to the main dining room today."

"I know eating can be awkward for him, but he seemed to enjoy the conversation."

"Maybe."

"You know Grandpa is a simple guy, he just loves when everyone is together. Although there was that one new face . . ." He looked at her. "That Mrs. Volkov was kind of interesting. She sure had big stories. She's been to a lot of places."

Beyond not wanting to gossip, Rosalie wasn't up to talking about her. She summarized her this way: "Katerina feels the need to impress."

"You don't say," he said sarcastically. "I could tell just by looking at her. She's a pretty woman, but all the jewelry and makeup..."

"She tries a bit too hard."

"Maybe that's it," he said.

They watched as some other residents saw their guests out the door.

Evan stood. "I do need to go." He pulled her into a hug and she marveled that she had a grandson who was nearly a foot taller than she was.

Once Evan left, she realized how tired *she* was. But before she could go back to her apartment, she headed back to check on Lonnie.

She paused at the entrance to the assisted living wing. If he was sleeping she didn't want to accidentally wake him. So she checked with the nurse's station.

She was assured by Jessie that he went to bed without a hitch.

Good. Now it was her turn.

** ** **

Rosalie was awakened by her cell phone ringing and vibrating on the bedside table.

"Hello?" she said.

"Mrs. Clemmons, this is Jessie. Would you please come down to—"

"What's wrong?"

"Just... please..."

She was fully awake now. "Jessie, tell me what's wrong."

Rosalie heard a shuddered breath. "I'm so sorry, but Mr. Clemmons has passed away."

Rosalie bolted to sitting. "Away? No. No. How can that be?"

"He pushed the call button around his neck, but by the time we got there..."

She flung her legs over the side of the bed. "I'm coming!"

*** *** ***

Rosalie didn't remember getting from here to there, but found Lonnie's apartment crowded with aides and nurses blocking the bed. As soon as she entered, they stopped talking and left, leaving Jessie behind.

"I'm so sorry," she said.

"Let me see him."

Jessie stepped outside and let Rosalie have time alone with her husband.

She stared at him for a long moment: his gray hair that was still black at the temples, the deep lines in his forehead, the dimple in his chin, and his rough whiskers. When was the last time she'd truly *looked* at him? Studied his face? In her mind's eye her image of him wasn't so old. But he *was* old. They both were, and the reality of it shocked her. Mentally she felt like they were both fifty, but visually there was no denying they were decades older.

And now... he was so still. He looked like he was asleep, he was at peace, tranquil. If only she could nudge him and say, *Hey, hon. It's time to get up.*

But Lonnie wasn't there anymore. This wasn't her Lonnie.

Although her thoughts were rooted in her faith and belief in heaven, Rosalie took his hand to comfort him. But there was no warmth there. No strength to pass on to her, and no reaction to her own warmth.

She began to cry as she fully grasped that this was real. This was happening. Rosalie peered heavenward and whispered, "Why did You take him? He's needed here!"

The room remained silent, with no response from the Almighty or her husband.

What was she going to do?

I need to ask Lonnie what to do. He'll —

Her chest tightened.

Lonnie couldn't help her anymore. Lonnie couldn't be her rock. Her love. The very breath of her being.

Lonnie's breath was gone. His strength had been extinguished. He could move no more, touch no more, laugh no more.

She stroked his hair away from his face—which was pale and slack as if the departure of his soul had left behind an empty shell. Then Rosalie leaned down to kiss his lips. But at the last moment she kissed his cheek instead. She didn't want the last memory of her beloved to be an unrequited kiss.

She heard a commotion in the next room. This time, their time—their final time together—was short.

Rosalie took his hand between hers and held it to her chest. "I love you, dear man. You've been my life for forty-eight years. I don't know how to live without you." New tears flowed, yet she brushed them away. This was not the time to cry for herself.

There would be a lifetime of that.

Chapter Twenty-Four

Accosta

> You keep track of all my sorrows.
> You have collected all my tears in your bottle.
> You have recorded each one in your book.
> Psalm 56: 8

Wake up!
Accosta bolted upright.
It was still dark.
She checked the bedside clock: 3:16. She nodded at the special number and repeated the verse from the book of John that she always recited when she awakened at that time. "'For this is how God loved the world: He gave his one and only Son, so that everyone who believes in him will not perish but have eternal life.'"

That said, she lay down again. But she couldn't get comfortable. After a few minutes of tossing about she sat up a second time. "Yes, Lord?"

The image of Rosalie came to her mind.

"Rosalie needs me?"

Rosalie needs Me.

Accosta got out of bed and quickly dressed. She didn't want to frighten Tessa if she woke up and discovered she was gone, so she wrote on a sticky-note: *I'm fine. Be back soon.* She put it on the door, took up the bracelet that held the apartment key, and quietly opened the front door. It took a little finagling to get her walker out to the hall, but she managed, locked the door, and turned toward Rosalie's apartment.

When she got there, she hesitated about knocking on the door. It would be hard to do without waking every other resident nearby. Yet she knew Rosalie needed help. She *knew* it.

Accosta was just about to knock when an aide came down the hall.

"Mrs. Rand, what are you doing out and about?"

Accosta pointed at the door. "God woke me up and told me that Rosalie needs help. I was—"

The aide put a hand on her arm and nodded. Her expression was one of sorrow. "God was right."

"Is she okay?"

She shook her head slowly. "It's Lonnie. He passed away."

Accosta gasped and put a hand to her chest. "Is Rosalie with him?"

"She is."

"Then that's where I need to go."

** ** **

Accosta waited in the small living room of Lonnie's apartment. The bedroom door was closed. The aides had told her Rosalie was in with her husband.

Accosta remembered her own husband's death. The initial shock, and then the endless cycle of disbelief, pain, disbelief, pain. It was odd how long it took for her to comprehend that he was truly gone. Was Rosalie going through that now?

"It's good you're here, Mrs. Rand," Jessie said. "She'll need someone to be with her."

"I expect that's why God sent me."

Jessie's eyebrows rose. "Sent you?"

"Told me to wake up."

"Told you?"

Accosta understood how some people thought she was crazy for being so blunt, but she'd also decided she didn't care. *Not* giving God credit was worse than dealing with any disbelieving reaction. Besides, she wanted people to know that God *did* do such things.

"He nudged me to wake up and I bolted upright. I tried to lay back down, but He put an image of Rosalie in my head. Maybe you could ignore those kind of nudges, but I couldn't. I can't." Accosta spread her arms as if to say, *And so I'm here.*

Jessie's expression softened from skepticism to someone wanting to believe.

Accosta said a quick thank-you prayer that God would go the rest of the way and nab her heart.

Just then the bedroom door opened and Rosalie came out. Accosta stood. "I'm so sorry, dear lady."

Rosalie fell into Accosta's arms and cried.

** ** **

The two of them went back to Rosalie's apartment.

Rosalie stood in the small foyer as if she didn't know where to go.

"Why don't we sit down," Accosta said. When Rosalie looked from the dining table to the living room but didn't move, Accosta put a gentle hand on her back and led her to the couch.

Rosalie perched on the end of a cushion. "This has to be a dream. Isn't it a dream?"

Accosta ran a hand up and down her back. "No, dear, I'm afraid it isn't."

Rosalie sighed deeply. "Last night after seeing Evan out I went to check on Lonnie, but when the nurse said he went to bed easily, I went home." She glanced at Accosta. Her voice cracked, "I should've checked on him."

"Are you thinking you could have saved him?"

Rosalie hesitated. "Maybe."

Accosta did *not* want Rosalie to live with that guilt for the rest of her life. "Jessie told me he used his call button. The nurses came and helped him—as much as they could."

Rosalie nodded, staring into the air. Then she said, "I pushed him too hard yesterday, making him come to the main buffet to eat. Afterward we took a stroll outside, then looked at photos with Evan for too long. Lonnie was exhausted." She touched her eyes. "I could see it in his eyes."

"You're telling me he spent the last day of his life celebrating Thanksgiving and spending time with you and his dear grandson, reliving fun memories from his life?"

Rosalie sniffed and managed a bittersweet smile. "It *was* a good day."

"It's a day you can hold in your heart from now on."

She nodded and her tears welled again. "From now on . . ." Rosalie looked pleadingly into Accosta's eyes. "What am I going to do from now on? How can I keep going without him?"

Accosta remembered the same overwhelming feeling of panic. "You'll take it one day at a time. And you're not alone. I'm here. Tessa's here. And all your other friends. We won't let you flounder. God won't let you flounder either."

Rosalie faced Accosta, her eyes wild. "Why did God take him? He was only seventy-eight. There was never any indication that Lonnie wouldn't get through his rehab and move back here with me."

Accosta wished she had a good answer. "I don't know why God took him."

Rosalie scoffed. "I don't know if that's encouraging or depressing. You, who are so close to Him . . ."

Accosta wasn't sure she liked the pressure Rosalie was putting on her faith, and yet, it was true. She *was* close to God. She wanted Rosalie to be too.

She pulled her friend under her arm and said, "Here's a verse for you. 'The eternal God is your refuge, and underneath are the everlasting arms.' His arms. Holding you up."

Rosalie leaned against her and together, Accosta and the Almighty held her tight.

** ** **

After tucking in Rosalie for the night and making it back to her apartment, Accosta got ready for bed. Again. It was still early morning and she was exhausted. Yet she couldn't rest until one more thing was accomplished.

She got out her Worry Box and chose a pink index card. On it she wrote: *Pray that Rosalie's broken heart is mended.*

Accosta bowed her head and repeated the prayer, adding it to the dozens she'd sent up during this very long night.

Then she filed the card in the Worry Box with the other prayer needs, and put herself to bed.

Chapter Twenty-Five

Scranton

> Forget yourselves long enough
> to lend a helping hand.
> Philippians 2: 4

There was a knock on the door. After his disappointing Thanksgiving, Scranton had not wanted company. That's why he'd called the dining room and feigned illness for the past three days in order to get delivery. Hopefully, this was his breakfast.

Scranton got up from his recliner and messed up his hair a little, ready to play the part. By the time he answered the door, his shoulders were slumped and his expression was one of exhaustion and pain.

He was surprised to see Mrs. Halvorson holding his breakfast tray. Usually it was one of the wait staff.

"Good morning, Mr. Stockton."

He hurriedly brushed away his surprise and went back to being sick. "Morning." He cleared his throat and coughed convincingly.

She brushed past him and set the tray on his dining table.

"Thank you," he said.

"You're welcome." She didn't move to leave. "It's been three days so I'm going to send a nurse to check you out."

No! "No need," he said. "I'm feeling a bit better."

She cocked her head and gave him a sideways look. "Do you have a fever? Body aches?"

Although he'd wanted everyone to think he was sick, he wasn't that kind of sick. "No, no, none of those," he said.

She studied him for a moment, making him feel uncomfortable. "Then we can expect you in the dining room for dinner?"

Apparently his time playing the recluse was over. "I'll try."

"You do that, Mr. Stockton. And if you change your mind about having a visit from the nursing staff, let me know."

As soon as she left, he took the tray to his recliner. Coffee, orange juice, oatmeal, sausages, fruit, and an English muffin. Perfect. He put sweetener in his coffee and started eating.

Actually, he was surprised they'd let him go this long. He hadn't planned on the sick act, but after his disastrous Thanksgiving, missing the buffet, missing his family, and finding himself at a burger joint, he'd been in a funk.

The funk wasn't just because of that one day either. He wasn't happy at Happy Trails. There were too many people. He didn't like living with people all around.

He wanted just one person—and he couldn't have her.

The house he'd shared with Olivia had been their private oasis. Sure, they had friends, but every evening when he came home they closed the door on the world and focused on each other. Right before she died, Olivia had pegged it: "You are my everything." That's how he'd felt about her too.

Of course they'd loved Shelley and Craig and BB—that was a given. But it came down to one fact: you didn't get to choose your relatives, but you did choose your spouse. Your person. He and Olivia chose each other. Over and over again, through all seasons of life, they chose each other.

They'd had a few years alone before Shelley's birth, and then again after she was grown. He'd been very relieved Olivia wasn't the type of mother to grieve when their child left the nest. She'd encouraged Shelley to find her own way, and they were pleased with the results. Which meant they'd been excited about the chance to remake their lives as a couple.

They'd traveled a bit more, but they were limited with Scranton's busy trial schedule. Their big dream was to go on a 128-day round-the-world cruise.

But then cancer crept in.

They'd been hopeful at first. Women beat breast cancer all the time. But for some reason Olivia wasn't one of those women.

She'd taken the news far better than Scranton. God had a place saved for her in heaven, and she'd get to see her parents and her brother who'd died in Vietnam—eternally twenty-two.

He didn't care about being with relatives in some far off place. He wanted Olivia here, now, with him.

When she'd needed more care, Scranton cut back his hours to be with her. But it didn't matter. Even though it went against who he was as a man, he couldn't save her. It wasn't fair.

To which she'd replied, "Was it fair that Jesus—a perfect, innocent man—was convicted of crimes and put to death on the cross?"

Of course not, but still . . .

Scranton had never been a praying man, but the cancer had forced it on him. Yet obviously, he hadn't done it right because Olivia still died. And he was left alone.

He'd tried to stay in their house, but he simply couldn't be there without her. So when the memories threatened to consume him, he sold it all and moved to Happy Trails.

What an idiotic name, for an idiotic place.

He went back to his breakfast, eating every bite as though it was his last meal.

** ** **

When Scranton went to the dining room that evening he wore a chip on his shoulder. Yet when nobody asked how he was feeling, he felt it slide off like a useless appendage.

They hadn't missed him any more than he'd missed them.

So be it.

When it was his turn to be seated, he spotted Rosalie sitting alone. There were dirty dishes at the other places, but she was still there, picking at her food.

"I'd like to sit with Rosalie, please."

The hostess looked in her direction. "She's already eaten, Mr. Stockton."

"Doesn't matter." He strode past her to Rosalie's table. "May I join you?" he asked.

She seemed surprised to see him. "I'm just finishing up, but . . . of course."

He took a seat, setting the dirty dishes aside. Then he caught the eye of a waitress and beckoned her over. He ordered his meal before turning to Rosalie.

"There now," he said. "So, how have you been? How's Lonnie?"

She blinked at him. She looked pale. Her eyebrows dipped in the middle.

She was in pain.

Before she could answer, a couple came to their table. The woman put her hand on Rosalie's shoulder. "We just want to tell you how sorry we are about Lonnie. He was a delightful man."

Sorry? Lonnie? Was?

As soon as they left Scranton tried to make up for his ignorance. "I'm so sorry. I didn't know. I've been in my apartment since Thanksgiving."

"It's ok." She folded her hands in her lap. "Were you sick?"

He felt guilty for pretending. "I'm fine now. What happened to Lonnie?"

"He had another stroke Thanksgiving night." Her eyes did not fill with tears, signaling that she'd repeated these words enough times to numb herself to their full meaning.

Scranton put his hand on hers. "I know how much it hurts."

She studied him for a moment, then nodded. "You do. How long since your wife died?"

"Nearly two years."

"Do you ever get over it?"

He was torn between encouragement and truth and settled for a combination. "Over it, no. But you do get on with it. With life."

She sighed deeply and waved at a woman who blew her a kiss as she left the dining room. "I don't see how that's possible right now."

"Of course you don't. Right now you survive day to day. Hour to hour."

"Minute to minute."

Her pain reignited his own. "When is the service?"

"Tomorrow. At Grace church at eleven."

"I'll be there." He was surprised by his words but felt them settle in. It was the right thing to do to be there for Rosalie like others had been there for him.

His salad came but he made no move to eat it. "How can I help?"

This time she touched his hand. "People keep asking me that. But honestly, I don't know right now."

"That's fair." He thought of what he might have to offer her. "If you need any legal advice or help with the will or . . . whatever . . . I'm here."

"Thank you, Scranton. I appreciate that." She pointed at his salad. "Please. Eat."

Another couple came over to give their condolences, at which point Rosalie excused herself.

"I'll see you tomorrow then?" she asked.

"You will."

After she left, Scranton picked at his salad, but got a doggie bag for the rest of the meal.

Grief was not conducive to his appetite.

Chapter Twenty-Six

Rosalie

> Their days of labor are filled with pain and grief;
> even at night their minds cannot rest.
> Ecclesiastes 2: 23

Rosalie sat with a glass of orange juice at the table in her apartment. For the hundredth time since Lonnie's death, she noticed his placemat in front of his chair. She reached out to touch it. "It's like you're gone, but not gone."

She looked around and saw Lonnie everywhere. Not only in framed photos, but in his reading glasses, his coat on the coatrack, and the fishing magazine on the coffee table. Oddly, she didn't mind that these mundane items ignited emotions in her. Right now it was painful, but someday . . . she knew there would come a time when these items would elicit memories she could enjoy in her mental scrapbook. But not today. Not yet.

Although she'd gotten used to being alone in the apartment when Lonnie was in assisted living, today was different.

Today she would bury her husband.

She looked outside and saw soft snow falling. Lonnie loved snow and would relish the wet kind that could be made into snowballs. He would hold one in his hand and grin at her, and she would squeal and tell him he'd better not. He never threw it at her. But he did like gripping her neck when his hands were cold, making her shoulders rise up, making him laugh.

It was fitting he would be laid to rest in ground covered with snow. Yet Rosalie was glad she'd opted out of a graveside service. The temperatures had been frigid since Thanksgiving. Most of their friends and extended family were old. She didn't need to worry about anyone falling or catching their death.

Ha. Very funny.

Rosalie knew she should eat something, but the mere idea was distasteful. Since her heart was empty, her stomach should be too.

If only her mind could empty itself. Its busyness had kept her from satisfying sleep as thoughts of past, present, and future kept raising their hands, vying for her attention. More than once she mentally interjected, *I need to talk to Lonnie about this.*

Reframing her life would take time. She'd been a daughter, a wife, a mother, a grandmother, and now —

The clock struck the half-hour. Evan was picking her up soon. She set her juice in the fridge and went to get dressed for her latest role: widow.

** ** **

Rosalie held Evan's arm as they walked up the center aisle of the church. She was pleased with the attendance, but was not surprised by it. Lonnie was a loved man. Respected and valued. Who could ask for anything more?

I don't want anything more, I just want him *more — for more years.*

Evan let her go in the pew first. Rosalie nodded to their extended family who sat in the pews behind hers. She hadn't seen some of Lonnie's cousins in years. It was rather sad that families waited until too late to keep in touch. She was as guilty as they were.

It was also sad that Rosalie and Lonnie's daughter, Cheri, and her husband couldn't be here. They'd been notified of Lonnie's death, but they were at sea in the Far East and by the time they reached a port and secured a flight, they would miss the funeral. Cheri had felt so bad about it. "You know I'd love to be there, Mom."

Rosalie knew. And actually, seeing them a few weeks from now might be better. She needed time to adjust and grieve on her own.

But today was a time for public grief. Too many eyes were on *her* — which made her uncomfortable. If only she could adopt the old-fashioned style of covering her face with a dense black veil. She'd never thought of it before, but such fashion *did* allow a widow some privacy.

Rosalie saw Lonnie's casket in front of the altar. Suddenly, she saw the symbolism of it all: Lonnie's life, offered to God in death as it had been in life.

The pastor came out and stopped in front of her. He took her hands and said, "Shall we start, Rosalie?"

She nodded.

And so it began. One last event together.

** ** **

Rosalie sat at a table and let others come to her. She was glad for the chair as her legs weren't working right. She felt as unstable as a toddler.

A ham slider, potato salad, and fruit ambrosia sat uneaten on a plate — and would remain so. She had no intention of eating, and was almost glad the constant stream of people made her unable to do so.

Everyone was so kind and she enjoyed the stories people shared. Yet she wondered how many people had complimented Lonnie in life?

Who knew that a funeral could teach her so many lessons?

Tessa and Accosta came by, accompanied by Scranton. The ladies sat and Scranton stood nearby.

"It was a lovely service," Accosta said. "'I Surrender All' is one of my favorite hymns."

"It certainly was Lonnie's," Rosalie said.

"I'm going a little more upbeat at mine," Tessa said. She lifted her arms, closed her eyes, and began to sing, "'Victory in Jesus, my Savior, forever. He sought me and bought me with His redeeming blood.'"

"Sing it, Tessa!" Accosta said.

She opened her eyes, and lowered her arms. "Sorry, Rosalie. I like your choices too."

Leave it to Tessa to liven things up.

Scranton gestured toward her plate. "I'd tell you that you need to eat, but I know better. I didn't eat at Olivia's funeral, and not much after either." He touched his midsection. "The grief diet."

Accosta nodded. "People brought so much food to our house that I ended up giving it to neighbors. But you will want to eat eventually."

Rosalie wasn't so sure. "We'll see."

One step at a time.

Chapter Twenty-Seven

Rosalie

> He gives power to the weak
> and strength to the powerless.
> Isaiah 40: 29

Funeral planned: check.
Funeral attended: check.
Husband buried: check.
Check. Check. Check.

On the morning after Lonnie's funeral Rosalie stood in front of the fancy coffee pot, staring at it. Lonnie always made the coffee. And during his time in assisted living she'd shared coffee with him in his room—the aides had been good enough to make a pot every day.

She'd noticed a lot of little things that Lonnie had done throughout their day. Besides the coffee, he'd opened the blinds—tilted just so to keep the direct sunrays at bay. They'd always tackled a crossword puzzle together. Rosalie had tried one on her own but had failed miserably. Lonnie would have immediately known a ten-letter word for "fleecing." Rosalie couldn't seem to get past the thought of sheep. Only with Tessa's help had she found the right word: defrauding. He'd also turned down the bed at night, smoothing the covers back in two perfect triangles. She could slip into her side like a letter going into an envelope.

Small things. Things of no consequence. Yet small things added up to create a life. Two lives.

The doorbell rang. Rosalie was expecting Tessa and Accosta to pick her up for breakfast. In the week since Lonnie died, they'd been attentive friends. They seemed to know when she wanted to be alone and when she needed company.

She opened the door.

"Ready?" Tessa asked.

Accosta elbowed her. "Good morning, Rosalie."

Tessa nodded. "Yes. Good morning, Rosalie."

The two of them always made Rosalie smile. "Good morning to you both."

"Shall we go?" Tessa asked.

"In a minute. I know this is silly but . . . would you mind showing me how to run the coffee maker?"

Tessa looked surprised. "Of course. But I'm really surprised you don't know—"

Rosalie took a breath. "Lonnie always made it."

"Ah," Accosta said. "Then let's teach you."

Pour water in, set the K-cup in place, choose the ounces, and press start.

Rosalie hated every step. They were Lonnie's steps. Not hers.

On their way out, Tessa paused in front of a huge flower arrangement Rosalie had taken home from the funeral. She fingered a leaf. "I noticed Cheri wasn't at her father's funeral. It's too bad she and her husband couldn't get home for it."

Rosalie didn't like the hint of condemnation in her voice. "I told them not to. They're halfway around the world on a trip they've been planning for years. Them interrupting their trip wouldn't bring Lonnie back to us."

"I think they made the right decision," Accosta said.

Tessa shrugged. "I suppose."

"Don't you worry. They've called me every day," Rosalie said.

"I wouldn't want to pay *that* phone bill," Tessa said.

Rosalie couldn't win.

Accosta bent down to smell the carnations and roses. "When do they get back?"

"In a couple weeks." She didn't want to talk about it anymore. "I'm sorry, but can we go? I'm hungry."

Rosalie let them leave first, locking up behind. The dining room was more empty than usual. Snowy days were often that way. It's like people preferred to hole up in their apartments.

When their juice and coffee had been served, Tessa placed both of her hands flat on the table. . "So then, Rosalie, how are you really doing? Are you relieved yet?"

Rosalie took a sip of her coffee. "Yes. It's good to finally know how to make coffee."

"No, no," Tessa said. "Relieved that the funeral is over."

"Oh. That." She wasn't sure if *relieved* was the right word, yet in a way...

Accosta chimed in. "I remember after my husband's funeral, I felt proud that I'd done the good thing, laid him to rest, and let friends and family pay their respects."

Rosalie appreciated the way Accosta expanded on Tessa's blunt question. "I *am* glad it's over, and that it went well."

"It was lovely," Tessa said. "A good turnout too."

Turnout? It was a funeral. Again, Tessa's choice of words seemed brusque.

"And with the funeral done and past, you *could* say that today is the first day of the rest of your life," Accosta said.

Rosalie shuddered. "I can't think that way yet. It's too overwhelming. The first day of the rest of my life, without Lonnie?" She shook her head adamantly.

Tessa slapped her hand on the table. "Today is today," she said.

It seemed an odd statement. Of course today was today.

Once again, Accosta clarified. "You don't need to worry about the rest of your life. You only need to take one day at a time."

One day. Days turning into weeks, weeks to months, months to years . . . years without Lonnie.

None of it made much sense. "Lonnie gave my days purpose — especially after he retired."

"You had purpose before he retired" Tessa said.

"I did, but before then most of our days were spent separately: his at work, and mine at home taking care of Cheri, or doing volunteer work at the Nearly New shop and church. I worked at a fabric store for a short while too."

"See there? Purpose," Tessa said. "You need to find your new purpose, one day at a time." She nodded at Accosta. We've both been there, and done that."

"And made it through to the other side," Accosta said.

"Retirement is a season, and so is widowhood," Tessa said. "Give it time. God will show you what's next."

Rosalie certainly hoped so.

Their fruit cups came. Rosalie took her coffee cup off of the saucer and put all the honeydew melon pieces on it.

"What are you doing?" Tessa asked.

It took her a moment to answer. "I always gave Lonnie the honeydew and I took his cantaloupe." She picked up the saucer and dumped the melon back into her cup. "I don't need to do that anymore." She felt an unbalanced sadness about it.

Accosta touched her arm. "I don't know how many times I scooped up two bowls of ice cream."

"Or bought two *kinds* of ice cream," Tessa said. "Chocolate chip for him and lime sherbet for me."

It fit. Lime sherbet. Tart, like Tessa.

Tessa speared a strawberry and pointed it at Rosalie. "Remember to ask for help. Don't depend on people sensing what you need."

Accosta looked offended. "You have such a dim view of people, Tessa. Most people are more than willing to help."

"You're right," she said. "They're more than willing—if you ask. I'm just saying most people won't think about offering."

Rosalie knew that wasn't true. "I've had dozens of people tell me to let them know if I need anything."

Tessa spread her hands. "Exactly. *You* have to let them know."

There *was* a subtle difference. "I do need one thing."

The ladies' eyes lit up. "What?"

"I have some questions about finances and Scranton offered to help. I'm going to take him up on it."

Tessa spread her hands as if it had been her idea. "And there you go."

One step at a time.

** ** **

Rosalie rang the doorbell to Scranton's apartment.

He looked surprised to see her.

"Hi, Scranton. I was wondering if I could talk to you a minute?"

"Of course." He led her into his living room.

There weren't many pictures on the walls, or pretties sitting about. But then she remembered he'd moved in after his wife had passed away. Most men weren't good at decorating.

"How are you doing?" he asked.

She shrugged. "Fair to partly cloudy."

He smiled. "I like that phrase. I may use it a few times myself."

"You're welcome to it."

They shared an awkward moment, then he said, "You wanted to talk to me about something?"

"Finances."

"Ah. The will?"

She nodded. "Everything is left to me as the surviving spouse, but what I need is more simple. Rudimentary even."

"Such as . . . ?"

"I don't know much about the kinds of accounts we have: 401K? Stocks? Savings. Checking." She sighed deeply. "Lonnie handled all of that. He even did our taxes. We never had a financial planner. I'm embarrassed to say that I don't even know how to balance a checkbook. That's a thing I need to do, right?"

He looked shocked, but quickly changed his expression to one of understanding. "I'd be happy to help. When?"

"Now?"

He chuckled. "Now is perfect."

** ** **

Rosalie's dining room table was covered with neat piles of paperwork: bank statements, stock and tax papers, as well as utility bills and their Visa bill.

She'd made notes and felt comfortable with most of it. She'd even balanced the checkbook after he'd shown her how.

Scranton was on the phone with the Social Security office. "All right. I'll have her fill out the forms for widow's benefits. Thank you." He hung up.

"That seemed too easy."

"It's never easy. But it is worth the trouble. You'll get one hundred percent of his benefits."

"I will?"

"Eventually. Do you have a printer? I'll print out the form."

Rosalie showed him the computer and printer and within minutes Scranton brought the form to the table. Thirty minutes later it was filled out.

"Send this along with a death certificate and you're set."

She felt a twinge of panic. "The funeral home gave me one, but how do I get copies?"

"I already ordered five from the state office of vital statistics."

"Free?"

He shook his head. "No, but it's handled."

"Tell me how much and I'll pay you back."

Scranton looked her straight in the eye. "It's handled, Rosalie."

He was a very kind man. "I can't express how much I appreciate all this," she said.

"I'm glad I could help." He looked at the piles. "Do you want help putting all this away?"

"No, I've got it."

He stepped toward the door, then faced her. "I hope getting some of the financial items checked off your list makes you feel a little better."

She nodded once. "It has. You've left me feeling more in control—of this, at least."

"Good. Let me know if you need anything else. And don't be nervous about what's to come. You can do this."

After he left, Rosalie carefully sorted the piles into file folders that she slipped into newly marked locations in a file drawer. She liked the feeling of neat-and-tidy, and of accomplishing something tangible.

Scranton was right. She could do this.

Chapter Twenty-Eight

Evelyn

> So be strong and courageous,
> all you who put your hope in the Lord!
> Psalm 31: 24

Ringo finished measuring the appliances in the kitchen. "Refrigerator, thirty-two inches."

Soon-ja stood nearby, writing on a clipboard. "I'd sure like a bigger fridge." She turned toward Evelyn who was washing dishes. "No offense, but with the baby coming I think I'll need the room."

Evelyn didn't mention she'd made three meals a day for herself and all of the boarders with that fridge. "I understand," she said. "We thought about updating the appliances but never got around to it."

Wayne dried a plate, nodding toward the dishwasher. "The dishwasher is kind of temperamental."

"He most certainly is," Evelyn teased.

Soon-ja smiled. "You mean your dishwashing services don't come with the house, Wayne?"

"Alas, they are being transferred to Happy Trails."

Soon-ja went back to the measurements. "Ringo, can we do something in order to get a bigger fridge?"

Ringo stood back and studied the situation. On one side of the fridge was a wall, and the other side was flanked by cabinets. "We'd have to lose half of this cabinet."

"Can you do that?" she asked.

"Do you doubt me?"

They exchanged smiles. "I wouldn't dare," she said.

Evelyn glanced at the cabinets, then shared a wistful smile with Wayne. There had been a lot of measurements taken, and ideas noted for possible changes. She wasn't sure if knowing about the changes made it harder or easier to let go.

"Let's measure the wall in the sunroom where I want to put my desk," Ringo said.

The couple left. Wayne put his hand on the back of Evelyn's neck. "Deep breaths."

She nodded. "I'm happy for them but letting go of Peerbaugh Place is tough. They're changing so much."

"But keeping a lot too. Plus, this kitchen was due for an update."

He was right. "It was due about twenty years ago," she said. She stopped washing the dishes and turned around to look at the room. "Why didn't I ever follow through?"

Wayne turned around too, and they both leaned against the counter. "You're a contented woman."

"Am I?"

"Aren't you?"

She thought about it for a moment. "I'm not sure if I'm contented or just afraid of change."

He chuckled. "Change is coming, ready or not."

Evelyn sighed. "Is moving the right decision?"

She was glad he didn't give her a quick answer, but a measured one. "Change is tricky because we won't fully know whether it's right or wrong until we're in the thick of it."

"And then it's too late."

He shook his head. "Maybe too late to go back, but not too late to get on the right road, even if we're on the wrong one." He bumped shoulders with her. "God won't abandon us. If we got this decision wrong, He'll make it right."

"I know."

"Then stop worrying. We prayed about the move. There were signs nudging us in that direction and things fell into place."

"Like an apartment opening up at Happy Trails, and Ringo and Soon-ja wanted to buy Peerbaugh Place."

"Exactly."

Evelyn nodded, acknowledging all of it. "We did get a fair price without having to go through open houses and showings."

"God made all this as easy as possible."

He had. Evelyn took a deep breath, drinking in the truth. "I guess there's only one thing to do."

"What's that?"

"Tell Him thank you."

Wayne took her hand and raised his arms toward heaven. "Thank You, Jesus!"

Evelyn laughed. "Thank You, Jesus!"

They pulled each other into a hug. "I'm so glad I have you," Evelyn said.

"Ditto."

They stood that way a full minute, finding strength in each other.

Then Wayne pulled back. "I know what we need to do."

"What?"

"Grab your purse and come with me."

** ** **

Evelyn and Wayne stood at the checkout counter at Saylor's Furniture. Andy Saylor—third generation to the Saylor business—checked off their purchases.

"A couch, chair, ottoman, recliner, coffee and end table, dining room set with a small buffet, plus a king bed, two bedside tables, and a long dresser with a mirror." He glanced up from the list. "Did I miss anything?"

Wayne checked with Evelyn, who shook her head. "That's it," Wayne said.

That's enough. More than enough.

"When can they be delivered?" Wayne asked.

"That's the best part, everything you picked out is in stock so it can be delivered tomorrow. Does that work?"

Tomorrow? Tomorrow!

She recalled Wayne's words in the kitchen earlier: *"God made all this as easy as possible."*

He most certainly had.

"Tomorrow is great," she said. "Thank you."

And thank You, Lord.

When they got in the car Wayne let out a long sigh. "Mission accomplished."

Evelyn was a little queasy about it. "I never thought our mission was to spend thousands of dollars."

He looked at her, incredulous. He counted on his fingers. "How much did you think seventeen pieces of furniture would cost?"

"Not that much," Evelyn said. "The last time I bought furniture was...pretty much never."

He put his hand on her knee. "I promise it will be all right. We are not spending above our means. We made good choices—both design-wise and finance-wise."

But Evelyn's heart beat wildly in her chest.

"Ev. Take a breath."

She drew a breath in, then let it out—twice. It did make her feel better. "Sorry, but this is all new to me."

He grinned. "New and exciting, yes?"

She leaned closer and kissed him. "Yes."

*** *** ***

Wayne finished drying the last of the dinner dishes and wiped his hands. "Want to watch an episode of 'Mad Men' with me?"

Evelyn wiped off the counter. "No thanks. I've got some writing to do."

Wayne's eyes lit up. "Writing?

"Writing about Peerbaugh Place—about all the tenants and such."

He folded the dish towel and hung it over the oven handle. "What brought this on?"

"Moving. Let's just say I'm feeling a lot of feels right now."

"And you *feel* the need to write them down?"

"Exactly."

He turned toward the sunroom, then stopped. "If you'd rather I didn't watch TV, I could do something else. Something quieter."

"No, no. Go ahead. I'll go in the parlor."

He kissed her forehead. "Have fun."

She wasn't sure about that.

Evelyn heard Wayne shut the doors of the sunroom. The low hum of the TV began. She sat in her favorite Morris chair in the parlor and opened her notebook. Where to start was the hard part.

Feel the feels.

Evelyn nodded. She'd never felt so many emotions as she did right now. Maybe the best thing to do was start with *now*, and *then* visit the stories from the past.

Right or wrong, she just needed to begin and worry about the order of things later.

And so she took a cleansing breath and set her pen above the paper. And then, almost beyond her power, the pen started moving across the page. *Leaving Peerbaugh Place scares me to death. Yet I've never been more excited...*

Chapter Twenty-Nine

Evelyn

> For everything there is a season,
> a time for every activity under heaven.
> A time to cry and a time to laugh.
> A time to grieve and a time to dance.
> Ecclesiastes 3: 1, 4

Evelyn scanned the goblets in the hutch. "I'm not sure about these."

Piper stopped wrapping great-grandmother Nelson's china to see what her mom was talking about. "Do you think you'll use them at Happy Trails?"

"I might use eight." She mentally counted off her friends: Accosta, Tessa, Mae and Collier, herself and Wayne, Piper and her husband, Gregory . . .

"I'll ask it another way," Piper said. "Your dinners are included in your monthly rent, so how many times are you going to cook for a crowd?"

Since dinners were paid for . . . "Not many. You, Gregory, and the kids maybe."

"Maybe."

Evelyn took out a goblet and held it toward the light, enjoying the design of the cut glass. She just wasn't sure whether she should keep it.

"Do the goblets have sentimental significance?"

"They were a wedding present from Aaron's parents."

"Then keep eight of them and leave the rest."

It was a good solution. Evelyn wrapped them up and put them in a box. Next . . . "Sherbet dishes." She sighed.

Piper laughed. "Have you *ever* used those?"

Evelyn thought back. "Maybe once."

"Then leave them. Or . . . where's your phone?"

"In the kitchen."

Piper got it. She took a picture of the sherbets. "See? Now you can remember them without having to store them. Do that with all the things that are questionable to move. Keep the memories, leave the stuff."

Evelyn laughed. "I should make a cross-stitch of that saying."

As they got back to work Evelyn found it easier to make decisions by taking a lot of pictures. "It's good Ricky and Soon-ja bought the house with most of the furnishings. Maybe they'd like the pretties that I'm not taking."

"You could ask. Or you could sell them."

Evelyn hoped it wouldn't come to that. Taking photos, writing descriptions, posting them online? Then shipping? It was a lot of work.

She put a lid on the box of crystal. "I have to admit that moving into a new place *is* kind of exciting."

"I'm sure it is. And how nice you have familiar faces waiting to greet you. And I heard Mae and Collier are considering Happy Trails too."

"Someday. Mae isn't in any hurry."

"The point is, your old friends will always be your old friends."

Evelyn chuckled. "*Old* friends. That's for sure."

Piper rolled her eyes.

As Evelyn looked around the dining room she marveled at the wonderful constancy of friendship. She touched the dining table lovingly. "Oh, the hundreds of meals that were shared around this table. Tessa would always tell us about something she'd just learned—I know about Elizabethan history because of her. And Mae would be sarcastic and spar with her, but always make us laugh. And Audra would try to teach manners to her daughter, while little Summer would take it all in."

"Kids are sponges, that's for sure."

"God has been very good to all of us."

Piper pumped a fist in the air. "Sisters forever!"

And ever.

** ** **

Evelyn stood at the edge of the parlor of Peerbaugh Place and watched Wayne tape a box shut.

"There we go," he said, straightening up. "The last one. We are finally done."

In so many ways.

He looked at her. "What's wrong?"

She shrugged. Despite saying she was excited about the move, her answer to his question was too complicated to put into words.

He took hold of her upper arms. "I know it's hard, Ev."

"Very."

"But it's the right thing to do."

"I know. It just happened so fast. We made the decision on Thanksgiving, and now it's a couple weeks later and we're doing it. It's done and there's no going back."

"Having a real estate daughter and a banker son certainly helps speed things up."

"And Ringo didn't ask for an inspection."

"He knows where to find us if they need us. Wayne said. "Plus, they made it easier by letting us leave a lot of stuff here."

Evelyn drew in a deep breath. "That, they did." She blew out the breath and added, "It's all a good thing." Maybe if she kept telling herself that . . .

His eyes met hers. "Everything will be good because we're doing it together."

She fell into his arms. "You always know just what to say."

He ran his hand up and down her back. "Because it's the truth."

Evelyn nodded before stepping away from him. "I *am* ready to let go. But that doesn't change the fact that there are thousands of memories swirling around in this house. Aaron and I had a wedding shower here. I rocked Russell in that very chair and helped him with his arithmetic on the dining room table. Then Russell met and married Audra and adopted Summer. They told us right here in the parlor. Summer was only five when she moved in here with her mom. Now she's seventeen!"

"Time passes quickly."

"Too much so." She sat on the loveseat. "We've had so many tenants: Mae, Audra, Tessa, Piper, Heddy, Lucinda . . . and then

Accosta and everyone from the hospital." In her mind's eye she saw her original sister circle of ladies dancing to an old record and—

"You're smiling."

Evelyn went to the old-fashioned turntable and chose a specific song. "I was remembering . . ." She set the needle on the vinyl and the Beach Boys' "Surfin' Safari" rocked the room.

It was impossible to be still. Evelyn took Wayne's hand and they did the twist as if they were twenty. When they stopped they were out of breath. "Whenever I dance I remember how much I love it. We need to dance more often, husband."

"Then we will. Happy Trails hosts a dance every Friday." He swung her under his arm one last time, then pulled her close. "Is it a date?"

"Most definitely."

Evelyn moved to put on another record, but the doorbell rang.

Evelyn fluffed her hair and answered it. It was the moving men. So much for dancing.

As the movers did their job, Evelyn did hers. Without looking back she linked her arm with her husband's. Then she walked out the door of one season of her life, to open the door of another.

*** *** ***

After the movers finished moving Evelyn and Wayne's possessions to Happy Trails, Wayne pulled Evelyn into the hallway and shut the door of their apartment.

"What are you doing?" she asked. "I'm in the middle of—"

He put his finger to her lips, shushing her. "I want to carry you over the threshold."

Evelyn checked up and down the hall, glad there were no witnesses, but she lowered her voice just the same. "You most certainly will not. I won't let you risk hurting yourself the first day we're here."

She could tell by his eyes that he reluctantly agreed. She put her hand on his cheek. "How about we walk in together?"

He eyed the door. "It's not wide enough."

"For side by side, but how about . . . ?" Evelyn put her back against Wayne's front, and pulled his arms around herself. She felt his breath in her ear. "Like this."

Wayne nuzzled his cheek against her hair. "Excellent," he said. "I like it. Open the door."

She opened the door and they walked in together. After Wayne shut the door he turned her around for a proper hug. "Welcome home, my darling woman," he whispered.

"Welcome home, my dearest husband."

A kiss sealed the moment.

** ** **

"How do we still have so much stuff?" Evelyn said as she arched her back, moaning with the pain of lifting and putting things away.

Wayne came in from the other room. "I'm feeling it too. In fact . . ." He took her hand and led her to their new couch where they sat with a *whoof*.

"Ahhh. That's better."

Evelyn slouched down to support her head against the cushions. "I'm afraid if I close my eyes I'll be done for the day."

"Nothing wrong with that." He slouched down too.

There was a knock on the door. Evelyn started to get up but Wayne blocked her with an arm. "Come in," he called out.

Tessa came two steps in, peered at them, and said, "Get going, you slackers."

Accosta followed her in with her walker. "Ease up, Tessa. Moving is a big job."

Tessa glanced over her shoulder at her roommate. "It wasn't for you."

"That's because I didn't have much to move."

Evelyn looked at the stacks of boxes. "I thought *we* didn't have much, but I was wrong."

Wayne stood and offered Accosta a seat. "Thank you, kind sir." She sat in the Morris chair — one of the few pieces they brought with them.

"Would you like to sit too?" Wayne asked Tessa.

"No, thank you. I am fine standing here as long as I have this." She lifted her cane. "Besides, we aren't staying long, we just wanted to check in."

Evelyn sat forward on the edge of the cushion. Even though she'd known Tessa for over a dozen years, she still felt like a student trying to please her teacher. "I thought I planned where everything's going to go, but I'm not sure anymore. ."

Accosta studied the space. "I expect you'll have all the boxes emptied in a jiff."

"That's the plan," Wayne said. "And the rest of the new furniture is coming this afternoon."

Tessa pointed at the empty bedroom and dining area. "Did you buy a table and chairs?"

"And a buffet too," Evelyn said.

Tessa continued to scope out the space. "Your old table would have been too big in here."

Tessa always acted like she'd thought of something first. It usually didn't bother Evelyn *that* much, but today it rubbed her wrong. Luckily she caught herself before she reacted badly. Instead of arguing with Tessa or pointing out that she and Wayne were quite capable of measuring things, Evelyn simply said, "You're right." Then she changed the subject. "I hope we settle in as well as you did, Accosta."

"I know you will. I am enormously grateful to be here and I'm sure you will be too."

"I'm glad it's—"

Tessa shook her head. "You didn't ask me how I've settled into our arrangement."

Okay . . . Evelyn would ask the question, but hoped Tessa wouldn't be rude. "So then, Tessa. How have you settled in?"

"I have settled in quite well, thank you. It's nice to have someone to talk to, and Accosta and I have enjoyed many insightful discussions during our Bible studies."

Evelyn glanced at Accosta to check her reaction. But as usual Accosta's demeanor was peaceful and content.

"I agree," Accosta said. "On all accounts."

Tessa tapped her cane twice on the entry tile. "Well then, that's that. We will see you at dinner. Five-fifteen sharp."

Yes, ma'am!

Wayne saw them out, locking the door behind them. "I think I'm more exhausted now than I was five minutes ago."

"Ditto and double ditto," Evelyn said. She beckoned him back to the couch and they snuggled.

"If I haven't ever told you, you're the best roommate ever," she said.

He kissed the top of her head.

It was comforting to go through life on the same page.

Chapter Thirty

Kay & Evelyn

> Do not judge others, and you will not be judged.
> For you will be treated as you treat others.
> The standard you use in judging
> is the standard by which you will be judged.
> Matthew 7: 1

Kay heard voices and commotion out in the hall. She peered through the peephole of her front door and saw delivery men carrying a large dresser. When they walked out of her sightline she opened the door to watch.

The door to the apartment three down from hers was open. She'd seen someone moving in, but hadn't met them yet.

At just that moment a man came by, walking toward the apartment.

"Hello," he said.

She smiled her best welcome smile. "Hello."

He stopped and held out his hand. "I'm Wayne Wellington."

"Katerina Volkov." He was kind of cute. Shortish, but he had a nice smile. "You're moving in?"

"We are."

We. Great.

"Would you like to meet the wife?" He gestured toward the apartment.

"Of course." Kay hoped she was friendly. It would be nice to claim the newest residents as friends.

Inside the apartment the wife was directing the delivery men how to place the dresser. She was short like Wayne, and cute with rosy cheeks.

When she saw her husband she looked relieved, "Wayne, does this look all right, centered on this wall?"

"Looks great to me."

The men left for another load. "A new dining room set and we're through."

"It's the first we've ever bought," his wife said. Then she smiled at Kay. "Where are my manners? Forgive me. I haven't moved since I was twenty, so it's a little overwhelming. Hi, I'm Evelyn." She held out her hand.

Kay shook it. "I'm Katerina. Volkov."

"An interesting name," Evelyn said.

"Volkov is Russian. There's Russian royalty in our line."

Evelyn seemed a little surprised. It *was* a Russian name, so why did she respond like that? Kay felt a little stitch in her gut. She'd seen a pattern in people's reaction to many of the things she said about herself. They'd pause just a moment, then look away.

They were probably jealous.

Wayne put an arm around his wife's shoulders. "Wellington is British, through and through. We have no royalty in our line, but obviously we're named after the general, the Duke of Wellington."

"He was a prime minister," Evelyn said.

"And defeated Napoleon at Waterloo." Wayne chuckled. "So I *wish* we were related."

Evelyn smiled at him. "You're hero enough for me, husband."

Kay felt a wave of envy. He was cute, she was cute. They were adorable together.

"Would you like to sit down?" Evelyn said. "You'll be our first guest."

Kay sat on the couch, which was pretty comfortable.

"Which apartment is yours?" Evelyn asked.

Kay pointed down the hall and gave the number. "I moved in alone. My husband died on a Mediterranean cruise."

There was the usual pause. Then Evelyn said, "How tragic."

Kay sighed deeply. "Very. Every year we went on a cruise to a different place. Nicolae was an amazing man of the world."

"It sounds like it," Wayne said.

Their reactions were normal—what she was used to, but this time Kay felt a twinge of regret for her words. The whole cruise and world stuff was getting old—even to her. "Sorry," she said. "None of these details is here nor there at the moment. I'm just really glad to have you here. I was the latest newbie, so now, I get to pass the crown on to you. Crowns. Two crowns."

They both chuckled. "We will wear them proudly," Wayne said.

Kay felt better about this last exchange than the earlier ones. They were good conversationalists and seemed to like her.

The sounds of moving men could be heard in the hall. They stood in unison.

"We'll have to eat a meal together once you're moved in," Kay said.

"We'd love that," Evelyn said. "Do you know Tessa Klein and Accosta Rand?"

Kay felt a twinge of disappointment. "I do."

"They're our dear friends."

Of course they are.

Kay skirted past the movers and went back to her apartment. It would have been nice to have new friends who needed a friend as much as she did.

** ** **

The furniture movers were just finishing up when Tessa walked into Evelyn and Wayne's new apartment.

"Busy bees," Tessa said as she surveyed the main rooms.

"Do you like the new pieces?" Evelyn asked.

Tessa ran her hand along the back of a dining chair. "Very nice. Very tasteful."

Evelyn wasn't sure that was complete approval, but with Tessa she took what she could get. "Come see the bedroom set."

As Wayne saw the moving men to the door, Evelyn saw him slip each of them a twenty. She was glad he tipped them. She never would have thought of it.

Tessa sat on the edge of the king bed. "Very comfy. And huge."

"We're used to a queen but decided to splurge since we had space for it."

"I always wanted to get a king because my husband snored like a freight train, but we didn't have the room."

Evelyn went to the bedside table and picked up a remote. "And look." She used it to tilt the top portion of the bed. "It adjusts so we can watch TV in bed or read."

"Very fancy. You two really *are* starting a new life."

There was something disapproving about her tone. "We are. Actually, we've never had any furniture that's just ours."

"It's a new beginning," Wayne said from the doorway. "In so many ways."

Evelyn gave him a special smile.

Tessa pointed her cane at the dresser. "I like the wood — though the sleek style is kind of modern for you."

"That, it is," Wayne said. "We figure this is probably the first and last furniture we buy so we might as well try something totally different."

"They call it Danish modern," Evelyn said.

"I've heard of that." Tessa finally nodded. "I approve."

Evelyn felt ridiculously relieved. She shouldn't care what other people thought. But she did.

Speaking of other people . . . "Actually, you're not the first to see it," Evelyn said. "A neighbor, Katerina, came by and introduced herself."

Tessa's right eyebrow rose. "What do you think of her?"

It seemed an odd question. "She seemed nice," Evelyn said.

Wayne raised a finger. "Her late husband was descended from Russian royalty."

Tessa did a double-take. "Royalty, you say?"

"That's what she said."

She shook her head back and forth. "That's a new one."

"A new what?"

"A new embellishment."

"So it's not true?" Wayne asked.

Tessa shrugged. "Can't really say for sure. Let me summarize Katerina this way: She likes to raise herself up by mentioning the places she's been, her possessions, her wealth, and even her charities."

"She probably has some interesting stories," Evelyn said.

"She doesn't tell stories. She gives fancy facts." Tessa shuffled her shoulders . "Or perhaps I just haven't heard the stories to go along with the facts. Either way, I should let you make your own conclusions."

Evelyn *had* made one observation. "She was certainly dressed up more than I thought we'd have to dress here."

"You do *not* have to dress like she does. Or wear as much jewelry. Or makeup." Tessa waved her hand. "I believe there comes a time in a woman's life when less is more."

Evelyn hoped that was true because she only wore the simplest makeup—though she *had* started to draw in her brows as they were fading into nothingness right before her eyes.

She saw Wayne checking his watch. "We need to get back to the house. Our things are moved, but we want to do a good cleaning for Ringo and Soon-ja."

"But what about dinner?"

He glanced at Evelyn. "We'll take a raincheck."

She was relieved. "I know I won't be able to sleep until the cleaning is all wrapped up."

Tessa got up from the bed. "Very good. I'll check back tomorrow."

As soon as she left, Wayne said, "I love Tessa dearly and don't mind the information about Katerina, but sometimes I wonder what she says about us."

Evelyn gave him a quick kiss. "Let her talk. I, for one, plan on being scandalously happy here."

He pulled her closer. "Scandalously?"

"You never know, husband."

Chapter Thirty-One

Rosalie

You can make many plans,
but the Lord's purpose will prevail.
Proverbs 19: 21

Rosalie tried to read a book, but kept reading and re-reading the same paragraph. She finally tossed it aside. Lately she couldn't concentrate on anything. It's like her mind was made of a thick mush which prevented any distinct thought from getting through.

She stood and stretched, hoping the movement would clear her brain.

Get out of your apartment.

It was a strange thought, but she realized it could be a good one. Although residents of Happy Trails had been kind and had stopped by many times in the past three weeks, she hadn't left except for meals. Without Lonnie's presence to enliven the space, the walls were closing in.

She checked the time and thought of her options: the building's van was taking a group shopping at Target; the chorus was practicing — she sang alto and had already missed two rehearsals; and there was a book club meeting but she hadn't read the book. Actually she wasn't sure she wanted to participate in anything as much as just be *out*.

So she smoothed her hair with her fingers, put on her shoes, and walked toward the Game Room. When she saw the puzzle table, she knew it was the perfect choice. She and Lonnie loved doing puzzles, though they approached them differently. She liked to sort the pieces into puzzle trays according to color, and he just liked to turn them over. The end result was the same and they alternated methods.

The community puzzle was half done. There were a few boats to do, but mostly there was a lot of sky left. *Chickens.* Rosalie actually liked big expanses of one color because she sorted the pieces according to shape. It made it far less difficult. She had names for the shapes: a whirligig, man, soup bowl, cross . . .

As she began sorting, the bell of her sleeve caught on a piece and a bunch of pieces were swept to the floor. "No!" With a groan she knelt down and began putting them back on the table.

"Having fun?"

She looked up and saw Scranton. "My sleeve's to blame."

He knelt beside her and the pieces were returned to their proper places. She was pleased when he sat at the table. "Well then. What were you working on?"

"The sky."

He glanced over the blue pieces she was sorting. "It's all yours. I'll work on the sailboat."

They worked in silence for a few minutes. Then he asked, "How are you doing?"

"Okay, I guess." She sorted a few more pieces before continuing. "As you know, it's hard transitioning from two to one."

"I understand completely. When Olivia died I felt lost. Still am, part of the time."

She appreciated talking to a partner-in-grief. It gave them a special bond. "I was twenty when Lonnie and I married. How old were you and Olivia?"

"I was twenty-two and she was nineteen."

"All of us babies."

He bobbled his head. "But all of us grew up."

"Together," she added.

He nodded.

"My entire adult life was lived with Lonnie. Actually, he was the only man I really dated. So what am I supposed to do now? He was my entire world."

"What about your kids?"

"Kid. One daughter and son-in-law. They're great, but they're busy with each other and work. Other than a few stints with part-time work, I was a homemaker. I loved to cook. Now two meals a day are cooked *for* me. And without Lonnie to cook for…"

"Olivia made the best apple pie. What's your specialty?"

"Cakes. I'm pretty good with a pastry bag and buttercream."

"Sounds good to me."

"What's your favorite?"

"Olivia made me red velvet, but I also like white cake with white buttercream—like people have at weddings. You?"

"Chocolate with chocolate."

As they discussed their favorite foods, Rosalie got an idea. She'd make Scranton a cake.

Just thinking of it gave her a new purpose.

But first, she'd finish the sky.

** ** **

Rosalie knocked on Scranton's door. She listened for a few moments and heard shuffling. As the door opened, Scranton glanced at her, then down at the cake. His eyes lit up.

"Surprise!"

"Wow. For me?"

"Yes, for you. A white wedding cake with buttercream frosting. A thank-you cake for helping me with the financial stuff."

"You didn't have to do that—but I'm glad you did. It looks delicious. Come on in." He motioned toward a small dinette table. "Set it there. I'll get plates and forks." He headed to the kitchen.

"And a knife," she said.

He returned with everything they needed, plus a carton of strawberry swirl ice cream and a spoon.

"Perfect," she said. "Want me to do the cutting?"

"Please. I'll add the ice cream."

Together, the two pieces were served. They sat at the table. She was eager to see his reaction to the first bite.

He did not disappoint, but closed his eyes. "Mmm. Cake is definitely your specialty."

"Thank you, sir."

He pointed his fork at the red piping along the edges, and the spray of red roses. "And you *are* good with a pastry bag."

"It all started when I took a baking class thirty years ago. It takes a lot of practice."

"I'm sure."

"Do you have your wife's recipe for apple pie? I could help you make one."

"I suppose I do." He got up and came back with a recipe box. His fingers walked over the cards until he pulled one out. "Here it is." He handed her the card.

Rosalie looked over the recipe. It looked pretty straightforward except for one addition. "Cardamon?"

"I don't even know what that is," he said.

"A spice. I've never used it, but I think it's kind of like cinnamon. Maybe it's the ingredient that made the pie so good. Do you have any?"

"I haven't a clue." They both went to the kitchen and searched through Olivia's spices. "Here it is!" he said.

"Do you have apples?"

Scranton shook his head. "I'll get some and we can take a stab at it—but I've got to eat up this cake first." They returned to the table and began eating again. "Actually, good as it is, I don't know how I'll ever eat this entire thing."

"Have friends over."

Scranton's silence made her wonder if he had friends at Happy Trails. She tried to remember who she'd seen him with. The list was small. "You could have Katerina over."

He shook his head adamantly. "She is not a friend—though she'd like to be."

Rosalie felt sorry for the woman. Ever since Katerina's party, there'd been more talk against her than for her. She'd certainly gotten off on the wrong foot. "There's got to be someone you want to share cake with. I know Tessa and Accosta would love to have a piece."

"Maybe." He ran his fork through the frosting but didn't eat it. "I've made a few mistakes since moving here."

She saw a look of regret cloud his expression. "Such as?"

"Never mind."

"No, no . . . don't shut yourself off like that."

He scoffed. "An apt choice of words."

She briefly touched his hand, then pulled it away. She could see the hurt in his eyes. "I'm on your side. I promise."

"I don't know why I'm telling you this, but . . . I've done my best to keep to myself—as much as the staff will let me."

"The staff?"

"Meals. I don't like making small-talk so meals are excruciating. They won't let me eat alone in my apartment. They want me to socialize."

He made the last word sound excruciating. "I understand what you mean about the meals. Most days I'd prefer eating by myself. Especially now, being a single. I always had Lonnie to make conversation with our tablemates. I could just sit there and chime in once in a while, but now that he's gone, meals exhaust me."

His eyes brightened "I feel exactly the same."

There was an easy solution to both their problems.

At the same time they said it, "Let's eat together."

They laughed, and agreed to start their twosome at dinner that night.

"I'm sure glad God nudged me out of the apartment this morning."

"What?" Scranton asked.

She told him about her sudden idea to get out and do something. "I ended up at the puzzle table. Where I swept a bunch of pieces on the floor."

"Just as I was walking by."

She liked the sequence of events. "I'd say it was a coincidence, but I don't believe in them."

"Why not?"

"Because coincidences are just God working undercover." She swept her hand toward the cake. "And here we are. Two introverts who love puzzles and cake."

"And who need a dinner companion."

"Exactly," she said. "God is good. Very, very good."

He nodded. "Even as a lawyer who's used to making arguments, I can't argue with you."

Chapter Thirty-Two

Scranton

Don't be afraid, for I am with you.
Don't be discouraged, for I am your God.
I will strengthen you and help you.
I will hold you up with my victorious right hand.
　　　　Isaiah 41: 10

Scranton stood in his closet and pored through his tie rack. He still had dozens of ties from his courtroom days. Beyond work, there were few occasions to wear them. Even in church, men went tieless. Although ties *were* slightly uncomfortable, he liked the look, and the respect that came with wearing one. Though the firm had adopted Casual Fridays, he'd argued that people acted differently when they were dressed up. Or down. He'd been overruled. Collarless shirts and rubber-soled shoes. What was the world coming to?

It irked him that society had dumbed down what clothing was proper to wear. He was appalled when he saw pajama bottoms in public. And most young women he saw — women in their prime — didn't seem to care about their hair either. They didn't let it hang down in all its glory, but pulled it back in ponytails and messy-buns to get it out of the way. There was no pride in appearance anymore.

He heard Olivia's voice in his head: *Don't judge, honey. We wore our share of ripped jeans, miniskirts, and granny dresses. Our parents were appalled too.*

Maybe so, but that didn't explain away times where the bad-fashion choices of youth carried over to older generations. Gray-haired women wearing leggings and flip-flops? Old men in tee-shirts, and wearing their shirts untucked?

It was what it was. He couldn't fight the world.

Today he was going to the office so he put on a white shirt — classic was always a good choice. After Olivia's death he'd taken a little time off, but had eventually gone back to work full time. That is, until his partners suggested he cut back to three days a week. "Ease into your retirement, Scranton." He'd done so reluctantly. After all, over his lifetime he'd had zero time for hobbies, so he had absolutely nothing to do the other two weekdays. Plus weekends without Olivia were excruciating. When he'd first told them he was moving to Happy Trails—an unfortunate, insipid name—they'd congratulated him on selling the house and making the "wise" move. They'd told him to come in once a week as a consultant—another insipid word.

Today was not his usual day of the week, but the senior partner, Lance Burroughs, had summoned him.

It was nice to be needed.

He chose a royal blue tie for the occasion—Olivia's favorite.

** ** **

The reception desk at Burroughs, Blake, and Stockton was draped with pine garland. A nine-foot Christmas tree stood in the corner, covered in gold and silver balls and thousands of white lights. Happy Trails had turned into fairyland as well. Both locations made him feel guilty about not putting up any decorations.

Whatever.

"Good morning, Mr. Stockton. How are you today?" asked the receptionist.

He set his briefcase on the counter. "Very good, Connie. And you? How are your little boys? Are they playing basketball this winter?"

She smiled "Alex is, but Eric has decided he likes hockey."

"Good for them," he said. "Have a nice day."

"You too."

He walked down a long hall toward Lance's corner office. When he passed his own office, he turned in to drop off his briefcase.

He stopped in the doorway. His ornately carved desk had been replaced with a modern one in stark black and glass. His leather tufted guest chairs had been usurped by two royal blue chairs with skinny legs that looked like they would break if anyone over a hundred pounds sat in them.

What was going on?

He kept his briefcase, upped his pace to Lance's office, waved at his secretary, and went right in.

Lance stood. "Scranton. How nice to see you."

Scranton hooked a thumb over his shoulder. "Who authorized new furniture in my office? I hate it. It's way too modern."

Lance offered him a chair and they both sat down. "That's what I wanted to talk to you about." He smoothed his tie against his chest. "I know you don't like to mince words so I won't either. Bottom line . . . it's not your office anymore."

Scranton's head jerked back. "Whose office is it?"

"John's."

"John Weederman?" A squirrely yes-man with an eternal three-day beard.

"We're making him a partner."

Scranton's heart beat double-time. "When was this decided?"

"Last week."

He pushed against the armrests to sit forward. "As a founding partner, don't you think I should have been asked my opinion?"

"You're a retiring founding partner."

"I'm still a consultant. I'm still a part of this firm."

Lance pressed his hands on his executive desk and Scranton wondered why *he* got to keep *his* desk.

"That's why I called you in today." Lance stood and closed the door—never a good sign.

Between the door and Lance's return to his desk, Scranton knew what was going to happen. He desperately tried to think of a way to stop this rolling boulder from landing on top of him.

But couldn't.

Lance retrieved some papers, handing them to Scranton. "We would like to buy you out. Here are the terms of the buyout. As you can see—in recognition of your position and hard work for thirty-six years—we are being extremely generous."

Scranton didn't look at the papers. "You and Blake have been here nearly as long as I have. Are you being bought out?"

"Our time will come. As of right now we both work full-time." He straightened a pen on his desk. "And with what you've been through with your situation with dear Olivia . . ."

"You have no right to call my wife 'dear.'"

Lance raised his hands. "I meant no disrespect. None. It's just that life has dealt you some difficult situations where you had to pivot. Fortunately you've been able to ease your way out of the rat race. We thought you might like some seed money for the next season in your life."

Although he didn't really want to look at their offer Scranton skimmed through the papers. The sum *was* generous.

But still . . . "I don't like how you're making this decision for me."

Lance shook his head. "It's an offer. We are beholden to all you've done. I still am shocked by how three green lawyers could start a practice and bring it to this level. Isn't it time to reap the harvest?"

Scranton stared at the pages in his lap. He didn't need the money. The sale of their home had bought him into Happy Trails, and his wise investments easily paid the monthly fees. What would he do with this sort of money?

His first thought was, *Go on a world cruise with —*

With no one. Olivia was gone.

"I'm sorry if this seems sudden, Scranton. We assumed you sensed it was inevitable."

Had he? Or had he been so wrapped up in himself that he hadn't thought about the future?

Whether he knew or not was immaterial. This was happening. He could fight it and let it happen later — or . . .

Surrender.

"Hand me a pen."

** ** **

When Scranton got back to his apartment he shucked off his nicely-shined shoes, ripped off his tie, and tossed his suit and shirt on the bed. He yanked open a drawer he rarely opened and took out a pair of sweatpants and a sweatshirt that Olivia had bought him when they'd briefly joined a health club.

It was time for lunch. He spotted Rosalie's cake, got out a fork, and took the entire thing to his recliner. He turned on the TV and purposely stopped on a soap opera. Maybe he'd get addicted to it and vicariously live out the rest of his life through the storylines.

It was better than the life he'd been dealt.

Chapter Thirty-Three

Kay

> Truthful words stand the test of time,
> but lies are soon exposed.
> Proverbs 12: 19

In the hallway, Kay saw a couple she'd met on an outing to see a play last week. She only knew them because they'd sat next to her at the theatre. Bill and ... Dorothy?

Since she wasn't sure about their names, she hurried to catch up with them — which she did when they stopped at the elevator.

"Hello again," she said.

Their smiles were a bit tentative, but they did smile. "Hi, Katerina," the wife said.

"Are you two available for dinner?"

They exchanged a look between them. Bill answered. "I'm sorry, we're meeting another couple."

As was everyone else she'd asked. Kay tried not to let her disappointment show.

The elevator door opened. Bill waited for her to enter, but she glanced at her watch and said, "Oops. I forgot something. I'll see you later."

She slowly walked back to her apartment. Why was she being shunned? She couldn't think of anything she'd done to offend people yet every meal presented a problem: who could she eat with?

She looked up when she heard a door open. The newbies Evelyn and Wayne came out to the hall. She walked faster toward them.

"Hi," she said. "Heading to dinner?"

"We are," Wayne said. "And you?"

"I was just heading that way. Care to join me?"

Evelyn only hesitated a moment. "We'd love to."

Bless them.

*** *** ***

Kay tried not to glare at Scranton and Rosalie sitting together with the man she'd nicknamed Wrinkles. Rosalie looked awful. Yes, she'd recently buried her husband, but just the same . . .

Yet if she looked so bad, why had Scranton latched onto her?

Actually, Scranton seemed a little worse for wear himself. He looked... old. She checked out her own hands. The veins were pronounced, the skin at her wrists wrinkled. No matter what she wanted to believe she was old too.

While they read the menu, Kay realized Wayne was talking about the people who'd bought their house. People who had ridiculous names: Ringo and Soon-ja.

Then both Evelyn and Wayne looked past Kay — who had her back to the entrance. Kay turned around and saw the hostess coming toward their table. She was focused on Kay.

"Yes?"

"The front desk just called and said your daughter, Tif, is here?"

She can't be. She lives in Idaho. Why is she here?

"How nice," Evelyn said. "We'd love to meet her."

Kay pushed her chair back. "I'll go down and —"

"Invite her to join us," Wayne said.

That was the last thing Kay wanted, but she had little choice. Frani was waiting for an answer. "Of course. Invite her up." Her mouth was suddenly dry. She sipped her water.

"You don't seem happy about her visit," Evelyn said.

Kay forced her face to look pleased. "I'm just surprised."

"How long has it been since you've seen each other?"

"A year?" Or more. Tiffany knew nothing of Kay's new life as Katerina. *I should have gone down to see her first. To tell her . . .*

"Where does she live?" Wayne asked.

"Idaho," Evelyn answered the question, which must mean she'd heard it from someone else.

Why did I ever mention her to anyone?

It was too late for regrets. Kay took a fresh breath and continued the lie. "Tiffany is a successful chef in Boise. She owns a three-star restaurant and —"

Again, Evelyn and Wayne looked behind Kay. And Wayne stood. Kay's stomach flipped. She turned around and saw her daughter—who was wearing tight jeans and a green velvety top that had crystals on it, forming the shape of a dopey reindeer.

Tiffany's mouth was open in shock. "Really, Mom? I'm a three-star chef?"

Oh dear. She'd overheard.

Kay hurried to introduce them. "Tiffany, this is Evelyn and Wayne Wellington . . . this is my daughter, Tiffany."

"Tif." She nodded at the couple. "Nice to meet you."

Wayne got up to pull out the empty chair. "Would you like to join us for dinner?"

"I'm not sure just yet." But she sat down and leaned her arms on the table. "Mom, why did you tell them I was a chef?"

Kay had no idea what to say.

"And by the way, nice wig."

Kay felt her cheeks grow red. "If you can't be polite, I think it's best you—"

Tiffany put her hands to her chest in that dramatic way she'd done since she was a child. "*Me? I'm* not being polite?" She looked at Evelyn. "I am not a chef. I run a Dairy Sweet with my husband."

"Oh," Evelyn said. "That's nice. I love ice cream."

"Everybody does. But it's obviously not nice enough for my mother. Right, Kay? The people at the front desk said you're going by Katerina? Where did that come from?"

Kay shoved her chair back from the table and dropped the napkin on her plate. She looked at the Wellingtons. "I'm really sorry about this."

As Kay rushed out of the dining room she heard Tiffany say to Evelyn and Wayne, "You two should feel privileged. Mom is never sorry. Nice to meet you."

Tiffany was coming after her so Kay nearly ran down the hall toward the elevator. It was on another floor. She checked around. *Where are the stairs? I should take the—*

Her daughter caught up with her, spinning her around to face her. "What was all that about?" She flipped a strand of the wig. "And this? Really? Are you sick?"

Kay didn't know what to do. She didn't want to argue in the hall, but didn't want to take Tiffany back to her apartment either. She wanted her gone.

When she spotted the door to the stairs she made a beeline for it. Tiffany followed her in. The door clanged closed behind them. She leaned against the railing, winded from all of the commotion. "No, I'm not sick, but I'm suddenly not feeling well. I'm living my life the way I want to live it, and that's that. You need to leave, Tiffany. Please."

Tiffany scoffed. "What is all of this about? We haven't seen each other in a year and you brush me off like I didn't exist? And lie about me? About yourself?"

"It's complicated."

"It'll be even more complicated when people find out about your son, Con the con."

"Stop." Kay started up the stairs.

Tiffany followed her. "I will not stop. I bet you've told people he's a lawyer or a doctor. Which is it?"

"His name is Connery and he's a pharmacist." Kay stopped on a landing to catch her breath. She hated the way their voices echoed in the stairwell.

Tiffany cackled. "He's into drugs, that's for sure. And doing five years for it."

Kay forced herself up the last set of stairs. She put her hands on the push-bar to open the door.

Tiffany put her arm across the threshold and stopped her. "What do you have to say for yourself, Mom?"

Kay felt trapped. There was no way out. And so she began to cry. "I started a new life. So what if I embellished it a bit?"

Tiffany's eyebrows dipped. "Are we really that awful that you thought you needed a new life? I understand how Con is a disappointment, but I never thought I was." She lowered her voice and blinked slowly. "What have you told them about Rod and the kids?"

"Nothing. Really. Nothing."

Tiffany's eyebrows dipped. "Great. They don't even exist. That's probably worse."

Kay's chest tightened. "You know what, Tiffany? You got me. Are you satisfied?"

Tiffany huffed. "Don't act like this is something I wanted. *You're* the liar." She gave her mom a smug smile. "You wanted a new life? As Ka-ter-in-a? Sheesh, Mom. Really?"

Kay couldn't handle any more. Her whole world was coming apart. She whispered. "Please go."

"Gladly." Tiffany pushed the door open with a clatter. "I'm so glad I came all this way to surprise you. See you never, Mother." She stormed away.

Kay made a conscious effort to relax her hands, which had formed into fists. She wanted to fall into a lump on the floor, but she couldn't give into it. Not until she got home.

She opened to the door to the hall and saw Accosta and Tessa.

Great. Just great.

"Katerina? Wait!"

She hurried to her apartment, locked the door, and collapsed into nothingness.

Chapter Thirty-Four

Accosta

> I will not allow deceivers to serve in my house,
> and liars will not stay in my presence.
> Psalm 101: 7

Accosta and Tessa were stopped in their tracks when they heard Katerina's voice echoing from nearby. She was arguing with another woman. They'd been on their way to the dining room when the harsh words had made them hang back, out of sight.

Suddenly a young woman burst out of the stairwell and stormed past them.

"Oh dear," Accosta whispered.

"There was nothing dear about any of that," Tessa said.

A few moments later, Katerina came out of the stairwell too. She hurried past them.

"Katerina? Wait," Tessa said.

She did not slow down and there was no way for Accosta with her walker and Tessa with her cane to catch up to her.

Evelyn came hurrying down the hall from the elevator. "Have you seen Katerina?"

"She just flew past," Tessa said.

"She was arguing with another woman," Accosta said.

Evelyn nodded. "Her daughter came to visit and overheard her mom saying she was a chef, which I guess isn't true."

"Then what is true?," Tessa asked.

"She runs a Dairy Sweet."

"There's nothing wrong with that." Accosta hated airing Katerina's dirty laundry in the hall. "I'm sure there's a good explanation."

Tessa scoffed. "I'm sure there's a good *lie*. Katerina is a wiz at embellishments."

Evelyn seemed torn. "Should we go after her? See how she is?"

"Maybe we should give her a minute to collect herself?" Accosta said.

"Give her a minute to get her stories straight is more like it," Tessa said. "Why can't she just be herself and stop with all the mumbo jumbo?"

Evelyn sighed, as if pushing the uncomfortable situation away. "Have you eaten?" she asked.

"We were on our way," Accosta said.

"Come join Wayne and me. We were sitting with Katerina when she left. We were just getting ready to order."

"I accept," Tessa said. "It will give us a chance to compare notes on the mysterious Katerina."

Accosta disagreed. "It will give us a chance to come up with a plan to get that poor woman to be herself and stop living in pretendland."

** ** **

While Evelyn, Wayne, and Tessa compared notes on Katerina and how to help her, Accosta prayed.

Although Tessa seemed to take satisfaction in Katerina's predicament, and Evelyn and Wayne seemed stunned by it, Accosta felt a huge weight of sadness. Why would someone create so many lies? Everyone knew the truth always came out. So now, with various truths being bandied about, Katerina must feel horrible. Accosta silently prayed Psalm 34: 18. *The Lord is close to the brokenhearted; he rescues those whose spirits are crushed.*

"The question is," Tessa said, spearing a piece of lettuce, "what are we going to do about her?"

"Do we have to do something?" Evelyn asked.

"Of course," Tessa said. "It's our duty to uphold truth, so others don't fall prey to such deception."

Their responses suited them perfectly: Evelyn, the non-confrontational empathizer, and Tessa, the give-me-the-facts teacher. The judge.

Wayne buttered a roll. "Be careful, ladies. There's a proverb that says, 'It is safer to meet a bear robbed of her cubs than to confront a fool caught in foolishness.'"

"She's a fool, all right," Tessa said.

"She's foolish," Evelyn said.

Tessa pointed her fork in the air. "She cannot get away with deceiving people—and herself."

"So saith, the mighty Tessa?" Wayne asked.

Tessa raised her index finger—which let everyone know she was going to quote scripture.

"'Those who sin should be reprimanded in front of the whole church; this will serve as a strong warning to others.'"

"A warning not to sin?" Wayne said. "How about, 'Do not judge others, and you will not be judged.'"

Tessa quoted back at him, "'If people are causing divisions among you, give a first and second warning. After that, have nothing more to do with them.' I know Katerina's been called on a few of her lies—and still she keeps lying."

"So you want to shun her completely?" Evelyn asked.

Tessa lifted her chin defiantly. "'If someone is caught in a sin, you who live by the Spirit should restore that person.'"

Wayne cocked his head. "In this battle of the verses, I insist you include the last word in that verse."

Tessa suddenly became absorbed in cutting her chicken. "I don't know what you're talking about."

Wayne smiled at her. "Yes, you do. Say it."

Tessa set her knife and fork down with a clatter. "Fine. The missing word is 'gently.'"

"We are to restore that person *gently*," Wayne said.

Accosta had her own verse to share. "'Do all that you can to live in peace with everyone.'"

The table went silent—which was a miracle of peace in itself.

Evelyn nodded eagerly. "I like that approach. We go talk to Katerina—"

"Kay," Tessa said.

"Kay," Evelyn said. "We talk to her gently and find out why she's lying. There has to be a good reason."

"There'd better be," Tessa said.

"Do you want to go after dinner?" Accosta asked. "We can check and see if she is okay as well."

"Agreed," Tessa said.

** ** **

The three ladies walked to Kay's apartment without Wayne. They'd all agreed it was probably best to confront her as women to woman.

But Kay didn't answer their knocks. Or the doorbell.

"She must have gone out," Accosta said.

"Or she's avoiding us," Tessa said. "I'll call her." Her phone rang and rang. Tessa hung up.

"Why didn't you leave a message?" Evelyn asked.

"I was going to say, 'we want to talk to you, pronto', but I didn't want to scare her away."

"You could've said, 'We're worried about you,'" Accosta said.

Tessa shrugged. "We can talk to her tomorrow. Her lies aren't going anywhere and neither are we."

Accosta reluctantly agreed. Besides, it would give her time to pray more—for all of them.

Chapter Thirty-Five

Kay

> What sorrow for those
> who are wise in their own eyes
> and think themselves so clever.
> Isaiah 5: 21

There was a knock at her door.
Again.
The doorbell rang.
Again.
Tessa called out, "Katerina? Kay? We need to know if you're all right."
Again.
Her phone rang.
Again.
She didn't answer.
Again.
Kay lay in bed, hugging her pillows—for the second straight day. She hadn't dressed, showered, or even gone to meals. She'd binge-watched "The British Baking Championship" and "Project Runway." She'd lived off of Cheerios, crackers, and soup.

The trouble was, she had no idea how she would ever be able to show her face again. If a few people were talking about her before, now everybody knew about her lies. Her shame.

She closed her eyes, letting the ever-supportive Tim Gunn tell the designers to 'make it work.'

Fat chance.

During the long hours alone with her thoughts, she'd come to a conclusion. She had narrowed it down to four choices. Number one, she could pack up a couple suitcases and sneak out under cover of darkness, leaving a note that said she was sorry and to send her things to…

Where? She'd used her share of the house equity to buy into Happy Trails. She had nowhere else to go. Sharon might agree to take her in for a short time, and maybe her stuff could be sent there until she got another apartment. Being homeless was not a good look.

The second choice would be to act like nothing was amiss. She could get all dolled up and stroll into an event like the Christmas party. She'd enter as the diva she'd created herself to be. But the thought of seeing people whispering behind their hands made her stomach roil.

The third alternative was to send a blanket letter to the residents of Happy Trails, saying she was sorry. She would try to explain why she'd lied to them. Yet that proved problematic because try as she might, she could not think of any good reasons. She'd started this new life with confidence but when it came to the why . . . it all seemed silly now.

The fourth choice was to stop eating and let herself fade away to nothingness. Eventually someone would notice the foul smell coming from her apartment. They'd break in and find her dead. At least she wouldn't be around to face further humiliation and pity.

The contestants on the fashion show clapped and cheered. The sound of celebration depressed her. Kay had no reason to celebrate. She shut the TV off.

The silence wrapped around her like a shroud. Her pain couldn't seep out and peace couldn't seep in.

She reached for her phone, turned on a music station, and fell back against the pillows, pulling the covers around her neck.

Barbra Streisand began singing. *Why can't you just tell me the truth? Hard to believe the things you say . . .*

Kay sucked in a breath. It was like the song was talking about her!

You change the facts to justify . . . Don't lie to me.

She threw off the covers and sat up in bed. The song was haunting, the anguished call of someone hurt by lies and deception.

But my lies haven't hurt anyone.

The image of her daughter came to mind. They hadn't hurt anyone except Tiffany. And maybe Sharon. If not exactly hurtful, making her best friend pretend to be the hired help was demeaning.

Which was hurtful.

Suddenly there was a strong knock on the door. And a voice that wasn't Tessa.

"Katerina? It's Mrs. Halvorson. Please answer the door, or I'm going to use my key to come in. We need to make sure you're okay."

A wave of panic sped through her. Come in? She was in her pajamas, the kitchen was a mess, she was without makeup.

And no wig!

She scrambled out of bed, trying to find a robe, but as soon as she put her arms in the sleeves, the door opened.

Mrs. Halvorson walked in. As did Tessa, Evelyn, and Accosta.

Kay ran her fingers through her super short hair that most likely resembled a child's hair after a night's sleep.

"Katerina?" Tessa called out from the entry.

She had no choice. She stepped out of the bedroom. "I'm here. I'm fine."

Kay saw their eyes move from her face to her hair. And her red and green flannel nightshirt and furry pink robe. Weeks of hard work looking smart and pulled together flew out the window.

"I'm glad you're all right," Mrs. Halvorson said. "You haven't been at meals. Your friends were worried."

Friends? I have friends?

"You could've at least taken my calls," Tessa said.

"I . . . I was under the weather. But you see I'm okay. Thanks for your concern, but—"

Tessa turned to Mrs. Halvorson. "If you don't mind, we'd like to have a little chat with our friend."

Mrs. Halvorsen nodded and turned to leave. "Let me know if we can do anything to help." She closed the door behind her.

The other ladies moved to the living room. Katerina hurried to intercept them. "I'm perfectly fine," she said, stepping between Tessa and the couch. "There's no need to stay. Really."

Tessa nudged her aside with her cane. "We'll be the judge of that." She sat. As did the other two.

Kay had never felt so exposed. She tied the belt of her robe tighter. "If you'll give me a moment to get decent . . ."

"No need," Tessa said.

"I like your short hair," Accosta said. "It's sassy."

Kay knew she was lying, but appreciated her words just the same. Accosta was always so kind.

Evelyn looked around. "I like what you've done in your apartment."

"Thank you."

Tessa pointed her cane at a chair. "You might as well sit, this is going to take a while."

"What are you talking about?"

Tessa glanced at the other two, and they nodded in unison. "We're here for an intervention."

That was ridiculous. "I assure you I am not on drugs, nor do I drink too much."

"Never said you did," Tessa said.

"No, not at all," Accosta added.

Tessa pointed at the chair again. It was amazing how this tiny, elderly woman had such power over her, but Kay sat. "I'm sitting. Now what?"

"Now you come clean. Now you tell us the truth about who you are, because we know you aren't who you pretend to be."

Accosta gave her a reassuring smile. "Just tell us about *you*. The real you. The one we see glimpses of beyond the wig and fancy clothes."

Kay glanced longingly at the bedroom. If only she could slip back to bed.

Tessa shook her head, getting impatient. "If we have to go through the lies one by one, we will."

That might be simpler because Kay had lost track.

"Okay then," Tessa said. "Is your name Katerina Volkov?"

That was an easy one. "My name is Kay. Plain old Kay Volkov."

"Nice to meet you Kay. And you're far from plain," Evelyn said. "You have excellent taste."

"And wigs. I'm assuming your hair now isn't fake." Tessa shook her head as if wigs disgusted her.

Kay could not let that comment go. "They are as real as I want them to be. You and Accosta wear lots of hats. No one faults you for that. No one should fault me for my wigs." She ran both hands through her hair. "My real hair has thinned so much it doesn't hold a curl or even a perm. So when I moved here I decided to wear wigs."

"There's nothing wrong with that," Evelyn said.

"They *are* very smart looking," Accosta said.

"Moving on." Tessa sat up straighter. "Is your husband's name Nicolae?"

This one was embarrassing. "Wallace. Wally to be exact."

"Those two names conjure up completely different images," Evelyn said.

"That was the point. I wanted to imagine anyone but Wally as my ex-husband."

"You always mentioned your late husband. Is Wally living or dead?" Tessa asked.

And here we go . . . "The only thing late about Wally are his alimony checks. I've been divorced for a year. He married a much-younger woman and is annoyingly happy."

"I'm so sorry," Accosta said. "That's extremely hurtful."

"It's devastating. After we celebrated our forty-sixth anniversary, I kind of expected us to be married for life."

"Wow," Evelyn said. "Throwing away nearly five decades is pretty dramatic."

"My biggest regret is being blind to what he was doing, the affair he was having. Make that plural. Affairs. Surely you ladies have regrets about your marriages."

Evelyn raised her hand. "My first marriage wasn't happy. Aaron was very controlling."

"Did you divorce?"

She shook her head. "He died in a car accident."

"I'm sorry," Kay said.

Evelyn shook her head and shrugged. "After the initial shock and mourning I was rather relieved he was gone. To this day I regret feeling like that."

"I'd like to feel that way. I thought our marriage was good, but obviously, Wally didn't agree with me. I regret being so blind."

"I'm so sorry," Accosta said. "Being surprised probably makes the divorce extra hard."

Evelyn pulled a throw pillow into her lap. "Maybe good will come from your divorce?"

Kay spread her hands. "Yeah. This is real good."

"It can happen," Evelyn said. "It did for me When Aaron died I had to earn money, so I opened my home to boarders. That's how I met these lovely ladies."

"And many others," Tessa said.

"And many others. And I met Wayne. He's the best husband a woman could have."

"You got a good one, that's for sure," Accosta said.

"Do you have a marriage regret, Accosta?" Tessa asked.

She sat quietly for a moment, fingering a button on her blouse. "Not a marriage regret, but I do regret not keeping in touch with my son and his family as much as I should."

"That's not all your fault," Evelyn said. "The phone lines go both ways."

"I know. But still . . ."

Kay appreciated their openness. "How about you, Tessa? What are your marriage regrets?"

She leaned both hands on her cane and peered at the ceiling. "Hmm. I can't think of anything right off."

They all chuckled.

"Well, I can't. When I think of something I'll let you all know."

Accosta turned her attention back to Kay. "Can you tell us more about who you really are, Kay? We really want to know."

Kay wasn't sure about this. Once the truth was out, there was no turning back.

She noticed a picture of the Eiffel tower. "All the bragging I've done about travel? I've never been to a foreign country."

"At all?" Tessa said.

"At all."

"Where did you live before moving to Happy Trails?" Accosta asked.

"An hour east. In Missouri. Wally and his new wife wanted to stay in the house—*our* house. I didn't want to live anywhere nearby, where I might run into them. So I moved out on my own for the first time ever. I lived in an apartment for a year, but that wasn't as satisfying as I'd hoped it would be." They stared at her blankly. "Everyone was young, always partying with their loud music. It wasn't a place for me to make friends."

Accosta nodded. "My old house was in a neighborhood where most of the houses were being divided into apartments, and yes, there was a lot of noise. And a lot of young people. I didn't fit in anymore. Evelyn and Wayne saved me from all that."

It was nice she understood. "For the last few months in the apartment I started to think about moving. And then I got a brochure in the mail about Happy Trails and . . ." It would sound dumb. "I liked the name Happy Trails because I was searching for happiness. It almost seemed like . . . like . . ."

"A nudge from God?" Tessa asked.

"I don't know about that."

"You not knowing about that doesn't erase the fact it's probably true."

I don't know about that and I don't know about Him either.

Accosta grabbed her hand. "We're glad you're here."

Were they? But Kay said, "Thank you."

The silence seemed to simmer. Maybe the confession time was over.

But it wasn't.

"What about your children?" Tessa asked. "Since your daughter isn't a chef, I'm assuming your son isn't a pharmacist?"

Connery's situation was a sore spot in her heart. She stood and took a step away from her judge and jury. "The truth is, Connery is a con and Tif went to school to be a chef, but dropped out to get married and run an ice cream stand four states away."

"I like ice cream," Accosta said.

Which is neither here nor there. "I had big plans for them and they . . . they . . ."

"Let you down?" Evelyn asked.

"Yes. Yes, they did. Connery was the sweetest boy. We used to play Monopoly for hours, and laugh and laugh. And Tiffany was so smart. She flew through school with all As." Her heart was heavy for what could have been. "Somehow I failed them."

"You did *not* fail them," Tessa said. "Young adults make their own choices."

Kay wasn't willing to let her guilt go. "I failed as a parent and I failed as a wife. *I'm* a failure."

Tessa patted the cushion beside her. "Come over here right this minute."

Kay shook her head. "I'm okay here."

Tessa slapped the cushion. "Come over here now, I say."

Reluctantly, Kay took the seat beside Tessa. She braced herself for either a scolding or a rap on her knuckles.

She did not expect Tessa to set her cane aside and hold out her arms, drawing Kay into a hug. Tessa felt so frail. There wasn't an ounce of fat on her. Yet her hug was strong. It felt good.

"You are *not* a failure," Tessa said, patting Kay's back. "I understand why you stepped away from that pain."

You do? Kay lingered in Tessa's arms. When was the last time she'd been hugged? Too soon, Tessa let go.

"I'm so glad you understand. I needed to start fresh. Recreate myself. Be special for once in my life."

Evelyn chuckled. "By giving yourself a glamorous husband and over-achieving children?"

It seemed a bit silly now, and yet . . . "Yes."

They shared a silent moment, then all laughed. "Go big or go home, eh, Kay?" Tessa said.

She smiled a wistful smile. "I thought if I played the part hard enough, and well enough it would make me feel good about myself, about my messed up life."

Tessa scoffed. "Perhaps you overplayed it?"

"Maybe," Kay shrugged. "I wasn't blind. I saw how people reacted when I bragged but I couldn't stop myself."

Tessa put a hand on her knee. "Most people are smarter than you think. Savvy people sensed there was something off about your stories."

"Did you feel good about your Katerina life?" Accosta asked. "Special?"

"Not really. It was exhausting." Kay felt that exhaustion now. Her shoulders slumped.

Tess put an arm around her. "It was exhausting because you weren't being yourself. Now listen here, Kay, Accosta and I have a couple decades on you—and you too, Evelyn. One thing we've learned is that there's a lot of peace and joy in just being yourself. Life's too short to put on airs."

Accosta nodded. "'To thine own self be true.'"

"Which Bible verse is that?" Evelyn asked.

"It's Shakespeare. 'Hamlet' I believe," Tessa said.

"Ooh, ooh," Accosta said, leaning forward. "I have another one: 'All the world's a stage, and all the men and women merely players.'"

Tessa nodded approvingly. "Very good, dear. It suits the moment well." She looked at Kay. "Don't you think it's time to play the part of a genuine woman, a part that reveals the real Kay Volkov? I have a feeling that woman is special in her own unique way."

The idea of ridding herself of all the artifice was suddenly overwhelming. Kay began to cry.

Three sets of arms held her as she let Katerina die and brought Kay back to life.

Chapter Thirty-Six

Rosalie

> Two people are better off than one,
> for they can help each other succeed.
> Ecclesiastes 4: 9

Rosalie answered her door. A young man was there with a luggage cart full of boxes marked *Christmas*.

"Bring 'em in, Jason."

He rolled the cart inside. "Where would you like me to stack them?"

Rosalie felt a sudden surge of panic. Was she really going to decorate for Christmas? Alone? "Is it possible to just leave them on the cart? I'm not sure how much I'm going to use."

"Sure thing, Mrs. Clemmons. Let me know when you're done and I'll come get the cart — and whatever else you want put back in your storage space."

After he left, Rosalie took note of the seven boxes and the tabletop tree covered with a trash bag. When she and Lonnie lived in a house there'd been twice as many boxes. Since moving to Happy Trails they'd always emptied these seven, but this year . . .

When she removed the tree bag, a few ornaments fell onto the carpet. One was in the shape of a seashell — a souvenir from Hawaii. Another was delicate and much older. It was a glass Christmas star they'd bought when they'd honeymooned in the Ozarks. So many ornaments, representing so many memories.

On the buffet, she moved a vase aside and set the tree in its place. She began to fluff out the branches — which had always been Lonnie's job. But then she stopped mid-fluff as a full-blown revelation popped into her mind. "I don't want to do this without him."

She stared at the boxes on the cart. The thought of unpacking them, setting the pretties out, finding space for the pretties whose place was being usurped by Christmas . . .

"I can't do it."

Rosalie waited for someone to argue with her, to spur her on. If Lonnie were alive, that's what he'd do. *You can do it, Rosie. You want the place pretty for Christmas, don't you?*

Did she? Since moving into Happy Trails their family didn't spend Christmases in their apartment. They all spent the holiday at Cheri and Jay's house, with Evan. They were due back from their Far East trip soon — Rosalie couldn't remember what day they'd said. She wasn't even sure what day it was most of the time. The point was, without Lonnie to enjoy the decorations there seemed little reason to mess with them.

No reason at all.

She put the tree back in its trash bag and pulled the drawstring tight. She put it back on the luggage cart and called Jason to come get it.

A few minutes later he was at the door. "That was fast."

"Yes, it was. I think it's best to forego decorating this year."

She watched his face change from confusion to understanding. "I get it, Mrs. Clemmons. I miss him too."

"Thank you Jason. Sorry to make you go through so much work."

"It's no trouble at all," he said.

She held the door open so he could wheel the cart into the hall. "If there's anything you need — anything at all, you call me."

People were so kind. "Thank you. But I'll be all right." *Eventually.*

Rosalie leaned against the door and took a good look at their — her — apartment. Lonnie's keys were still in the bowl by the door, and his jacket still hung on the hall tree. His favorite peppermints were in a bowl by his recliner, and his coffee mug that was emblazoned with an L hung from the mug rack. If anything, she should spend her time going through the apartment to get rid of his things.

Her chest tightened and she shook her head against the thought. There was time enough for that. A lifetime for that. Right now she needed things to stay the same, sans Christmas, sans a purging. She needed to stay frozen in time, with Lonnie.

She noticed the vase was not where it belonged on the buffet. She moved it back into its place.

There. That was better.

If not better, it was—she was—where she needed to be at the moment.

** ** **

After getting her mail, Rosalie stopped by the Christmas tree that stood in the foyer of Happy Trails. Scattered among the ornaments and lights were little angel cutouts with names on them. It was late in the season and there weren't many left. She took one off the tree. A boy named Ramone, age six, wanted "anything dinosaur." She smiled at his request.

"What's got you smiling?" Scranton asked as he walked by.

She held out the tag. "I haven't done this for years, but this little boy's Christmas wish is calling to me."

He read the tag. "Your calling is dinosaurs?"

"It is, because it makes me remember my grandson, who used to be a dino-holic when he was little. So I'm choosing this one."

Scranton nodded and handed it back to her. Although they'd shared a few meals, he'd been standoffish the past few days.

"Maybe you should pick one too," she said.

"I don't think so. I'm not feeling very Christmasy this year."

"I understand completely. I started decorating my apartment but sent it all back to storage. I decided not to put up a single thing. Is that wrong?"

"Of course not. I'm not decorating either," he said. "And don't let other people tell you how to grieve. If you tell them anything, tell them to mind their own business."

He'd been testy for a few days. She'd asked what was wrong, but hadn't received an answer. Yet it was clear something had happened. "Maybe we should both take an angel," she said. "Maybe buying something for a child will spark that Christmas spirit in us."

He just stood there, staring at the tree.

She touched his arm. "Listen, Scranton, I'm finding it hard to be joyful too. Without Lonnie . . ."

HIs eyes softened and he did a swift shake of his head. "I'm sorry. You have far more reason to be struggling than I do."

Perhaps. "But you *are* struggling just the same. My new grief doesn't make your old grief any less valid. Are you ready to tell me what's going on?"

He looked at the tree, then her, then the tree again. Then he plucked off an angel. "Let's do this."

** ** **

Rosalie and Scranton sat on a bench in the mall, shopping bags at their feet. They ate ice cream cones.

"I haven't had a cone in ages," she said as she enjoyed the cherry chip.

"Me either." He pointed at her cone, and she caught a drip before it dropped. "Do you have wrapping paper at home?" he asked.

"I do. We can wrap up the toys when we get back." She thought about their toy store experience. "I couldn't believe the number of dinosaur toys there were. There sure are a lot more choices than when we were kids."

"And so much of it is electronic," he said. "What was your favorite toy growing up?"

She didn't have to think long. "My baby doll. Joanie. My mom made her clothes and hats and even a bridal gown."

"For a baby doll?"

Rosalie shrugged. "All my dolls had bridal gowns. What was your favorite toy?"

"Hands down, my Erector Set."

"My brother had one of those. It came with a motor?"

"It did. I'd drive my mom crazy building cranes that could lift up forks and spoons and saltshakers and . . . I don't know why I was intent on messing with kitchen stuff, but I was."

Rosalie thought of childhood Christmases. "We only got one toy. Nowadays kids get too many."

"Everybody gets too many presents." Scranton bit into his cone. "I worry that the toys now don't encourage kids to use their imaginations. Kids expect everything to be on a screen, already created. With lots of noises and sound."

Rosalie agreed—to a point. "Evan liked—still likes—video games, but he also used to draw up these complicated worlds with monsters and teleporting machines and . . ." She sighed. "What can we do? The world is constantly changing. I sometimes think we're being left behind."

"Hmph." He squirmed in his seat.

"Did I hit a nerve?"

He ate the last bite of the cone and brushed off his hands. He angled toward her. "My law firm is buying me out."

"That's wonderful. Congrat—"

He shook his head adamantly. "Nothing wonderful about it. They're forcing me out."

"Oh." This would certainly explain his bad mood. "When did you find out?"

"A few days ago. I went into work and they'd gotten rid of all of my stuff. Someone new took over my office."

"That's a low blow."

"More like a knockout punch. I talked to one of my partners—*my* partners—and he finished me off. He told me I was out."

"He said it like that?"

Scranton shuffled his shoulders. "The result is the same. They don't need me anymore."

And there it was. The bottom line. "They said that?"

He tossed his napkin in the trash and sat down again. "They were nice about it—after all, we're lawyers. We know how to spin a sentence."

"But isn't it rather drastic? Why don't they just cut your hours?"

"I already did that. There was nothing left for them to cut when I only worked one day a week. When Olivia was really sick, I'd cut back my hours to care for her, and when she died, I was a . . ." He obviously didn't want to admit that he'd fallen apart.

"A mess?"

"Completely. You are doing so much better with your loss than I ever did."

She looked at her lap. "Outwardly maybe, but inside . . ."

"You'd like to scream?"

"Loud and long."

Scranton watched the people walking by. "I suppose we could do it, right here, right now."

Rosalie was appalled at the idea. "I never . . . I couldn't do that."

"Me neither. But I like the thought of it." He sighed. "Afterward she was gone I kept my hours cut back. When I couldn't stand being alone in the house anymore and moved to Happy Trails, I cut my hours to just a couple days a week, then just one." He hesitated. "If I'm honest with myself I knew this was coming. I'd checked out ages ago." He brushed a cone-crumb from his knee. "What did you do in your before-years?"

She was surprised by the question. "Before I got old?"

He chuckled. "Exactly."

Rosalie saw a mother pushing a baby in a stroller. "I was the quintessential housewife and mother. I brought up our daughter, Cheri, and volunteered for everything from Girl Scouts to the May Day party." She hurriedly added, "I know that doesn't sound like much but—"

"Don't say that. I hate how the world disparages women who stay at home."

She appreciated his opinion. "Actually, from talking to Cheri—who is an OB nurse—a lot of women would love to go traditional but they can't because of finances. It's an expensive world out there."

"That, it is."

Rosalie thought of something else. "I did bring in a little money making cakes for people."

"That, I believe. The one you made me was amazing. You had a business?"

"Not officially. Just a side hustle. But I loved it."

"You should do it again. I'd pay good money for that cake. The people at Happy Trails could keep you busy."

Maybe too busy? "I'll think about it." She changed the subject. "Did Olivia have a job?"

"She was a fifth-grade teacher. You should've seen the church at her funeral. It was filled to the brim with old students."

"What a wonderful testament to her life."

"It was." He sat with his memories for a moment. "The only good thing about being bought out is the money. They're paying me well."

"That's a good thing."

He gave a reluctant nod. "When I let myself be logical, I get it. It makes sense and is wise and good for the firm. But when I allow myself to *feel* it . . . being a lawyer was my identity. To not be a lawyer on top of not being a husband anymore . . . Who am I?"

All the usual placating answers filed through Rosalie's brain, yet stayed there unspoken. Scranton didn't need platitudes right now. What *did* he need? *Help me here, Lord.*

"Sorry," he said. "I sound weak and needy."

"You sound human."

"So? Who am I now?"

Rosalie stood to toss the last part of her cone away—mostly to buy herself some time. She sat back down and took his hand. "First off, you're my dear friend."

He squeezed her hand. "I appreciate that more than you know. But what else am I?"

"You're an adventurer."

"What?"

"You've embarked on an unknown journey, exploring new territory."

He chuckled. "You, my dear lady, are an optimist of the highest degree."

She laughed with him—but for a different reason. "Lonnie was the optimist in our family. I was the pessimist. Talk about weak and needy..."

Scranton studied her face for a minute. "You've never seemed weak to me."

She scoffed. "I was so clueless about the logistics of life and money. I could never have waded through the estate stuff if you hadn't helped me."

"You learned quickly."

"I'm learning to do all sorts of daily life-things that I didn't have to do with Lonnie around. I even made coffee." She took in the bustling mall where shoppers rushed here and there in their quest for the perfect Christmas present. "I won't say I was a cat in a corner, and in truth I wasn't completely helpless, but over the years I stepped aside and let Lonnie run our lives."

"I didn't know him that well, but he never seemed like a take-charge kind of person."

That definition was *not* Lonnie. "He wasn't like that, never pushy or demanding. He was just . . . capable. He had things handled — for both of us."

"The two of you made it work."

She expelled a breath. "We did. Good or bad, we did. Just like you and I are doing now."

"I never imagined myself living in a retirement home."

"A retirement *community*."

"Yes. That. And now that I'm there . . . I'm not sure I belong. Most people seem so at ease. They're excited about the activities." He shook his head. "I don't *do* activities."

She didn't like his attitude, but wasn't going to call him on it. And yet.... "Why don't you get involved? Do you — this may sound harsh — but do you think you're too good for the activities?"

His left eyebrow rose. "Not too good, I just have no desire to... He shifted his eyes while he thought of the right word. "Be a joiner."

"Were you going to say 'waste my time?'"

He raised his hands in surrender. "You got me."

Rosalie saw a gaggle of preteen girls hurry past, giggling all the way. "Do you know how to have fun, Scranton?"

"Of course."

"By doing what?"

His forehead furrowed. He was actually trying to think of a good answer to her question. He finally said, "I have fun, but I'm not a fun guy."

Rosalie chuckled "You could be. What did you used to do for fun?"

"Win cases."

"Beyond work. What did you and Olivia do for fun?"

He stared at a huge mobile hanging from the mall's ceiling as if the right answer was floating there.

Finally, he said, "We traveled."

"Good one. Traveling *can* be fun. You can still do that."

"I certainly have the money for it now."

Rosalie guessed that Scranton had never worried about money. "Maybe the reason God moved you into Happy Trails is so you could relax that stodgy demeanor of yours and—"

"I am not stodgy."

"Serious, then."

He seemed to accept that, but added, "And who says God moved me into Happy Trails? *I* signed the contract. *I* paid the money."

Gracious, the man was all facts and figures. "However you ended up at Happy Trails, it's your home now. Find your fun. There are lots of activities—"

"I have no desire to sing in the chorus, or play cards or bingo or—"

"Do puzzles."

"I actually don't mind puzzles. But Bingo? That's a game I cannot stand. You will never catch me playing Bingo."

"Why not?"

"It's the lost cause of recreation, playing a game that requires no skill whatsoever."

"But it's fun. I won $23.50 last month."

He made a face. "No thanks." He stood. "Shall we head back?"

They gathered up their purchases and walked to the car. On the way, Rosalie silently made a vow that one day she'd get Scranton to play Bingo—for his own good.

Chapter Thirty-Seven

Evelyn

> Those who use the things of the world
> should not become attached to them.
> For this world as we know it will soon pass away.
> 1 Corinthians 7: 31

"Evelyn, what are you doing?"

Wayne's question pulled her out of her thoughts. "I don't understand the question. I'm just sitting here."

"Exactly." He stood in front of where she was sitting. "You've been sitting in the living room for a half hour, staring into space. What's wrong?"

She blinked at him a few times, trying to gather her scattered thoughts. "I'm not sure."

He sat beside her on the couch. "Are you feeling okay?"

"Yes. I mean, no. But yes." She hated sounding so flakey.

"You'll have to give me more than that."

She forced herself to sit up straighter, hoping the movement would spark a clear thought.

And then it came to her.

"I miss Peerbaugh Place."

He patted her knee. "Me too."

She was shocked. "You do?"

"Well, yeah. A little. It was so comfortable and homey. And I had my shop in the garage and—"

"They have a woodshop here. In the lower level somewhere."

"I know they do and I need to check it out." He angled his head to look at her. "So what do you miss? Surely not the leaky windows or the worn carpet."

Evelyn shook her head. "I miss the purpose of it. The helping people part. Serving people."

Wayne nodded his head knowingly. "You have a servant's heart. It stands to reason you need people to serve."

Her mood seemed clearer now. "Gracious, I don't even have to cook anymore. We're eating breakfast and dinner in the dining room."

"I thought that would be a relief."

"It is. Yet . . . when am I going to make my famous pot roast or lasagna?"

He rubbed his stomach. "You can make either of those any time. I'm game."

"I appreciate that. But it's more than cooking. When I had a house full of tenants and guests there was always something to do to help somebody with something. Here . . . everyone is taken care of." She got to the bottom line of it: "I feel useless."

"Give it time," he said. "Once you get to know people you'll find ways to help. You won't be able to stop yourself."

He was right. He was always right.

Wayne's eyes lit up. "Wait here a second." He went to the desk and brought back a three-ring binder with a rainbow of sticky-notes on the pages. "Here. Do this. Work on your book."

Evelyn flipped through a few pages of her Peerbaugh Place notebook. She hadn't written in it since the day Ringo and Soon-ja were over, talking about all the changes they wanted to make; since the day she and Wayne bought new furniture for the first time ever. It would be good to get back to it.

"I do have time now . . ."

"Yes, you do. The best way to keep the memories of Peerbaugh Place alive is to write them down." He touched the notebook. "Do it."

She nodded — to him and to herself. Then she picked up where she'd left off.

** ** **

Evelyn carefully unwrapped each piece of the nativity scene and arranged them on the coffee table. She paused as she unwrapped the baby Jesus. "I hope you like your new home." She placed Him in the manger, then set the empty box aside.

Wayne was hanging ornaments from a new skinny tree they'd bought last weekend. After he hung the last ornament, he stepped back. "There. How's it look?"

The blinking colored lights and shiny ornaments helped Evelyn feel more Christmasy. "Very pretty. Very different."

"I'll say. There's more, but I'm not sure they'd fit. I didn't use half the ornaments." Wayne put the lid on the still-full ornament box. "I will say I do like the ease of this one over our nine-footer having to be hauled up from the basement and put together. And *it* wasn't pre-lit."

If she was honest, Evelyn was also glad about the smaller tree. She'd liked having the big tree decorat*ed*, but didn't necessarily enjoy decorat*ing*. And there were multiple Christmas trees around Happy Trails. They did a bang-up job with the decorations.

Wayne opened a box of porcelain elves. "Where shall I put these?"

"I have no idea. I used to have a particular place for everything, but now I'm starting from scratch. Just put them wherever you want and I'll rearrange when you're done."

"You got it."

Evelyn focused on her collection of sleighs. One of the runners had broken off, so she glued it on, holding it until it seemed strong. Then she arranged the sleighs on the corner of the kitchen counter. When she was done she turned around and saw Wayne putting one last angel in the center of the dining table.

"There!" he said. "All finished. That wasn't so hard."

She couldn't be mad at him—he'd done exactly what she'd asked. But...

"Don't you like what I've done?" he asked.

She sighed. "It looks like Christmas threw up in here."

"Hey!"

"Sorry, but . . ." She walked through the dining and living spaces and stepped into the bedroom. "Clearly we have too many decorations."

"Maybe. Unless you want to live in a Christmas store." He swept an arm toward the dozens of decorations he'd placed in the living and dining areas. "Now you can see everything and choose what you want. I'll pack up what you don't use and we can give them away."

More giveaways.

Wayne left to get the mail. As she went through the angels, candles, Santas, Wise Men, and snowmen Evelyn was reminded of the difficult time she'd had going through decades of possessions before the move. Here she was again. Yet now it was less stressful. She felt broken in, and more ready to choose her favorites.

Soon the dining table was littered with the leftovers, and the chosen items were neatly displayed around the apartment. She put her hands on her hips and took one last look. "That should do it."

When Wayne returned with the mail his eyes swept over the giveaway pile. "You're giving away more than you're keeping. I'm impressed."

She was rather impressed herself.

While it didn't take long to pack up the extras and do a little tweak here and there, it was exhausting.

Wayne and Evelyn fell onto the couch with expulsions of air and moans.

"We did it," she said.

"That, we did." Wayne took in all the decorations. "It looks nice too. Not cluttered. Just right."

She agreed. "Next year will be easier. I'm going to take pictures of where I put things so I don't have to reinvent the wheel."

Their doorbell rang. They looked at each other, but Evelyn got up to answer it.

It was Tessa and Accosta. Their faces were serious.

"Hi . . ." Evelyn said tentatively. "Is something wrong?"

"We don't know for sure," Accosta said.

Tessa waved her hand. "*I* know because I talked to her. Kay called and wants us to come over right away."

"Okay . . ."

"*Us* includes you, Evelyn."

Evelyn glanced back at Wayne. "Did you hear?"

"I did. Go on. Let me know if I can help."

And they were off.

Chapter Thirty-Eight

Kay

> Fix your thoughts on what is true,
> and honorable, and right, and pure,
> and lovely, and admirable.
> Think about things that are excellent and worthy of praise.
> Philippians 4: 8

Kay paced in front of the door wearing a navy suit with a patterned blouse. She'd carefully chosen a chunky silver necklace, bracelet, and earrings. They had to like her new look. Had to.

"Sit down," Sharon said. "You look beautiful."

Kay paused in front of a wall mirror. She touched her hair — *her* hair, not a wig. She saw *her* eyelashes, not fake ones. "I feel absolutely naked."

Sharon finished packing up the makeup case she'd brought over. "I think the better word is *genuine*." She secured the clasp. "You wanted a new you, you got her." She gave Kay a sideward glance. "Actually, I gave you back the old you. The Kay *I* know."

"I hope I look better than her."

Sharon put hairspray, gel, and other supplies in a tote bag that said: *All I need is coffee and mascara*. "Don't put yourself down. I love the old you and frankly can't relate to the Katerina persona you layered on — and I do mean *layered*." She waved her hand toward Kay's outfit. "This is much more 'you'. Though I still think the jewelry is a bit much."

Kay gazed down at her clothes. "I look classic. Put together. The clerk at the store said so."

"I'm not saying you don't, it's just a little much for a day look."

The doorbell rang and Kay's stomach flipped. "They're here," she whispered.

"Then open the door," Sharon whispered back.

There was no more time to second guess any part of her look. Kay took a deep breath and opened it. "Hi," she said.

Tessa, Accosta, and Evelyn just stood there, staring at her.

"Wow," Evelyn said.

"I second that wow," Tessa said.

Accosta nodded.

"Are you going to let us in?" Tessa asked.

"Of course."

The ladies took seats in the living room and were introduced to Sharon.

Tessa gave Sharon a once over. "I recognize you from somewhere."

Sharon shared a look with Kay. "I was the waitress at Kay's party."

It sounded as bad as it was, but Kay was quick to explain. "She helped me out. She's been my best friend for years."

Tessa made a circular motion near Kay's head. "So all this is your doing, Sharon?"

"It is. I'm a beautician."

Tessa nodded. "A good one."

"I agree," Accosta said.

"I think you look beautiful," Evelyn said.

Out of nowhere, Kay felt hot tears start to fall. It was embarrassing. "I...I'm sorry."

"Oh, honey. You don't need to cry," Evelyn said.

She felt like a fool. "They're happy tears," she said. "Relieved tears. I didn't know what you'd think, especially after knowing . . . her."

"Katerina?" Accosta asked.

Kay nodded.

The three ladies exchanged a look, but Tessa spoke. "We think you look lovely. Very real."

"We can see *you*," Accosta added.

Sharon nodded. "There's a quote from Coco Chanel that says 'Beauty begins the moment you decide to be yourself.'"

Tessa cocked her head. "Chanel, as in the designer?"

Sharon nodded. "The inventor of the 'little black dress.'"

"I've had a few of those," Tessa said.

"Me too," Accosta said.

"Me too," Evelyn said.

Kay was fascinated by their agreement. "To think that a simple idea like that would catch on to a myriad of women—"

"Over a myriad of years," Sharon said.

"A simple idea," Tessa repeated. "Good style is simple." She gave Kay a slow look. "Since you're in makeover mode, may I make a suggestion?"

Not really. But Kay said, "Sure. Fire away." *If you must.*

Accosta put her hand on Tessa's arm. "Be nice."

Tessa's eyes grew large. "Gracious, ladies. Give me a little credit. I *can* be kind."

Kay held back a chuckle. Tessa's version of "kind" was just as unique as the rest of her. "Go ahead," Kay said. "I can take it."

Tessa leaned forward on her cane. "Well then. I know you have all sorts of lovely outfits. But you're sometimes overdressed, which makes the rest of us feel underdressed and uncomfortable. It makes it seem as though you think you are better than the rest of us. There. I said it." She looked around the room. "I'm not wrong. You know I'm not."

"You're not wrong," Accosta said, softly.

Kay fingered her necklace. "What's wrong with what I'm wearing now?"

"Not a thing," Evelyn said. "If you're going to church or an important meeting. But around here..."

If they were comparing Kay to themselves, it was not a contest as to who was dressed the best. Tessa had a penchant for grandma cardigans and Accosta liked sweatshirts that had embroidered birds and flowers. Evelyn was wearing black pants, comfy slip-on shoes, and a knit tunic—not far from what Kay used to wear in her pre-Happy Trails life.

Sharon stood. "I think I know what you mean. Kay, stand up."

Kay stood.

"Take off your blazer."

She did.

"Untuck your blouse."

"I haven't worn tops untucked in quite a while."

"Do it," Sharon said.

Kay did as she was told.

"Now give me the jewelry."

Kay put a protective hand on her necklace. "What's wrong with my jewelry?"

"Not a thing—in itself. But combined? Indulge me."

Kay took off the necklace and bracelet. "Can I wear earrings?"

"Earrings yes, those earrings, no. Just a minute." Sharon went in the bedroom and came back with a pair of narrow hoops, and navy loafers. "Put these on."

Kay got the hoops in, shucked off her heels, and put on the flats. She looked down at her outfit. "It's too simple."

All four women were shaking their heads. "Not a bit," Evelyn said. "Remember, good style is simple. You look just right."

"Very nice," Tessa declared with a nod.

"Very pretty," Accosta said. "Very approachable."

Sharon pointed toward the bedroom. "Take a look for yourself."

Kay stood before the full-length mirror and the other ladies joined her in the bedroom. "I'm certainly not Katerina now. This looks like the old Kay."

"But a better Kay," Sharon said. "You're authentic. That's the perfect way to start fresh."

"Is it a fresh start if I already messed up the first fresh start? Or was it my second fresh start? I've lost track."

Accosta smiled at her. "You can start over as many times as you want. God doesn't keep count."

"He doesn't?"

"He most certainly does not. He wants you to be the best you can be."

"Agreed." Tessa glanced at her watch. "Let's try out your new look in the dining room," she said. "And then at the Friday Fling."

Accosta clapped. "Oooh. An unveiling."

"This I gotta see," Sharon said.

Kay felt her wrist where a bracelet should be. "I don't know about this. I feel so vulnerable."

Evelyn slid her hand around Kay's arm. "That's understandable."

Sharon agreed. "It is, because you're not hiding behind fake hair, too much makeup, and a costume of what you think a well-off

224

widow should look like." She shared Kay's reflection, smiling at her. "Just be Kay Volkov, my best friend. Okay?"

It would be hard to let go of this Katerina persona, but returning to being Sharon's best friend was a relief, like falling into strong, welcoming arms.

** ** **

The dining room hostess did a double-take at Kay. "Mrs. Volkov?"

Kay pretended nothing was different. "We need a table for five, Frani. If you please?"

"Will Mr. Wellington be joining you?" she asked Evelyn.

Evelyn had called Wayne, and he'd graciously bowed out. "Not tonight. It's just a girls' table tonight."

Frani smiled. "Right this way, ladies."

On the way to a table in the middle of the dining room, Kay felt like she was walking through a gauntlet.

As soon as they were seated, Tessa leaned close. "Now there's the way to enter a room."

Kay chuckled softly, but wasn't sure things were going as well as Tessa suggested. There was still a lot of talking behind hands and shifting eyes.

"Everybody's staring," she whispered.

"Let them stare," Sharon said. "You look great." She opened the menu. "What's good here?"

Their waitress was Summer. "Wow, Mrs. Volkov. You look really pretty tonight." She caught herself. "Not that the rest of you don't—"

"It's alright, sweetie," Evelyn said. "Kay does look particularly pretty. And this is Kay's friend, Sharon."

Summer's blush began to fade. "Nice to meet you. What can I get you to drink?"

Kay tried to act nonchalant as they ate their dinner, she tried not to look at the other diners. Turns out she didn't need to because one by one, they came to *her*.

Wrinkles stopped by during dessert, grinning ear to ear. "Well, look at you, Katerina. You shine as pretty as the star on a Christmas tree."

She felt herself blush. "Thank you, Joe. But the name's not Katerina." She held out her hand for him to shake. "It's just Kay."

Joe cocked his head, but then took her hand and drew it to her lips. "Nice to meet you. Kay." He gave her a wink and left.

"Well, well, well," Evelyn said. "That was an especially nice exchange."

Tessa watched him go. "Joe is a good man. He was a professor of economics at the university."

Although Kay came to Happy Trails with the intent of being the center of attention, now that she'd earned it for the right reasons she felt embarrassed. "I'm so sorry for the interruptions," she told the ladies.

Tessa flipped her concern away. "Soak in the compliments, my dear. This is your moment."

"Eat it up," Sharon said.

"It's your time to shine," Evelyn said.

Accosta touched her hand. "'Pride leads to disgrace, but with humility comes wisdom.'" She nodded once as if reinforcing the words.

The words swam through Kay's mind: pride, disgrace, humility, wisdom. She'd gone down a road of disaster. Could she really come out of it whole?

"What's wrong?" Accosta said. "You look like you're going to cry again."

Kay drew in the deepest breath she could manage. She did *not* want to cry in public. "I was so wrong to put on this charade." She looked at Sharon. "And I treated you so badly, nearly throwing away our friendship."

"Nearly, but not quite," Sharon said.

Her heart was beating so fast she had to press her hand against it. She looked at the other ladies. "Thank you for taking care of me, and for . . . for . . ."

"Staging an intervention?" Tessa said.

Kay smiled. "That's exactly what you did — and I'm grateful." She looked around the table at each lovely face. "I promise I will be — to use Sharon's word — *authentic* from now on."

"Here here!" Tessa said, raising her glass of iced tea.

The tinkling of glass against glass added a delightful soundtrack to the moment.

** ** **

Kay's pared-down style cut the time it took to get ready for bed in half. But she was still completely done in and exhausted. This morning she'd awakened as Katerina yet was going to bed as Kay. She'd awakened with lies and was going to sleep with the truth.

What a wild couple of days.

But as she reached to turn off the light, she stopped. There was something she had to do to cap off her transformation.

She slid out of bed and knelt on the floor beside it. She wasn't much of a pray-er, but guessed kneeling was the proper way to do it. She leaned forward on the mattress and clasped her hands. She bowed her head and closed her eyes.

Okay . . . now what? She cleared her throat and said His name. "Jesus? Are You there?"

She let silence swirl around her. Should she be waiting for an audible answer? Or was that too presumptuous? She was new to all of this.

"You don't have to answer me, but I'm going to assume You're out there. Somewhere. Sorry for not being in touch much." Her thoughts demanded honesty. "Actually, hardly at all. But I'm here now. I'm so sorry for all the lies I told. I tried too hard to be someone I'm not — I'm thankfully not." She took a fresh breath. "I may not know You very well, but I know lying is bad. Thanks for Sharon, Tessa, Accosta, and Evelyn. Most of the ladies only knew the fake me, but they didn't give up on me. And Sharon and Tif . . . I hurt my own daughter worst of all. Please forgive me and help them forgive me. And give me the strength to *be* me." She shook her head. "Not just *me,* but a better me than I've ever been. I'm not ashamed of who I am anymore. I want everyone to know me. I'm not sure what that means but — "

Come clean.

She jerked her head up. Had she heard real words or was it in her head? She froze, waiting for something more.

But there was no more.

Yet those two words were enough.

She had to come clean, not just to the ladies, but to everyone she'd lied to. But how could she do that?

She spotted a basket of Christmas cards and letters that she'd been looking through during her downtime in bed. Though Christmas letters had a bad name, she loved receiving them.

And sending them?

She'd discounted that tradition this year, as she wasn't sure how to talk about her divorce and moving to Happy Trails. And most of the people she usually sent to knew the real Kay. The people at Happy Trails were the ones she'd lied to.

Come clean. To them.

Kay got up off the floor and went to her computer. She had a Christmas confession to write.

** ** **

Kay didn't finish until two in the morning. She printed the letters and used a directory to personalize each envelope. Now came the task of delivering them.

She got dressed in jeans and a blouse, and put on her walking shoes. She put the letters in a tote bag, quietly walked down the empty halls, and slipped a letter under each door.

She didn't get back to her apartment until nearly three. "Can I hear an amen?" she told the room.

Soon after, Kay Volkov fell asleep with joy in her heart.

Chapter Thirty-Nine

Scranton

> Better to have little, with godliness,
> than to be rich and dishonest.
> Proverbs 16: 8

As Scranton walked from his bedroom to the kitchen he noticed something white on the floor of the entryway.

An envelope. Probably a Happy Trails reminder not to miss an elves extravaganza or a Santa shindig. He opened it up anyway.

> Dear Neighbors, I am writing to you to apologize for my deceitful behavior. My first name is not Katerina, but Kay. And my late husband, Nicolae doesn't exist. My ex- husband's name is Wally and we are divorced.

Without meaning to sit down, Scranton found himself sitting at the table. The letter was fascinating. It was like watching a trainwreck and not being able to turn away.

At the end of her confession Katerina — Kay — said:

> I went too far in my effort to start over with a fresh new life at Happy Trails. I created a make-believe life and in the process acted like I was better than everyone else. I am not better. I am far worse, for I am a fraud. Please forgive me for all the hurt I've caused. And if possible, I'd appreciate a second chance.

"Well, I'll be." Scranton looked up from the confession. As a lawyer he'd occasionally witnessed a client's *mea culpa* for their crimes. But none as eloquent as this one.

He carefully refolded the page and put it back in its envelope. He'd seen Kay at dinner last night — a completely changed woman. Her transformation from aging movie star to a pretty, mature woman took over the dinner conversation. Scranton had watched multiple people stop at her table to offer their compliments—and probably get a closer look. Though he hadn't known what caused her makeover, if the letter's confession was from her heart, then a renewed appearance solidified her new leaf.

He was impressed.

The mantel clock struck the half-hour. He was supposed to meet Rosalie in the dining room by now. He hurried to the elevator.

Two other couples had just entered and he slid in at the end and faced the door.

"I knew that Kay-person was lying about her trips to Europe," said a woman behind him on the right. "When I asked her about St. Peter's basilica in Rome, she kept talking about St. Paul's.'"

"St. Paul's is in London, right?" said another woman to the left.

"It most certainly is," said the husband.

Scranton couldn't let them get away with this nitpicking. He glanced over his shoulder. "Actually there *is* a St. Paul's in Rome, *Basilica Papale San Paolo fuori le Mura*. It was built on the place where the Apostle Paul was buried after being martyred." *So there.*

He smiled at the silence.

"Did *you* get a letter under your door?" the first woman asked him.

"I did."

"What do you think about it?"

The door began to open. Scranton turned enough to look at them eye to eye. "I think it was one of the most courageous acts I've ever witnessed." He smiled. "Have a good breakfast." He stepped out and headed toward the dining room.

Rosalie was reading some posters in the corridor. She turned when she saw him coming. "Why are you smiling?"

"I always smile at justice."

"For what?"

The two couples were walking by, so he brushed her question away. "What are you looking at?"

She pointed to the poster. "Here's all the Christmas events this week. See this? Santa Bingo. Just what you've been waiting for."

"I'll pass." He could not think of a worse way to spend his time.

Thankfully she didn't press. "Then how about helping deliver the toys for the angel project?"

"Actually go to people's houses?"

"That's where the kids live."

He wanted no part of it. "I'm not comfortable with that."

Rosalie shook her head, incredulous. "And I am? Come on, it will be good for both of us to do something charitable, beyond just buying a present."

He looked toward the dining room. The line for breakfast was getting longer. "If I say yes, can we go eat?"

"Absolutely."

He offered her a nod and his arm.

** ** **

"Over there!" Rosalie said from the passenger seat of Scranton's car. "That white house on the right with the Christmas lights on the bushes."

Her description could have applied to most of the houses on the street, but Scranton saw where she was pointing, pulled up front, and shut off the car. "What's the kid's name?" he asked.

"Kids plural. Randy and Sophia."

"Let's do this."

They carried the wrapped presents to the door and Rosalie rang the bell. "It's your turn to talk first," she whispered.

Before he could object, the door opened. A petite young woman with beautiful brown eyes saw the presents and smiled. "Hi."

Scranton cleared his throat and spoke, "We're here with Angel Gifts. For Randy and Sophia?"

"Thank you—" Suddenly she gave Scranton the strangest look, and studied his face. Then she nodded to herself and scowled.

What was that about?

A moment later she called over her shoulder, "Kids! Someone's brought you something."

Randy came running, tripping over air as if his feet were too big for his body. Sophia ran up behind him. She was about three. "Pe-sants?"

Their eyes zeroed in on the packages. "Those are for us?" Randy asked.

"They are," Rosalie handed them over. "Merry Christmas."

"Thank you." He peered up at his mother. "Can we open them?"

"Not until Christmas. But you can put them under the tree."

As the kids brought the presents to a tree in the corner, Rosalie and Scranton turned to leave. But then the mother said, "Mr. Stockton. Right?"

She knows my name? "Yes?"

She scoffed. "You don't remember me? My husband was a client of yours. God help him."

Her last comment made him want to end the conversation. Now. She *did* look a little familiar, but no name came to mind.

"Since you obviously don't remember, his name was Stan Rostenkowski. You urged him to take a plea by freaking him out with talk of doing worse time if it went to trial. We've regretted it ever since. Stan didn't know his friends were going to rob the liquor store when he dropped them off there."

A glimmer of a memory came back. "Aldo's Liquor?"

"You remember the store, but not Stan? That tracks. He's not here because of you."

Scranton didn't appreciate the accusation. "Actually, he's not here because he got arrested for driving the getaway car and taking a cut of the money. And lying to the police."

Stan's wife shook her head. "He changed his mind about the money and gave it back to the other two. We told you that."

It was all coming back to him. "That's not what the other two said. They said the robbery was your husband's idea."

"They lied." Her eyes filled with tears. The kids were staring at their mom.

Scranton felt Rosalie tug on his coat.

When the kids came to their mother's side, their eyes were sad and worried. "Mommy?"

She picked up Sophia while Randy leaned against her leg. "It's okay. They were just leaving."

Rosalie said, "I hope you have a lovely Christmas."

"Thank you, ma'am." She glared at Scranton. "If those presents weren't for my kids, I'd give 'em back to you."

This whole thing was surreal. Scranton came bearing gifts and was getting accused of not doing his job? He was a good lawyer. Sometimes a great one. This wasn't fair at all. And it was embarrassing to have Rosalie see it. "I'm sorry, but I did do my job, Mrs. Rostenkowski." What else could he say?

"Sorry doesn't get Stan back here with his family." She closed the door on them.

What just happened? Walking back to the car, Scranton handed Rosalie the keys. "Would you drive please?"

"Of course."

They rode in silence to their next stop, where Rosalie delivered the gift alone. When she returned she didn't start the car. "Want to talk about it?"

"Not really."

She hesitated, then said, "I think you need to talk about it."

He glanced at the house. Being parked out front was probably not a good idea. "Pull into that gas station a couple blocks back and I'll tell you." *Just a little.*

Within a few minutes they were parked, the engine off. Rosalie angled to see him. "Tell me about Mr. Rostenkowski."

"The memories aren't good ones."

"It was that bad?"

Scranton shook his head. "Not his case, but the combination of his case and what was going on with me at the same time as his case."

Her eyebrows rose in a question.

"First off, Rostenkowski's case was pro-bono work. I didn't charge them a thing."

"I'm not sure that matters."

"Probably not. But the firm requires our lawyers to take pro bono cases, and it was my turn." He remembered first meeting Stan and his very pregnant wife, Maria, who held a two-year-old Randy on her lap. Scranton had glanced over the case, and was annoyed by the guy's whiney denials and the wife's tears. *Sure, you're innocent. Everybody's innocent.*

"Honestly, I didn't have time to deal with his case. I was needed elsewhere."

"What was going on?"

He took a fresh breath. "Olivia had just been diagnosed with cancer and we were both a mess."

She touched his arm. "I'm so sorry."

Scranton gazed out the window as people came and went from the gas station, all busily going somewhere. It started to snow. Olivia would've called it a Christmas snow — gentle and fine.

"In my own defense, there was no evidence to support Randall's non-involvement. Just his word against everybody else's. And it wasn't his first offense. He'd been picked up for drugs a couple times. Pleading him out was the best choice."

"For you."

Ouch. Yet . . . was she right? With one breath in, then out, Scranton knew she was right. "For me."

"What was his sentence?"

"Six years." He was quick to add, "If there'd been a trial and his past offenses came up, it could have been double that."

"If he's telling the truth, any sentence is harsh, but that's a long one."

True.

Scranton rubbed his hands over his face. "Aahhh. Why did I have to make a delivery to their house — of all places? What an awful coincidence."

They shared some silence. He was so embarrassed.

Rosalie shook her head. "Maybe it wasn't a coincidence."

"How can you say that?"

Rosalie faced forward, looking at the snow. "I don't believe in coincidences. I believe there is a reason you delivered presents to that particular family."

"So I'd feel horrible?"

"Well . . . maybe. Sometimes God uses — "

He wanted to nip this conversation before it went further. "If God wanted me to feel horrible, I question His motives."

Rosalie squirmed in her seat. "Maybe He wants you to reassess that period of your life?"

"Whatever for? So I can simmer longer in my desperation and grief? That time was the beginning of a long and painful road that ended with God giving Olivia the death penalty. There's nothing to reassess. Court dismissed."

"I—"

He glanced in the backseat. "We're out of packages. We're done." In more ways than one. "Take me home."

** ** **

On the ride back from the Rostenkowski's Scranton felt himself teetering on the edge of a cliff. It would be easy to fall into the abyss of grief and regrets and anger. It would take more effort to take a step back and walk away from the negative emotions.

It had already been an emotion-filled day. Finding Kay's confession letter, defending her courage to naysayers, going with Rosalie to deliver presents . . . which he'd actually enjoyed doing. Then why had everything been ruined by delivering to a family who held a grudge?

Because they brought up memories of Olivia's cancer diagnosis.

Which made him snap at Rosalie.

Who recently lost her husband.

Who was doing everything she could to be his friend.

Bah humbug?

With a shake of his head Scranton forced himself to take a deep breath, hoping it would nudge him off that cliff.

"I'm sorry the afternoon turned out so badly," Rosalie said.

And there it was. The decision. Fall forward into his bad emotions or walk toward something better. Either way, none of this was Rosalie's fault.

Her generosity of spirit sealed his choice. "Don't be sorry," he said. "I've had a lovely afternoon with you, and the families appreciated the gifts. Thanks for suggesting it."

Rosalie expelled a sigh of relief. "You're welcome." She hesitated, then asked, "Will you be all right?"

"Yes." He almost believed it. He had to be all right. The past was the past. He had to pay attention to right now. Appreciate right now.

He had an idea. "So, Rosalie. Since you were kind enough to invite me to go on the deliveries, I'm going to invite you to go to something with me."

"What's that?"

He couldn't believe what he was going to say, but said it anyway. "It seems I have a hankering for Santa Bingo."

She laughed. "Really?"

Really? "Really."

She laughed again. "Since when does Scranton Stockton use the word *hankering*?"

"Since today. Since right now." He noted her profile as she drove. "You're a good influence on me, Rosalie Clemmons."

She smiled back at him. "Glad to be of service."

** ** **

"Bingo!" Scranton's hand shot up. "I have a Bingo!" He couldn't believe how excited he was.

A man came over and checked his card. "It looks okay. We have our first winner of Santa Bingo!"

Rosalie's eyes lit up. "What does he win?"

Win? *I get something?*

Mrs. Halvorson carried a huge bowl over, and held it close. "Take your pick."

The bowl was full of Christmas sweets: candy canes, little bags of Hershey kisses, M&Ms, peanut brittle, and chocolate Santas.

He was about to choose but instead turned to Rosalie. "You can choose for me."

She peered over the bowl like a little girl. "I choose the peanut brittle."

"Good choice," he said, even though it wasn't what he would have chosen.

Maybe that was the point.

They moved on to the next game. And the next. He didn't win again, but surprised himself by not minding a bit. Who would've thought a kids' game like Bingo could be fun?

After the games were over, he spotted Kay Volkov. She almost looked afraid of him. He hadn't been *that* mean to her. His thought was answered when he walked toward her and her face seemed panicked. "Hi, Kay," he said.

"Hi, Scranton." Her eyes flit around the room as if she needed someone to save her.

Answering an inner nudge he said, "I wanted to tell you how nice you look."

A wave of relief changed her expression as she smoothed her clothing. "Thank you."

He was pleased that she was pleased. But there was more he could do. "I also wanted to commend you for handing out that letter, clearing things up about . . . you know."

"My lies. I *do* know. I messed things up pretty bad."

"Not too bad. You made things right. That takes courage."

Her eyes peered up at him, hopeful. "Thanks for saying that, Scranton."

Speaking of making things right . . ." I need to apologize to you for my past rude behavior."

"Really? I mean, thank you. I know I brought it on myself and. . . thank you." She pointed at my prize. "Peanut brittle?"

"I let Rosalie choose, and offered it to her, but she said it was my prize and . . ."He was rambling.

They both looked across the room where Rosalie was talking with friends. "She's a very sweet woman."

"Yes, she is." He saw that Kay was empty handed. "Too bad you didn't win anything."

Kay scoffed. "I didn't win candy, but I still won tonight. I got to be myself." She looked around the room and smiled.

Scranton knew the feeling. "I never thought I'd say this, but Happy Trails is a good place to be."

She nodded. "It's home."

"That, it is."

"I'll see you soon," Kay said as she walked away. "Merry Christmas."

"You too."

Rosalie joined him. "Kay seemed happy. I know there's been tension between you."

Had everyone seen it? "We made up. I gave her some overdue compliments."

She smiled. "Compliments? Santa Bingo? What's got into you?"

"You."

Her eyes looked surprised. "Thank you, but I think it's more than that." She pointed upward.

God?

"You can deny it all you want, but I think God's working on you, Scranton—like it or not."

The jury was still out on that one.

Chapter Forty

Evelyn

Set your minds on things above,
not on earthly things.
Colossians 3:2

Evelyn put on her shoes and stood. "I'm ready."
Wayne finished buttoning his shirt. "Are you?"
She looked down at her clothes, checking for something amiss. "I think so."
He came to her, held her upper arms, and peered straight into her eyes. "Are you ready to spend time at Peerbaugh Place when it's not ours anymore?"
Oh that. She hesitated. "I want to be." She deflected her unease. "It's really nice that Ringo and Soon-ja invited Accosta and us for dinner."
"To show us what they've done with the place. Their new home."
"That too."
"It'll be all right, Ev."
He was making her sound weak. "I hope you know by now that I am not a crystal flower, ready to shatter. We sold the house, knowing they were going to change things."
"So we did." He studied her eyes for a moment, then let go. "All right then. Let's grab Accosta and go."

** ** **

"Haydeho, Evelyn!" Mae greeted them at the door, inviting them inside.
Evelyn hadn't known Mae and Collier would be at dinner, but was glad about it. Conversation never lagged with Mae in the room.

Ringo and Soon-ja welcomed them, took their coats, and led them into the parlor.

Evelyn stopped in the doorway. Gone was the hall tree and the oriental rug. Gone were her usual Christmas swags on the stairway. It really wasn't hers anymore. "Wow," she said.

"Is that a good wow or a bad wow?" Soon-ja asked.

Wayne put an arm around Evelyn's shoulders. She knew what she *should* say. So she said it. "A good wow." She touched the back of a gray sectional that faced the fireplace—which now had a huge TV mounted above it. A Christmas tree stood in the corner.

Little Ricky zoomed a toy airplane up and over the sectional so he could bring it to Collier. "Look, Grandpa, it's new. It's a Stealth Fighter."

While the men admired the aircraft, the women moved into the kitchen. Soon-ja was clearly excited. She stood next to a huge side-door fridge. "Ta da!"

"My oh my," Accosta said. "It's enormous."

"And it has a large chiller drawer." Soon-ja pulled it out.

"What a handy invention," Evelyn said.

Mae pulled out the freezer drawer at the bottom. "We sure could've used a big-un like this when there were five females living here, eh Evie?"

Soon-ja put her hand on her growing belly. "Remember, soon enough, we'll be five."

"How are you feeling?" Evelyn asked.

"Great. No problems at all."

"Good for you."

Evelyn was intrigued with the cabinets to the side of the fridge. Some of them were gone completely and others . . .

"Ringo redid the cabinets to make it fit," Soon-ja said. "I use the uppers for Tupperware and the lowers for serving dishes."

"Tell them what else you're adding," Mae said.

Soon-ja swept her hands across the middle of the room where a maple dinette sat with four chairs. "Instead of this table, Ringo's building me an island with seating on one side. I thought about putting the stovetop on it, but decided to leave it plain, one large slab of quartz. That way I'll have room to make bread and the kids can do their homework there, and—"

"And cupcakes," Ricky said. "You said we're going to make cupcakes."

Soon-ja crinkled her eyes at Ricky and nodded. "And cupcakes. Lots of cupcakes."

"Pink cupcakes," Zoe said. "With sprinkles."

"Any kind you want," her mother said.

Mae ran her hand over the old Formica countertops. "Are you getting quartz here too?"

"We are. And a double farmer's sink. Plus a new stove, oven, dishwasher, and microwave. And we're painting the walls a pale gray." She sighed. "It'll be spring before it's all done, but Ringo promises it will be done before the baby arrives. I'm so excited."

"You should be," Mae said.

"It will be beautiful," Accosta said.

They looked at Evelyn as if waiting for her to say something. Being polite warred with being upset at all the changes. "I'm glad you're happy."

The ladies didn't respond. They just stood there.

Ricky looked at them, then at Evelyn, then his mom. "What's wrong?"

Evelyn felt horrible for putting a damper on Soon-ja's show and tell. "Nothing at all," she told him. She forced herself to smile. "Have you redone the sunroom yet?"

"Not yet, but we have plans. Do you want to see?"

"Of course," Evelyn managed.

Soon-ja led the way.

Evelyn didn't really hear the details of turning the sunroom into an office because her thoughts were filled with memories of that room: her son drawing pictures on the coffee table; Tessa leading a Bible study there; painting the dark paneling a lovely celery green color; letting hospital-visitors sleep on the sofa . . . And how many books had she read while sitting in the wing chair — which was now piled high with file folders.

Beyond the details she wasn't listening to was one fact: it was no longer a sunny haven but was now a busy office. All the charm was gone. All the memories eradicated.

Evelyn felt the sting of tears and panicked. "If you'll excuse me." She hurried past the stairs and out the front door. She stepped through the snow to the side of the house before the sobs started. Even as she was crying she chastised herself. *Stop it, Evelyn! You're being ridiculous. It's not your house! They can do whatever they want to it.*

A few moments later Wayne found her, his face worried. "Ev. Are you okay?"

She fell into his arms. "I'm so sorry. So sorry."

He held her tight and ran his hand up and down her back. "It's all right. It will be all right."

She pulled back. "But it won't be. That's not my house anymore! It's too late! I've lost it forever."

"Well . . . yes." Wayne glanced toward the house. "I'm not sure what more there is to say."

"But this house was the foundation of my life. We got married here." The vapor of Evelyn's breath rose in front of her face. She was cold. Wayne had to be cold. Being outside in the snow was dumb.

"Now we're living together in a beautiful new home that will hold more memories, and create a new foundation."

His words moved her from the past to the present, and into the future. She needed to snap out of it. She swiped her tears and took a deep breath. "I've really made a muck of things, haven't I?"

"They understand. I understand. Hold onto the fact that Peerbaugh Place lives on."

"For new generations."

"Exactly."

She took a fresh breath of cold air. "Let's go back in."

"No more tears?"

"I can't promise, but hopefully not."

Evelyn never considered herself an actress but was proud of the job she did in the next few minutes. She smiled and even laughed at herself.

"We didn't mean to upset you," Ringo said.

"We love the house," Soon-ja said. "We were just—"

"Making it fit your family," Evelyn said. "As you should."

Mae put an arm around Evelyn's shoulders and squeezed. "The fact is, you can't unshake a milkshake, right, Evie?"

They all laughed.

But Evelyn took Mae's words to heart. What was done was done. She could act depressed and cry about it or she could appreciate what she'd had and enjoy her new life.

She chose the latter. She hugged Ringo and Soon-ja. "You're doing a wonderful job on the house. I wish you a lifetime of happiness here."

As they thanked her, Ricky ran into the room. "I'm starving. When are we going to eat?"

"Right now, bud," Soon-ja said.

Soon the dining room was alive with happy people enjoying each other's company, just as it had done thousands of times before.

This wasn't the end. It was a new beginning.

Chapter Forty-One

Kay

> The seeds of good deeds become a tree of life;
> a wise person wins friends.
> Proverbs 11: 30

Kay punched the elevator button on her way back to her apartment after doing errands. She found herself humming, but stopped. *I don't hum.* Actually, she didn't used to hum but since coming clean and letting her mistakes go, she almost *had* to hum.

She started the tuneless song again.

Another couple joined her: Ruth was in a wheelchair being pushed by her ever-present husband, Roy. She had a bandana covering her hair because she was going through chemo.

The elevator doors opened and they went inside.

"How are you feeling today, Ruth?" Kay asked.

"I'm hanging in there," Ruth said.

Roy touched his wife's shoulder from behind. "She's a trooper, that's for sure. She makes the nurses smile."

"I gotta do something with my time there." She gazed at her husband. "Our kids are coming in for Christmas Day, so that makes everything better." She found his hand and squeezed it. "When it comes down to it, family matters most."

"Well said," Roy said.

Ruth touched her head scarf. "I hope I don't scare the little ones away."

"You'll do no such thing," Roy said.

Ruth looked at Kay and seemed to want to say something else, hesitated, then said it. "We got your letter under the door."

"Oh."

"It was a good letter, that took chutzpa to write," Ruth said.

"I'm sure it was hard for you to do," Roy added.

"It was. But it was even harder not to be myself." She chuckled. "It was exhausting thinking about Katerina all the time." They reached their floor. "Have a nice visit with your family."

"We'll try." Ruth touched her scarf as Roy pushed her out of the elevator. "You have a nice day too."

As Kay entered her apartment she thought about the disparity in Roy and Ruth's "nice" days versus her "nice" days. What nice day could they enjoy dealing with Ruth's cancer? Christmas and cancer didn't belong together.

Kay set out the ingredients she'd purchased to make peanut brittle for the Happy Trails Christmas party tomorrow night. She put the rest of the groceries away. She couldn't get the image of Ruth out of her mind. As she put some toiletries in her bathroom, she caught a glimpse of herself in the mirror. She was still getting used to her pared-down look. Every morning she had to fight the impulse to put on more makeup or one of her wigs.

Wigs.

Wigs she didn't need anymore.

Kay rushed to the cabinet where her wigs were kept, the sight of them solidifying her idea.

Then she made a phone call.

* ** **

Roy opened the door. "Come on in, Kay."

She came in holding two wigs on mannequin heads. Ruth was sitting at the dining room table.

"Here they are," Kay said. "What do you think?"

Ruth's tired eyes gained new life. "I think they're gorgeous."

Roy joined the ladies. "I do too."

"Which one do you want to try on first?" Kay asked. "I also have one with a braided bun, if these don't suit you."

Ruth looked from one to the other, then she pointed at the sleek one. She untied her kerchief, revealing a head splotched with tufts of hair.

Kay felt so bad for her. Although she hadn't known Ruth before the chemo, she spotted a healthy Ruth in a few photos nearby. She'd had beautiful hair back then.

She could have beautiful hair right now.

Kay stood behind her and had Ruth hold the wig at the front center. She carefully pulled the wig on and adjusted it. She smoothed the hair in a few places. "It fits perfectly."

"Like it was meant for you," Roy said.

Ruth waved her hand. "Bring me my hand mirror, will you, hon?"

Roy went to the bedroom and returned with a mirror. Ruth touched the hair and gave it a good look-see.

"Do you like it?" Kay asked.

Ruth nodded, but her expression showed imminent tears. "It makes me feel like a woman again."

Roy's eyes were misty too. "You look lovely, just lovely."

Kay was touched by the look of love they exchanged.

Will I ever experience that kind of love?

She mentally shook the thought away. This moment wasn't about her. It was about Ruth.

"Do you want to try the other one on? It's a bit different so you can alternate."

Ruth shook her head. "I will not be greedy about this gift. This one is enough. This one is plenty. Give the other ones to another woman-in-need."

Kay nodded, feeling a tightness in her throat. "I'll do that."

She gave Ruth a few pointers on caring for the wig, and gathered up the extra wig to take home with her.

But not before Ruth held out her hand, firmly squeezing Kay's. "This was a very good thing you did today, Kay. You're a good woman."

Kay had been called a lot of things, but she'd *never* been called that.

Kay kissed her on the cheek and left.

Who knew that giving away part of herself would make her feel so full inside?

** ** **

As the day went on Kay wanted to extend the high she'd felt after giving Ruth one of her wigs, and receiving all the nice comments about her letter. Kay could personally attest to the idiom, "confession is good for the soul." For the most part, people had been appreciative about her apology. God had been very gracious about that.

She went through her mail. There was a Christmas card from Tiffany. Inside was a short printed-out letter telling about their lives. But no personal note.

I don't deserve a personal note. I hurt her. I –

She remembered Ruth's words: *Family matters most.* On the heels of this wisdom came a new thought: *apologize to your family.*

Kay read the card's message: *The gift of love. The gift of joy. The gift of peace. May all these be yours at Christmas.*

Love. Joy. Peace. Kay had been far too cavalier about these essential elements of life. She'd hurt those she loved. She'd lied her way through any chance of joy. And she'd eradicated peace by brandishing a selfish ego above everyone else.

With a nod, she made a choice.

Kay dialed Tiffany's number.

"Mom?"

Tiffany did not sound enthused. "Hi, honey. How are things going?" Her question sounded lame.

"Things are busy," she said. "It's Christmastime. We sell a lot of ice cream cakes."

"Sounds yummy. I'd like to try one sometime."

There was silence on the line. "To try one you would have to come visit."

The doorway leading back to her daughter had opened just a crack. "I'd like that."

"Really?" There was skepticism in her voice.

"Really. I mean, it's Christmas and . . ." She let the words come out in a flood. "I'm so sorry for offending you like I did. I don't know what got into me, trying to be someone I wasn't. And I pulled you into it, hurting you. I was thoughtless, cruel, and stupid."

"Yeah, you were. I still don't understand any of it. I know the divorce was hard on you—it was hard on me too. But to throw away who you were—who *we* were—by creating this different reality? That's as bad as Dad tossing out his old life and creating a new one with Janice. It hurts to be tossed out like we weren't good enough for you."

Her words stung, but she wasn't wrong. "I don't know what to say."

"Then let *me* talk. Since Dad destroyed our old life, you *did* need to start a new one. But that doesn't mean you should throw out who we were. You build on that and make something better."

She was totally right. "How did you get to be so smart?"

Kay expected Tiffany to say "you." But she had another answer.

"Rod's the smart one. He's taught me so much about life."

Kay willingly relinquished the credit. She liked hearing good things about her son-in-law. "He's a good man." *That I barely know.*

"The best. So . . . would you like to fly out here for Christmas? We'd love to have you."

Kay's throat tightened with emotion. "That would be wonderful."

"Actually, let me arrange and pay for the flight — it will be our Christmas present to you."

Kay was sure the price would be atrocious. "That would be much appreciated. Look into flights and let me know."

"Will do. Can you stay a few days? The kids don't have school, so it would be a great chance to get to know them better. We have a guest room waiting for you."

"I can't wait. Thank you for being so generous and so forgiving, Tiffany. Tif. It means a lot to me."

"No problem. We look forward to seeing you. We'll have a Merry Christmas, together."

Kay hung up, her heart full. Merry Christmas indeed.

Chapter Forty-Two

Rosalie & Accosta

The fruit of the Spirit is love, joy, peace, longsuffering,
kindness, goodness, faithfulness, gentleness, self-control.
Against such there is no law.
Galatians 5: 22-23

Rosalie stood in front of her closet, trying to choose something to wear to the Happy Trails Christmas party. She spotted the snowflake Christmas sweater she always wore, but hesitated. Lonnie always wore a white shirt with a snowflake tie to coordinate. Somehow it didn't seem right to add to that memory.

Which made her wonder if she should even go. Lonnie hadn't even been gone a month. *He* was the joiner, the one who lured her out of the house to go to concerts, parties, and church events. When they'd moved into Happy Trails, he'd been involved in the men's chorus, woodworking, golf outings, and every Bridge or Bingo night. The only reason she'd gone to Bingo the other night was because Scranton wanted to go. Needed to go.

To help her make the decision, she opened Lonnie's end of the closet and pressed her face into his shirts, drinking in his scent. *I miss you so much, my darling.* But with his scent she felt his essence — and his opinions. Should she go to the party?

Of course you should go, Rosie. Staying home isn't going to make things change, or make them better. Being out with people will. Remember what Helen Keller said: Life is either a daring adventure or nothing at all.

Rosalie wasn't sure going to a Christmas party was a daring adventure, but she knew that staying home was nothing at all.

And so she closed the door on his clothes and put on a red blouse and red drop earrings.

As she was slipping on her shoes the doorbell rang. "Come in!"

Scranton entered wearing a red and green plaid vest, a red bowtie, and a Santa hat. "Ho, ho, ho."

She chuckled. "You look marvelous."

"The hat's not too much?"

"Not at all."

"And you . . . you look very pretty, Rosalie," he said. "Red is a good color on you."

She appreciated the compliment. She missed Lonnie's compliments.

"Come see the cake I'm bringing." She showed him the chocolate sheet cake shaped like a Christmas tree, that was fully decorated with icing, edible beads, and nonpareils.

"It's too pretty to eat."

"Never." She noticed he wasn't carrying any food. "Are you bringing something?"

"It's already there. I bought a meat and cheese tray and crackers."

"You can't go wrong with that. Shall we go?"

** ** **

"Would you like to dance?" Scranton stood before her, his hand extended like a courtier.

Yes, Rosalie wanted to dance. She loved to dance. But . . .

She felt the weight of sudden grief.

He put his hand down and sat beside her. "We danced at the Friday Fling—with Lonnie's approval."

She kept her voice low. "But he died so recently. I don't know if it's proper for me to dance. It's too soon."

He nodded. "I understand. As familiar as I am with losing a spouse, I'm not versed in the rules of widowhood."

"There are no rules anymore," Tessa said from her seat across the table. "Sorry to eavesdrop, but I can't help hearing what I hear."

"No rules?" Rosalie was surprised by her leniency. "So no more wearing black for a year?"

"Gracious," Tessa said, pushing her poinsettia hat a half inch to the left. "Can you imagine abiding by those old rules? And not being able to go out? Widows have lost their husband and their life. They need to be with other people." She glanced at Scranton. "Widowers too."

"I agree," Accosta said, adjusting her matching hat.

"Me too," Evelyn said. "My tenants saved me from my grief. People need people."

Scranton raised his hand slightly. "Does that mean she can dance with me?"

The ladies laughed.

"If you want to dance, dance," Tessa said.

Scranton stood and offered his hand again. "Shall we dance this one dance? We can take them one at a time."

It seemed like a good solution. She let Scranton lead the way.

It was awkward at first, until Scranton twirled her under his arm before settling into a gentle rhythm.

She enjoyed the moment—and the atmosphere. Christmas lights twinkled all around the room, with shiny ornaments reflecting the light.

They danced near Kay and Joe. Rosalie offered her a little wave. She looked so much prettier now. And by the ecstatic look on her face, she was happier too.

"Are you having fun?" Scranton asked.

Rosalie was about to answer when she noticed people looking at them, and it wasn't because they were good dancers. Scowled faces and side eyes . . . the message was clear.

They don't approve.

No matter what her friends said, it was obvious some people didn't think it was proper for a recent widow to dance.

"Rosalie?" he asked. "You didn't answer my question. Fun?"

She didn't want to make a big deal about her observations—for Scranton was being so nice and she loved seeing *him* being social—but she wanted to sit down as soon as possible. "Yes, I'm having fun, but my knees are hurting. Can we sit?"

"Of course."

They returned to the table.

"That was quick," Tessa said.

"My knees are acting up." It was an excuse, even if it *was* true.

"Maybe it's the cold weather," Accosta said.

Wayne put his hand on Evelyn's shoulder. "We get aches with the cold."

Rosalie was glad they weren't doubting her. She wanted to change the subject. "Where is everyone spending Christmas?"

"You start," Accosta said, pointing at Rosalie with a smile.

"I'm spending the day at our daughter and son-in-law's house. Evan is bringing home a girlfriend he's serious about." It was suddenly hard to pretend everything was normal. "But Lonnie *won't* be there." Her voice broke, and Scranton touched her hand.

"We know it's hard," Evelyn said. "If there's anything we can do..."

The others murmured variations of their own offers to help.

Rosalie didn't want her grief-bubble to ruin the evening. "Anyway. I will be all right. I'll get through it."

"Yes, you will, dear lady," Accosta said. "The trick is learning to enjoy the *now* now."

"That's quite profound," Tessa said. "The *now* now." She nodded her approval.

Rosalie would try to remember that good advice. "How are you spending Christmas, Tessa?"

"No surprises with me. My daughter makes a great glazed ham that I wouldn't miss. My son-in-law makes wassail, and my grandson is coming with his wife and baby girl." She pressed a hand to her chest. "My heart will be full." She turned to Scranton. "What are your plans?"

"I'm also going to my daughter's house. They live a couple hours away and I missed being with them at Thanksgiving: Shelley and Craig, and of course my granddaughter BB."

"What an unusual name," Tessa said.

"It's really Bernadette."

Tessa nodded once. "That's an odd one too. But pretty."

Evelyn chimed in. "We're going to my son's house. There will be Russell, Audra, Summer, Piper, Gregory, and the twins. They all live in town. But..." Her smile faded.

"But what?" Rosalie asked.

She gazed wistfully at her husband. "It will be the first time we're not celebrating in Peerbaugh Place."

There were a few murmurs of empathy. "Why is Christmas so often connected with high emotions?" Rosalie asked.

"It just is." Tessa's words were surprisingly short. She glanced at her watch, then suddenly raised her hand. "Accosta, you never said how you're spending Christmas."

** ** **

Accosta smiled at Tessa. "I'm spending it with you and your family, Tessa—and I'm very grateful."

"What about your son and his family?" Evelyn asked.

It made Accosta sad thinking about it, but facts were facts. "Eugene and Mandy have to work on the twenty-sixth, and the kids are home from college and . . . Cincinnati is a long way away."

"Is it?" Tessa pushed herself to standing. She raised her hand and waved as if signaling—

Accosta gasped as Eugene and his family walked across the room toward her. *No. It can't be. They can't be!*

She stood to greet them, holding out her arms.

Eugene filled them. "Hi, Mom."

She held him tighter than tight and whispered in his ear, "Are you a dream?"

He let go and smiled at her. "Nope. I'm real. Merry Christmas."

His wife Pat, and Accosta's grown up grandkids took turns with the hugs. John was as tall as his dad, and Jane was a lovely young woman.

More chairs were added to the table.

Accosta couldn't stop looking at them. "How did you arrange all this?" she asked.

Eugene glanced at his wife. "We still have to work on the twenty-sixth, but we asked work if we could take off a few days before Christmas, and . . . well, here we are."

Accosta began to cry happy tears. "Praise God."

Tessa pounded her cane twice on the floor to get everyone's attention. "Here's the deal. I am going to go stay with my daughter starting tomorrow morning so you and the family can celebrate in our apartment."

Tessa was involved? "How did you . . . ?" Accosta glanced from Tessa to her son.

"I was the one who called them," Tessa said proudly. She winked at Eugene. "They were going to fly, but decided to drive instead."

"It's only nine hours from Cincinnati," John said. "We all took a turn."

Jane rolled her eyes. "Unfortunately, I ended up driving through the traffic of St. Louis. Yuck."

Her dad chuckled. "On the way back, I'll make sure I'm driving then."

Accosta still couldn't believe they were here. She inundated God with thank yous.

A new song began with the strains of violins. John stood up and held out his hand. "Wanna dance, Grandma? It's a slow one."

Accosta wasn't sure she was stable enough to do such a thing, but she couldn't refuse. John helped her to her feet and steadied her as they walked onto the dance floor.

"Don't worry, I've gotcha," he said as they began to dance.

The Etta James song was the right song for the moment and Accosta softly sang along as John rocked her back and forth. "'At last, my love has come along. My lonely days are over and life is like a song . . .'"

It was the perfect song for the most perfect moment.

Chapter Forty-Three

Kay

March

> Anyone who belongs to Christ
> has become a new person.
> The old life is gone; a new life has begun!
> 2 Corinthians 5: 17

Kay watched the last of her furniture being loaded into the truck. The men closed up the back and the driver brought her something to sign.

"We're taking it to Another Chance consignments on Elm, correct?" he asked.

"Yes," Kay said. "They know you're coming." She signed the work order and watched as ninety-percent of her belongings were driven away.

Sharon walked up beside her. "I'm still shocked you're selling everything. Some of that furniture is nearly new."

Kay felt a little flip in her stomach. It *did* make her nervous, but she put on a confident face. "I won't need it in Idaho."

"I still can't believe you're moving fourteen hundred miles away. Who knew a visit to see Tif at Christmas would turn into an invitation to move there? And I can't believe you accepted."

"How could I not? I haven't smiled and laughed so much in years. Decades, probably." She wrapped her arms around herself. "I haven't felt love like that either." Kay glanced at Sharon. "They love me. Can you believe it?"

Sharon put an arm around her shoulders and squeezed. "I can. We all love you. Now you have to work on loving yourself."

"I'm working on it."

Sharon looked down the street in the direction of the moving truck. "But all your stuff . . . I know Tiffany's garage apartment is completely furnished, but is it your style?"

"I don't care about style anymore."

Sharon laughed. "Those are words I never expected to hear from Kay Volkov."

And they *were* hard to say. But Kay couldn't back down. Moving away from Happy Trails to a new life close to her family was the right thing to do.

It was odd that three words from Ruth, the woman who accepted one of her wigs, had changed the course of her life.

Family matters most.

Sharon's husband Hank came out of Happy Trails carrying two boxes. "These are the last of 'em," he said. He put them in Kay's car. "I don't think there's room for an extra shoe."

Kay took note of her car containing all the trappings of her life. She'd gone from a large house to two small apartments, and now would be in an even smaller place.

Yet it was okay. It was good. It was time to be with her family. She could have a new life, while still being herself. Her best self.

Hank wiped his forehead even though the March air was cool. "You want to go back and check that I got everything?"

"And say goodbye?" Sharon added.

Kay only considered this for a moment. "I'm good." She pointed west. "I need to head thataway."

"Does Con know you're moving?" Hank asked.

"He does. I visited him last week."

Sharon scoffed. "Just because he's stuck here, doesn't mean you have to be." She had a second thought. "I don't mean *stuck*. Not like that."

"I know what you meant. Don't worry, he's good with it," Kay said. She opened her arms to her best friend. "Thank you for all you are and all you've done for me."

Sharon squeezed her tight. "Love you bunches."

Kay held back tears. "Love you bunches back." She let her friend go and pointed at Hank. "You keep your promise and both come out and see me."

He nodded. "Will do. Take care of yourself, Kay."

She ended the goodbyes by getting in the car. She spoke through the lowered window. "I'll send updates along the way." Then Kay pulled out, tooting her horn. She spotted Wrinkles taking a walk. She waved at him, and he gave her a bow.

Joe was a good guy. But she'd turned her heart and mind to other things.

So much so, that she nearly drove through a stop sign.

She slammed to a stop.

"Get a hold of yourself, Kay. You've got three days of driving ahead of you."

She didn't let herself digest the full implications of her trip until she was safely on the interstate. But as the miles slipped by, she smiled. She felt at peace. She'd made a good decision.

When she'd moved to her first apartment she'd wanted to capture a world she'd never experienced in her youth—and certainly didn't fit in now. At Happy Trails she'd shucked away her old life by pretending to be a different person

But now . . . she was starting over a third time and this time she *was a* different person. She was free of everything fake and was embracing everything real: family, faith, and the freedom to start fresh, while being exactly who she was.

Kay saw a red barn that had two words painted on its side. She smiled at the simple but perfect message: *Jesus Saves.*

That, He does. That, He did.

Chapter Forty-Four

Scranton

March

> Learn to do right; seek justice. Defend the oppressed.
> Take up the cause of the fatherless;
> plead the case of the widow.
> Isaiah 1: 17

The barista called out his name.

Scranton went to the counter and picked up two coffees. His was black. He wasn't into mochas and lattes. Just give him the hard stuff. And certainly not a chai tea — which is what he handed the kid who sat at the table with him.

"Thanks, man," the kid said.

Moe was the brother of a waiter at Happy Trails. He needed legal advice because he was on the cusp of losing his license for speeding.

Moe took a sip of his tea. "You see, I really need my license so I can get to work."

"You should've thought of that three speeding tickets ago."

Moe's eyebrows met in the middle and he stood up. "Aren't you supposed to be on my side? I don't got to take this, man."

"No, you don't. And I don't have to help you. Gratis."

"Huh?"

"For free." Scranton cocked his eyebrow at the kid.

Moe's shoulders dropped as he slid onto the chair again. He patiently listened to Scranton's instructions about what would come next. Or he seemed to listen. Long ago Scranton learned not to take responsibility for those he defended. He could help them, and try to get them to toe the line, but the rest was up to them.

As they were wrapping up he checked his watch. He had another appointment with a fellow resident at Happy Trails who had questions about probate. He stood. "I need to be going."

Moe stood too. "Thanks for all your help, Mr. Stockton."

Scranton took it as a good sign that Moe's salutation had changed from *man* to *Mr. Stockton*. "Learn something from this, Moe. I don't want to see you again."

"Got it. Thanks." He left the coffee shop.

Scranton was just leaving when his phone rang. The caller ID made him return to his chair. It was Stan Rostenkowsky's wife. He answered. "Yes, Maria?"

"Mr. Stockton. Stan called me last night from prison and I told him about your offer to help get him out."

"And he said . . . ?"

"Yes. Of course! He didn't quite understand how you, the lawyer who'd had him make the plea, would want to help him get out, but he's grateful."

Ever since seeing Maria and the kids while delivering the Christmas gifts, Stan's plea deal had sat heavily on Scranton's conscience.

"I'm not guaranteeing anything will come of it, Maria, but I'm willing to take a shot."

"It's more than we've had before," she said. "And to do it for free? We don't know how to thank you."

"Don't thank me until I get him out."

"When that day comes, we'll have a party and you'll be invited."

He couldn't imagine going. Yet, stranger things had happened.

"It still floors us that this all came from you bringing a few Christmas presents to our house."

"It was a nice coincidence."

"It was God," Maria said. "I know it."

Scranton did too, but wasn't ready to state it so plainly.

"We'll wait to hear from you," Maria said. "God bless you, Mr. Stockton."

Scranton hung up, then leaned forward on the table, shading his eyes with his hand. The weight of Maria and Stan's faith in him was heavy, yet the hope he felt, lightened the load. And Maria's

"God bless you"? He did feel blessed to have a chance to make things right. He added his own silent, *God help me.*

Then he remembered the time and hurried back to Happy Trails to meet with his next client.

Who needed Scranton as much as Scranton needed them.

Chapter Forty-Five

Rosalie

March

> You must each decide in your heart how much to give.
> And don't give reluctantly
> or in response to pressure.
> For God loves a person who gives cheerfully.
> 2 Corinthians 9: 7

Rosalie scooped pink frosting into her pastry bag.

Scranton stood at the end of the counter. "Don't worry if you spill some. I'll take care of it."

"I'm so glad," she said. "I was worried about that." Scranton and Lonnie both had a sweet tooth.

She twisted the top of the bag and held it at the right angle. Then she applied a scalloped edge of frosting with one hand and turned the turntable with the other.

"That is so amazing," he said. "It's so smooth."

"It takes practice, lots of practice."

"Are you putting roses on it?"

"A few. Lynn's husband said she loves pink roses." She nodded to the bowls of deeper pink and green frosting. "Do you want to stir the pink bowl a little? It's next."

Scranton stirred—and swiped the edge of the bowl with his finger. "It's ready to go. How many cakes have you made in the past few months?"

"This is my tenth."

"Looks like you have yourself a business."

"Not really. I don't charge people—kind of like you helping people with legal issues for free."

"Patsies, both of us."

She laughed and filled a smaller bag with the dark pink frosting. "I prefer to think of us as culinary and legal do-gooders."

"How about 'philanthropists'? That sounds better."

"Fancier for sure." She concentrated on piping roses on top of the cake.

"You bite your tongue when you concentrate," he said.

"Shh." Though she did try not to do it.

He swiveled back and forth on a stool. "You want to hear something strange?"

"Sure."

"Helping Stan and Maria gives me more satisfaction than I ever felt getting a defendant off when I was at the firm."

She finished a rose and looked at him. "Why do you think that is?"

"Because Stan was wrongly convicted."

"And your other defendants were guilty?"

He shrugged. "Some were. Some weren't. They deserved to be defended either way. I'm really hoping I can get Stan freed."

"That would be a very, very good thing."

He seemed to be thinking about something hard.

"What's going on in that mind of yours?" she asked.

Scranton blinked as if putting a period on his thoughts. "I've been thinking about God-stuff more often."

"God-stuff?"

"You know, faith and praying?"

"Oh. That stuff." Rosalie was glad to hear him talking about it. "What conclusion have you come to?"

He slipped off the stool and got himself a drink of water. Rosalie waited patiently. She didn't want to spook him.

Finally, he set the glass down and faced her. "Olivia was the one who handled God-stuff in our house."

"That's not unusual."

"And *you* talk about Him quite a bit."

"I guess I do."

He leaned against the counter. "Remember when you told me that God led me to Happy Trails?"

"I seem to recall you pooh-poohed the notion."

He shrugged. "I've been thinking about it a lot and I know why God led me here."

She wanted to fist pump him. "So you *are* admitting God got you here?"

He squirmed like a five-year-old, then stood still. "Do you want to hear it or not?"

She did a turn-a-lock motion in front of her lips. "I do. Tell me."

"The reason God brought me to Happy Trails was . . ."

"Yes?"

"Was to meet you." He took her hand and pulled her into an embrace. "You've given me a new lease on life, Rosalie Clemmons."

Her heart overflowed. In answer she leaned her head against his shoulder and whispered, "Me too, old man."

Scranton held her tight. Rosalie closed her eyes, realizing how much she'd missed being hugged.

But no more.

No more.

Chapter Forty-Six

Evelyn & Accosta

March

> When you pray, go away by yourself,
> shut the door behind you, and pray to your Father in private.
> Then your Father, who sees everything, will reward you.
> Matthew 6: 6

Evelyn put Accosta's walker in the back of the SUV and got in the car. "I like putting Easter baskets together for the kids at church, but it's a big job."

"It sure is."

"It's time to get back to home sweet home."

After a few minutes of driving, Accosta said, "Hey! You missed it."

"Missed what?" Evelyn checked out the buildings they'd just passed.

"Whenever we're out and about you always drive by Peerbaugh Place."

"I don't always—"

"You do. Every time."

Although Evelyn wanted to argue with her, she realized Accosta was right. For over three months she'd driven past whenever she'd been anywhere close. Even a few times when she wasn't close at all. "I guess you're right. You got me."

"What's different today?"

Evelyn tried to pinpoint it, but couldn't. "There isn't one reason. I just..."

"You just...?"

"The need to be there—to check on it—has faded."

Accosta slapped her hands together. "Praise the Lord!"

Evelyn glanced at her. "You've been praying about this?"

"Of course I have. Haven't you?"

She was ashamed to say she hadn't.

Accosta touched Evelyn's arm. "We both miss the before years there—before Happy Trails. They were happy years."

"Indeed, they were." Evelyn turned toward home.

"And we're living happy years where we are now," Accosta said. "Right?"

"We are," Evelyn admitted without a hint of hesitation.

Accosta began counting on her fingers. "I see you, Wayne, and Tessa of course, Rosalie, Scranton, Bill, Dean, Arthur, Mabel . . ."

Evelyn chuckled. "We have a lot of friends there."

"New brothers and sisters."

Sisters . . . funny you should use that term. "I do know a reason why the need to drive past has faded."

"What's that?"

"I've been working on my book about Peerbaugh Place. Reliving so many of the emotional moments has kept it alive, in here." Evelyn touched her heart.

Accosta rubbed her hands together in excitement. "I can't wait to read it. Do you have a title yet?"

"I think so. How does *The Sister Circle* sound?"

Accosta clapped her hands. "It's perfect! For sister circles are what we created. And no one can take them away from us."

"They wouldn't dare," Evelyn said with a smile.

** ** **

Before Accosta got ready for bed, she took two special boxes and set them on the bed. She had a victory to celebrate.

She found the right card in the Worry Box, held it between both hands, and read what was on it: *Please let Wayne and Evelyn be content at Happy Trails.*

She gazed heavenward and smiled. "Mission accomplished, Lord! Thank You!"

Then she carefully tore the card into many pieces, letting them rain down like celebratory confetti into the second box where the remnants of hundreds of other answered prayers mixed together in a blessed prayer potpourri.

She closed the lid, gave it a happy shake, and set it aside. Then Accosta drew another card from her worry box, bowed her head, and did what she did best.

The End

** ** **

Since we are surrounded by such a huge crowd of witnesses to the life of faith, let us strip off every weight that slows us down, especially the sin that so easily trips us up.
And let us run with endurance the race God has set before us.
Hebrews 12: 1

Dear Sisters,

You had to be there. That's a truism that fits aging to a tee. When we were young, we looked at old people when we had to. We glanced. We never really looked. Never saw them. We tolerated their slowness, listened to their complaints about aches and pains, and felt sorry for them—because they weren't young like us.

Now that I am old(er) I realize how little I truly understood about the process of getting old. Yes, there is the freedom of not having to work (though many of us *choose* to work), and the freedom of not feeling the need to wear makeup all the time, or post on social media, or feel guilty about getting our senior discounts. But there's also the hard facts about our aging bodies. Personally, we've dealt with cancer this year, ER visits, hospitalization, and I'm having back surgery in November. It's definitely time for a 65,000 mile tune-up.

We've also become aware that the world is no longer ours. Our grown children are busy: jobs, kids, sports, dance lessons, scouts, dentist appointments, carpool lines, never-ending laundry, meals, homework, church, and having very little time for themselves. Been there, done that. And yet, did we really do that? Our three married kids and their spouses *have* to work. Added to the stressors we faced in the 1980s and 90s, they have to deal with the dangers of the Internet, cell phones, social media, ever-changing morals, high crime, loss of innocence, predators, and drugs their kids might take accidentally. I truly thank God that we got to experience a world that was simpler and safer than the world is now. Not safe. But safer.

For instance, I remember going to Richman Gordman with all three kids and letting them run to the indoor playground in the center of the store. Without me, while I shopped alone. I wouldn't think of doing that today. Our kids walked to school. And I walked more than a mile to and from junior high with a heavy backpack and a violin (I know, I know, it was uphill both ways.) We rode our bikes without helmets. We didn't worry about being carefully "introduced" to strawberries and other foods. We didn't lock our doors. For instance, when I was growing up in the sixties our Skyline milkman would come into our kitchen without knocking, look in our fridge, and leave what we needed—all before we woke up for the day. Can you imagine that now? We played outside until the streetlights came on and always drank from the garden hoses. We had lemonade stands where we sold a glass for three-cents. As girls we were only allowed to wear pants to elementary school when it was cold out, but we had to take them off from under our dresses in the coat room before class. We dressed up for church. We went to the movies for 50-cents and bought a Slo-Poke sucker for a nickel. We held onto our innocence a lot longer than kids do now.

Enough reminiscing—which we oldies do love to do.

Back to aging. I remember my mother telling me when she was in her eighties that she didn't think of herself as old, but in her fifties. I understand what she means now. At age 65 a switch seemed to click in my brain where I realized other people saw me as an old woman while I still felt like someone who was 50. Bridging the gap of that reality is a work in progress that I don't like.

Another phenomenon I discovered from my mom is her realization that she didn't have unlimited time left. When we're younger than 50 we seem to ignore life's time limits. Oh, the years we waste thinking we have all the time in the world! Recognizing our time limit (and its inevitable expiration date) has made my husband and I prioritize what's important and what we really, really want to do. That's not a bad thing at all. I'm getting my back fixed now so we can hike in Switzerland for a 50th anniversary trip in 2024 (that we're taking a year early, just because with our health issues, sooner is better.)

The characters in *Senior Sisters* go through situations that are common to most of us. But here are a few "really true" notes about some anecdotes in the book:

- Evelyn and Wayne are worried about 93-year-old Accosta falling and breaking a hip—which is often inoperable for the elderly. I know this from experience. In 2020 Mom broke her hip at age 99 and a week later she was gone. *Miss you, Mom.*
- Scranton didn't enjoy the required sit-down meals at Happy Trails. My dad was like that. He was a good conversationalist, but having each meal take an hour or more often irked him. And he hated small talk (so do I.) But Mom? In the dining room

she'd stop at a half-dozen tables on the way to her place, chatting with everyone. Soon after they moved in, I was eating with them in the dining room. Dad pointed at Mom who was chatting on her way to join us and said, "*That's* why I wanted to move here. Your mother will thrive here." And she did. Dad died a couple of years later, but Mom lived there for nine years. Everyone knew Mrs. Young.

- Mae mentions mashing hard-boiled eggs on a plate, putting a pad of butter on top, and nuking 'em. My husband likes them this way. Frankly, I've never tried it because it sounds awful. Of course, *he's* never tried peanut butter on a BLT which comes from my side of the family. Or ground up Spam and dill pickles with a little Miracle Whip. Yum.
- Tessa's hats: Mom was an expert seamstress and often created matching hats. I didn't have a store-bought dress until I was in high school. She made my swimsuits, coats, prom dresses, my wedding dress, and clothes for my Barbies — the tiny sleeves are amazing! Although I can sew, I don't do it much anymore. Maybe I should. In my spare time.
- Kay's fake Bandolino shoes: at Millard Lefler Junior High in Lincoln, Nebraska, every girl who was cool had a pair of Bandolino leather, tie flats, with cutouts on the top and leather shoelaces. But they were expensive at Hovland Swanson's — more than my family could afford. But then a chain store offered non-leather copies for a fraction of the price. Mom let me get a pair of those. Why do I still remember this 55 years later?
- I've mentioned my mother a lot. She was an amazing woman. So much so that I wrote a novel inspired by her life: *An Undiscovered Life*. It's about a woman who wants her family to understand who she was in her *before* years — before them. She implements a very creative way to show them. I'm pretty sure we all can relate to wishing our family knew more about who we are.

- Kay's last scene, seeing a barn with "Jesus Saves" on the side. That barn exists on Interstate 70 in the Flint Hills of Kansas (though it might say "Trust Jesus", I can't remember for sure.)

Jesus Saves or *Trust Jesus* . . . both illustrate what's become my main priority in my senior years. Jesus. I really enjoy the process of growing closer to our Lord. I regret the years I wasted keeping Him at arm's length and I'm eternally glad He's so forgiving and patient.

As are you, dear sisters, for letting me ramble on about aging. May we all fully enjoy what life has to offer. Remember Psalm 138:8: "The Lord WILL fulfill his purpose in me." (not *might*, but *will*.) If you don't know what your purpose is, it's never too late to find out. Ask God about it. He's waiting to share it with you!

Blessings and good health to all,

Nancy Moser

A Special Bonus

I included this painting and poem in the back of my novel, *An Undiscovered Life*. It applies to *Senior Sisters* too.

Painting by Leonid Baranov

An Old Lady's Poem
Anonymous

What do you see, nurses, what do you see?
What are you thinking when you're looking at me?
A crabby old woman, not very wise,
Uncertain of habit, with faraway eyes?

Who dribbles her food and makes no reply
When you say in a loud voice, "I do wish you'd try!"
Who seems not to notice the things that you do,
And forever is losing a stocking or shoe.
Who, resisting or not, lets you do as you will,
With bathing and feeding, the long day to fill.
Is that what you're thinking? Is that what you see?
Then open your eyes, nurse; you're not looking at me.

I'll tell you who I am as I sit here so still,
As I do at your bidding, as I eat at your will.
I'm a small child of ten, with a father and mother,
Brothers and sisters, who love one another.
A young girl of sixteen, with wings on her feet,
Dreaming that soon now a lover she'll meet.
A bride soon at twenty – my heart gives a leap,
Remembering the vows that I promised to keep.
At twenty-five now, I have young of my own,
Who need me to guide and a secure happy home.
A woman of thirty, my young now grown fast,
Bound to each other with ties that should last.
At forty, my young sons have grown and are gone,
But my man's beside me to see I don't mourn.
At fifty once more, babies play round my knee,
Again we know children, my loved one and me.
Dark days are upon me, my husband is dead;
I look at the future, I shudder with dread.
For my young are all rearing young of their own,
And I think of the years and the love that I've known.

I'm now an old woman, and nature is cruel;
'Tis jest to make old age look like a fool.
The body, it crumbles, grace and vigor depart,
There is now a stone where I once had a heart.
But inside this old carcass a young girl still dwells,
And now and again my battered heart swells.
I remember the joys, I remember the pain,
And I'm loving and living life over again.

I think of the years, all too few, gone too fast,
And accept the stark fact that nothing can last.

So open your eyes, nurses, open and see,
Not a crabby old woman; look closer . . . see ME!

Verses in *Senior Sisters*
All NLT unless noted   (P)=paraphrased

Chapter 1	Providing for needs	2 Corinthians 9: 8
Chapter 2	God's plans	Jeremiah 29: 11
Chapter 3	Pain	Psalm 69: 29
Chapter 4	God saves	Isaiah 12: 2
	God's provision	Philippians 4: 19 (P)
Chapter 5	Prayer	Romans 8: 26
	Our desires	Psalm 37: 4 (P)
	God's generosity	Ephesians 3: 20-21
Chapter 6	Changes	Hebrews 12: 1
Chapter 7	Deception	2 Peter 2: 13
Chapter 8	Helping others	Proverbs 11: 25
Chapter 9	Arrogance	Psalm 31: 23
Chapter 10	Building each other up	Romans 15: 2
Chapter 11	Understanding	Proverbs 2: 2-3
Chapter 12	Encouragement	1 Thessalonians 5:14
Chapter 13	Fools and deception	Proverbs 14: 8
Chapter 14	Hospitality	1 Peter 4: 9-10
Chapter 15	Grief	Psalm 31: 9
	God has prepared a place	John 14: 2 (P)
Chapter 16	Praying	1 Thessalonians 5:16-18
	Meek	Matthew 5: 5 NIV
Chapter 17	Deceiving others	1 John 1: 8
	Don't lie	Exodus 20: 16 (P)
Chapter 18	Plans	Proverbs 16: 9
Chapter 19	Deception	Proverbs 14: 8
Chapter 20	Stubbornness	Psalm 81: 12
Chapter 21	Deception	Isaiah 28: 17
Chapter 22	Amazing things	Habakkuk 1: 5
	Praise	Psalm 92: 1-2, 4
Chapter 23	God's understanding	Isaiah 40: 28
Chapter 24	Sorrow	Psalm 56: 8
	Gift of Jesus	John 3: 16
	God's support	Deuteronomy 33:27 NIV
Chapter 25	Being selfless	Philippians 2: 4
Chapter 26	Grief	Ecclesiastes 2: 23

Chapter 27	God's help	Isaiah 40: 29
Chapter 28	Courage	Psalm 31: 24
Chapter 29	Seasons	Ecclesiastes 3: 1, 4
Chapter 30	Judging others	Matthew 7: 1
Chapter 31	Plans	Proverbs 19: 21
Chapter 32	God with us	Isaiah 41: 10
Chapter 33	Lies	Proverbs 12: 19
Chapter 34	Liars	Psalm 101: 7
	Brokenhearted	Psalm 34: 18
	Confrontation	Proverbs 17: 12
	Reprimand	1 Timothy 5: 20
	Judgment	Matthew 7: 1
	Warning	Titus 3: 10
	Restoration	Galatians 6: 1-2 NIV
	Living in peace	Romans 12: 18
Chapter 35	Deception	Isaiah 5: 21
Chapter 36	Helping each other	Ecclesiastes 4: 9
Chapter 37	Letting go	1 Corinthians 7: 31
Chapter 38	Good things	Philippians 4: 8
	Humility	Proverbs 11: 2
Chapter 39	Injustice	Proverbs 16: 8
Chapter 40	Focus on God	Colossians 3: 2
Chapter 41	Wisdom	Proverbs 11: 30
Chapter 42	Fruit of the Spirit	Galatians 5: 22-23
Chapter 43	Being made new	2 Corinthians 5: 17
Chapter 44	Seeking justice	Isaiah 1: 17
Chapter 45	Giving	2 Corinthians 9: 7
Chapter 46	Prayer	Matthew 6: 6
	Faithful endurance	Hebrews 12: 1

Discussion Questions for *Senior Sisters*

1. Chapter 1: The thought of moving into a retirement community is confirmation (in *their* minds) that Evelyn and Wayne are old. What made you acknowledge that fact? What constitutes *old?*
2. Chapter 2: Evelyn prays before her conversation with Accosta about the challenges caused by her physical limitations. Yet her prayers are wordless. "She trusted God to fill in the blanks." What do you think she means by this?
3. Chapter 3: Sharon and Kay discuss Kay's move. Sharon says, "You can call me 'old' — which is a matter of years — but don't ever call me 'elderly' — which is a matter of capability." Is that a good definition?
4. Chapter 6: Accosta and Evelyn look through old photos. Accosta says, "I've outlived my generation. Do you know how lonely that feels?" My own mother died at age 99 and outlived all her relatives and friends. She often talked about how hard it was. What do you think about this phenomenon?
5. Chapter 6: Accosta moves out of Peerbaugh Place and Evelyn says she finds it hard to deal with *lasts*. But Accosta says, "I refuse to think of lasts until after-the-fact. Until I'm already living in a first. By then, the pain is gone." How do you handle *lasts?*
6. Chapter 6: Accosta has moved out. Evelyn says, "My logical self lags behind my emotional self. I don't like change." How do you handle change?
7. Chapter 10: "Accosta knew that Mae and Tessa had the gift of gab while she and Evelyn were the listeners. The arrangement worked quite well. They balanced each other out." How do you and your friends balance each other out?
8. Chapter 11: Evelyn is exhausted getting ready for her party. It didn't used to be that way. What tasks have gotten harder for you as you've aged? How do you cope?
9. Chapter 11: Evelyn balks at the idea of moving out of her beloved Peerbaugh Place. How have you — or people you know — felt about moving because of age?

10. Kay became Katerina and most people did not respond well. Where did she go wrong?
11. Chapter 18: Evelyn and Wayne get nudges that let them realize it's time to move. If you've moved, what were your nudges?
12. Chapter 24: God wakes Accosta up in the middle of the night because Rosalie needs her. She says as much to a nurse, who balks. "Accosta understood how some people thought she was crazy for being so blunt, but she'd also decided she didn't care. Not giving God credit was worse than dealing with any disbelieving reaction. Besides, she wanted people to know that God did do such things." Have you ever had people balk when you've shared God-moments? How did you react to their doubt?
13. Chapter 24: Accosta has a worry box. Is this an idea you might consider?
14. Chapters 24-27: Rosalie deals with the aftermath of Lonnie's death. If you've been widowed, what advice can you give friends to help them know what is helpful, and what is not.
15. Chapter 28: Wayne and Evelyn see the new owners of Peerbaugh Place measuring and planning big changes. They discuss the huge can't-go-back decision of moving. "God won't abandon us. If we got this decision wrong, He'll make it right." Does change come easily for you? When have you made a wrong choice, yet God got you back on track?
16. Chapter 28: Evelyn and Wayne buy new furniture for Happy Trails—in a completely new style. Does that intrigue you? Or would you want to keep your old things?
17. Chapter 29: Evelyn is packing to move and finds it hard to downsize. Piper suggests taking a picture of giveaway items. "Now you can remember them without having to store them . . . Keep the memories, leave the stuff." What do you think about this idea?
18. Chapter 30: Evelyn and Tessa talk about Katerina's overdone makeup. Tessa says *less is more.* "Evelyn hoped that was true because she only wore the simplest makeup—though she had started to draw in her brows as they were fading into nothingness right before her eyes." Has this happened to you? (it's happened to me!)

19. Chapter 32: Scranton's firm buys him out. Do you think he should have accepted, or fought to stay involved? Do you have any tips about finding a new identity apart from your work?
20. Chapter 35 & 38: Kay is cornered by the ladies, who demand answers. She is forced to tell the truth. Do you think the ladies handled the intervention well? And Kay's physical transformation? What can we all learn from it?
21. Chapter 40: After seeing the changes to Peerbaugh Place Evelyn runs outside to cry. Wayne joins her and says he's feeling the pain too. Evelyn felt better sharing her inner turmoil. Name a time when you found comfort in sharing your big emotions, or when you shared someone else's.
22. Chapter 44: Kay found a way to use her Katerina wigs to help someone in need. God often brings good out of our pain. Name a time in your life when this happened to you.
23. Chapter 46: The verse topping the chapter is Matthew 6: 6: "When you pray, go away by yourself, shut the door behind you, and pray to your Father in private. Then your Father, who sees everything, will reward you." Accosta has a worry box and prays in private. And God hears her prayers. What do you think this verse means regarding praying together in large groups? Is private prayer better?
24. Chapters 43-46: Three months later… do you enjoy where the characters ended up? What would you have liked to happen to each character?

About the Author

NANCY MOSER is the best-selling author of 45 novels, novellas, and children's books that focus on discovering your unique purpose. Her titles include the Christy Award winner *Time Lottery* and Christy finalist *Washington's Lady*. She's written nineteen historical books including *Mozart's Sister, Love of the Summerfields, Masquerade, Where Time Will Take Me,* and *Just Jane*. *An Unlikely Suitor* was named to Booklist's "Top 100 Romance Novels of the Decade." *The Pattern Artist* was a finalist in the Romantic Times Reviewers Choice award. Some of her contemporary novels are, *If Not for This, An Undiscovered Life, The Invitation, A Steadfast Surrender, The Good Nearby, Crossroads, The Seat Beside Me,* and the Sister Circle series. *Eyes of Our Heart* was a finalist in the Faith, Hope, and Love Readers' Choice Award. Nancy has been married nearly fifty years—to the same man. She and her husband have three grown children, eight grandchildren, and live in the Midwest. She's been blessed with a varied life. She's earned a degree in architecture, run a business with her husband, traveled extensively in Europe, and has performed in various theaters, symphonies, and choirs. She knits voraciously, kills all her houseplants, and can wire an electrical fixture without getting shocked. She is a fan of anything antique—humans included.

Website: www.nancymoser.com
Blogs: Author blog: www.authornancymoser.blogspot.com
History blog: www.footnotesfromhistory.blogspot.com
Facebook: www.facebook.com/nancymoser.author
Bookbub: www.bookbub.com/authors/nancy-moser?list=author_ books
Goodreads:
www.goodreads.com/author/show/117288.Nancy_Moser
Pinterest: www.pinterest.com/nancymoser1/boards/
Twitter: www.twitter.com/MoserNancy
Instagram: www.instagram.com/nmoser33/

Visit the ladies again in . . .
Eyes of Our Heart

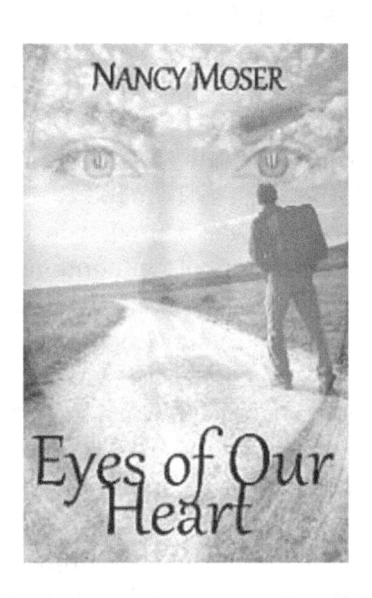

"Surrender" was the word Claire Adams used to describe her obedience to the Almighty. It sounded better than "submission" though the effect was the same.

Claire always prayed before she went to sleep, and hoped she got credit for praying off and on during the day too. As a successful middle-aged woman she didn't pray out of need for a material this or that, or even an emotional that or this, but prayed to be a better person, a better child of God.

It wasn't that she considered herself holy (heaven forbid) but she'd had enough God-moments in her life to want to know Him on a deeper level and make Him proud. Long ago she'd given up the notion of getting her own way, or even wanting her own way. From experience—having had equal moments of saying yes and no to the God of the universe—she knew that His way was the best way and it was easier and far more beneficial to just give in. Surrender.

But on this particular summer night, as Claire went through her bedtime ritual of removing her makeup and slathering on three types of wrinkle cream, she knelt at the side of her bed and offered prayers out of need.

She needed money.

Claire prefaced her request by thanking God for His many gifts: her charming three-bedroom home in a tree-lined neighborhood in Kansas City; her good health (ignoring her aching knees as they were an expected part of getting older); her status as a single, independent woman; and her ability to create mosaic artwork that provided a modicum of fame and financial stability.

Until recently.

Business had been slow. There were fewer customers willing to shell out thousands for a large wall piece when they could buy a wrapped canvas made from their own photo of a waterfall they'd seen on vacation, or purchase a framed landscape for fifty-percent off from their local craft store. The lack of business was the main reason she'd succumbed to covering bowls, lamps, and boxes with tile because they could be sold at a price the masses would accept. She had a gallery, but online sales and seasonal art shows were the new way to reach customers. Yet mosaics were heavy and hard to ship.

She rested her forehead on her clasped hands. "Father? As You know, business is slow. I need to sell more art or I'm going to have to close the gallery, let Darla go, or . . ." She hated to say the next because she really didn't want to offer God the alternative, but since He knew all the details of her life anyway . . . "Or sell the house and move to a smaller place. I know You have a plan and You'll do what's best, so I'll leave You to work out the details. I trust You. In Jesus' name, amen."

With a nod at the heavenly transaction, and a grunt as she pushed herself to her feet, Claire slipped into bed, leaving God to do His stuff.

**

Immersed in a dream, Claire moaned and rolled over in her sleep.

The dream voice said, "Make this for us."

Us? Who is us?

Before the question was answered she woke up. The glow of her bedside clock emanated a green, otherworldly glow. She reached for the lamp and flooded her bedroom with its cozy light.

That was intense. She remembered the dream vividly and reached for the paper and pen she kept nearby. She quickly sketched the image before it faded.

A cross made of arrows pointing outward.

Doves.

Pink roses and white daisies?

She finished her sketch and looked at it. "What *is* this?" She did not ask the question with joyful enthusiasm but with confusion and even a bit of disdain. This was *not* the sort of mosaic she created. She was known for impressionistic murals. On a smaller scale she covered furniture tops and created wall and table art that leaned toward geometric, whimsical designs.

Her drawing was whimsical all right. Nonsensical. Bizarre. No one would buy such a design. It reminded her of the Byzantine mosaics she'd seen in Turkey because there was a sacred overtone to the design. Although Claire's faith in her art was strong, this piece . . . it was not something her customers typically purchased.

"I need to make money," she said to her empty house.

Claire looked at the drawing and the quick notes she'd made to match her dream image. The arrows were aqua, the center circular area at their junction was black, the roses pink, and of course, the doves were ivory. White daisies were scattered within the arms of the arrows. These were not her colors. At all. Claire hated pastels. She was drawn to bold jewel tones. Pink and aqua belonged in little girls' bedrooms, not in her art.

She looked at the clock. It was half-past one, far too early for even Claire to get up. She set aside the sketch, turned off her light, and snuggled into her pillows hoping to dream of something sensible.

**

Claire woke in the morning refreshed, having had a dreamless sleep for the second half of the night. She drove to her studio to work on her newest project, a royal blue and gray wall mosaic of waves. Or sky. She wasn't sure yet.

Her cell phone rang and she answered. It was Agnes from her favorite Kansas City antique mall.

"Have time to swing by, Claire? I have a present for you."

"I love presents."

"Then get yourself over here. Soon. I need to get the stuff out of the way."

"Stuff?"

"You'll see."

Claire detoured to the mall. Agnes often gave her a heads-up about old trash that Claire made into treasures. Adding mosaic tile to the top of a 1930s dresser or covering a tin platter with tiles was fun and usually profitable.

Ten minutes later, she arrived and found Agnes at the front counter. "Come with me." Agnes led her into the back room, to the overhead door. Just inside were five 12" x 12" boxes.

"What's inside?"

"See for yourself."

Claire opened a box to find thousands of white and ivory tiles. Tiny pieces, most no bigger than one-fourth of an inch wide. "Are the boxes all the same colors?"

"I didn't check."

Claire opened each box and found one filled with black tiles, one with greens . . . All very usable. But the last two boxes made her pull up short. *No. No way.*

"What's wrong?" Agnes asked. "Those two full of gold or something?" She went to see for herself. "Pink and turquoise?"

"Aqua."

"Excuse me, Miss Artist. Aqua. They're pretty. Why are you staring at them like they're kryptonite?"

Long story. "Where did you get these?"

"I have no idea. They showed up outside this morning. I have no use for them. Thought of you. The price is right. Free?"

It took Claire a moment to respond. This was far too strange.

"I said they're free?" Agnes repeated. "You want them or not?"

"I want them. Thanks."

"Great," Agnes said. "Now come to the counter. I found a couple tin bowls you might like."

"Be there in a minute." Claire waited until Agnes had left, then stared at the tile. "Is this tile from You, Lord? Was the dream from You? Was the voice in the dream You?"

There was no other explanation.

Claire bowed her head, her thoughts a jumble. She let the implications rise and fall until she could breathe in a regular rhythm.

She lifted her gaze upward. "All right then. I have no idea why You want me to make this, but I'll do it."

@copyright 2020 Nancy Moser

Buy on Amazon

Made in United States
Cleveland, OH
09 April 2025